Laurel

Susan F. Craft

HERITAGE BEACON
F I C T I O N

PRAISE FOR *LAUREL*

Rich with history and the pulse-pounding trials of early America, *Laurel* is a heartwarming story of one family's Christ-like devotion and endurance made all the more authentic with its Native American theme. Author Susan F. Craft brings her passion for the south and its heritage to bear, weaving fact with fiction in a moving, memorable story. A welcome addition to the genre!

~**Laura Frantz**
Author of *The Frontiersman's Daughter*

The impeccable research of historical fiction author, Susan F. Craft, permeates every paragraph in the post-Revolutionary Era novel, *Laurel*. The story of a young mother whose daughter is kidnapped, and the subsequent search, will captivate readers with both unforgettable characters and adventures that sweep a reader to another time and place. Craft is brilliant in her marriage of both fact and fiction, as she weaves a story that captures your attention from first page to last. Ms. Craft has a gift with her pen, creating words that are both breathtaking and beautiful.

~**Elaine Marie Cooper**
Award-winning author of *Fields of the Fatherless*

In *Laurel*, Susan F. Craft weaves a tale of enduring familial love, sacrifice, and adventure that kept me reading late into the night. The stakes are high when a tiny child is kidnapped, but there's no peril Lilyan and Nicholas Xanthakos won't face to see their daughter restored. Readers of Craft's *The Chamomile* and new readers alike, will enjoy this exciting sequel set in the Carolinas during the first years after the Revolutionary War, a setting Craft brings to vivid life.

~**Lori Benton**
Author of *Burning Sky* and *The Pursuit of Tamsen Littlejohn*

Seldom do I come across a story that draws me in as skillfully as Susan F. Craft's *Laurel*. Her writing is so vivid and lyrical, her characters so real, I felt myself right there at our country's inception, experiencing the trials, dangers, and joys of those long-ago days. For my personal library, this one's a keeper!

~**Ann Tatlock**
Award-winning novelist and children's book author

LAUREL BY SUSAN F. CRAFT
Published by Lighthouse Publishing of the Carolinas
2333 Barton Oaks Dr., Raleigh, NC, 27614

ISBN: 978-1-941103-91-3
Copyright © 2015 by Susan F. Craft
Cover design by Goran Tomic
Interior design by AtriTeX Technologies P Ltd

Available in print from your local bookstore, online, or from the publisher at:
www.lighthousepublishingofthecarolinas.com

For more information on this book and the author visit: www.susanfcraft.com
and http://www.historicalfictionalightintime.blogspot.com

This is a work of fiction. Names, characters, and incidents are all products of the author's
imagination or are used for fictional purposes. Any mentioned brand names, places, and
trademarks remain the property of their respective owners, bear no association with the author
or the publisher, and are used for fictional purposes only.

Scripture quotations are taken from the HOLY BIBLE NEW INTERNATIONAL VERSION
r. NIVr Copyright c 1973, 1978, 1984 by International Bible Society. Used by permission of
Zondervan Publishing House. All rights reserved.

Scripture quotations from The Authorized (King James) Version. Rights in the Authorized
Version in the United Kingdom are vested in the Crown. Reproduced by permission of the
Crown's patentee, Cambridge University Press.

Brought to you by the creative team at LighthousePublishingoftheCarolinas.com:
Alycia W. Morales, Ann Tatlock, Rowena Kuo, and Eddie Jones

Library of Congress Cataloging-in-Publication Data
Craft, Susan F.
Laurel / Susan F. Craft 1st ed.

Printed in the United States of America

Acknowledgements

My heartfelt thanks to my children, grandchild, brothers, and sister, who each encouraged me in his or her own way.

Thank you to my mom, who inspired my passion for reading and to my dad, who stirred my enthusiasm for research and a love of history. I miss them.

Gratitude to my dear husband of 45 years, who puts up with my quirky writing schedule, who provides computer support 24-7, who drives me to locations of obscure Revolutionary War battlefields, and who tolerates my constant use of colonial American vernacular in our conversations. After all, who yells "huzzah!" when they've found something they've been searching for? I can do a r-r-right braw *Scots* accent, too. ☺

Above all, thanks to my Lord from whom all blessings flow.

When you harvest the grapes in your vineyard, do not go over the vines again. Leave what remains for the alien, the fatherless, and the widow.

Deuteronomy 24:21

CHAPTER 1

Blue Ridge Mountains, NC
May 1783

Inching forward on a ladder-back chair, Lilyan Xanthakos propped her elbows on her worktable and pressed a walnut shell into the pliant skin of a clay pot. Her face tight with concentration, she gingerly pulled out the shell and admired the pattern left behind.

"Finished."

Once again, her anxious gaze was drawn from her task to the road that meandered through the valley and wound its way up to the cabin.

What's keeping them?

She turned the pot toward the old man who sat beside her on the porch. "What do you think?"

Callum, his body wizened from years of hard living, hunting, and long-forgotten battles, stilled his rocking chair. He studied Lilyan's handiwork. "It's a fine pot, lassie. Like you. Beautiful, strong, dependable."

Adoration gleamed in his watery blue eyes, barely visible

beneath their sagging lids.

She accepted his compliment with a nod, expecting nothing less from the Scotsman who, long ago, had proclaimed himself protector of her and her younger brother after their parents died. Numerous times she had heard Angus McCallum called an insufferable curmudgeon, but he held such a special place in her heart she could not imagine her life without him. Granted, he had no trouble speaking his mind and did so loudly and often. His hot temper, which had drawn him into many fights during his sixty years, had cooled over time, but his opinions had not.

At breakfast, one of the vineyard workers mentioned he had heard General Francis Marion's men had deliberately not been invited to Charlestown, South Carolina's liberation celebration. They were *too rough and tattered.* That comment had ignited Callum into a round of fiery rhetoric and epithets that could have burned the ears off a donkey. In his eyes, Marion and his militia had won the war against the Brits.

Lilyan gathered her pottery tools—the clam and walnut shells for burnishing, the cord-wrapped spoon, corn cob, and peach pits she used to impress patterns into the pots—and rinsed them in a nearby bucket. She plunged her hands into the tepid rainwater and scraped the slick clay from underneath her fingernails.

As she scanned the valley road, she fought back a niggling fear that weighed like a stone in the pit of her stomach. "Why aren't they home yet? Golden Fawn knows I don't like for Laurel to go to bed so soon after she eats."

"Don't fret so. Your sister-in-law loves your baby girl as much as you do. She'd die before she let any harm come to her."

"Not such a baby anymore, Callum. Can you believe she'll be a year old tomorrow?"

Callum snorted. "A fine wee lassie she is. Been talking like a magpie for weeks. Took her first steps toward me, you know."

Lilyan smiled at the vision of her daughter, fiery red coils of hair bouncing on her head as she tottered for the first time on her tiptoes and fell laughing into the waiting arms of her *Lummy*.

She wondered again if she had made the right decision to allow Golden Fawn to take Laurel to visit her Cherokee family. The village lay only five miles away, but it was the first time her daughter had been out of her sight for any length of time, and the separation worried her more than she had anticipated. Her arms ached to snuggle her precious child against her breast, to bury her face in the sweet, silky curls, and to gaze into fern-colored eyes so like her own.

Wiping her hands on her paint-spattered, coarse linen apron, she rose and leaned against one of the log columns lining the front porch of the cabin. Before Lilyan and Nicholas had married, she'd entreated him to promise that her family would always have a place with them. Fulfilling that vow, he had built four cabins, connected to form a fortress with a center courtyard. Lilyan, Nicholas, and Laurel occupied the front cabin. The second housed her brother, Andrew, and his wife, Golden Fawn. Callum bunked in the third cabin alone because he "couldn't take nobody else's snoring." And the fourth accommodated Golden Fawn's twin brothers, with space for winter supplies. It had been a daunting task, but there wasn't much her adoring husband wouldn't do for her. As usual, when her thoughts turned to him, her heart tripped.

He's been out there long enough, she thought as she untied her apron and threw it over a chair. She took the spyglass from the corner of her worktable, slid it open, and trained it on the western side of the valley. The last rays of the afternoon sun danced across the tops of cedar trees, turning them into bright orange torches against the backdrop of hazy mountaintops. The rolling ridges reminded her of the ocean that dominated memories from her childhood. Except, instead of green, undulating waves, the peaks varied from shades of purple and morning-glory blue to a misty gray, one layer folding into the next as if God had raised a giant, silky coverlet in the air and let it billow down to the bedrock below. The mountains served as a stark contrast to the muscadine vines meticulously trellised in even rows, bursting forth in brilliant golden blooms that in three months' time—God willing—would yield their first crop of ebony-skinned grapes.

She moved the spyglass from the top terraces to search the one nearest the valley floor. Anticipating a glimpse of her little girl, she spotted her brother first, slump-shouldered, leaning his forehead against a wagon stopped on the vineyard path. He crawled onto the back of the wagon among the reels of twine and cuttings and clutched his sides as a spasm seized his frail body and sent him into a series of bone-rattling tremors.

"Andrew's coughing again."

Callum sank back into the chair and started rocking. "He's tougher than you think. Not many men could have lived through what he did. It's the Cameron blood in him, I vow."

Lilyan shifted her weight to focus the spyglass on her husband standing a few feet from Andrew. She watched him cut a piece of hemp and secure a cluster of vines to a stake. He had pulled off his shirt, exposing his bronzed chest and long, muscular arms. Strands of his soot-black hair had escaped from his braided queue and lay in sweat-drenched coils at the nape of his neck.

They had been married two years, but the war with England had separated them more than half that time. Now that the fighting was all but over, except for the final declarations, Nicholas was home for good, and Lilyan took great delight in watching her beautiful husband as often as she could. The moment he straightened and jerked his head to the side, she knew something was wrong. She sucked in a breath as he swung around and took off running. Gripping the telescope so tightly her knuckles ached, she stretched her body forward, trying not to lose sight of him as he sprinted between the trellises, slapping away vines that threatened to entangle him.

"What's amiss, lassie?"

"Something's startled Nicholas."

Callum pushed up from the chair with a groan and stood beside

Lilyan. The aroma of pinewood campfires and pipe tobacco wafted around her.

He cupped his hands over his brows and squinted into the distance. "Ach! My eyes don't work anymore."

Peering through the telescope, Lilyan could finally see what Nicholas raced toward—Golden Fawn's brothers.

"It's the twins. On the same horse. Smoke is slumped over. He's ... he's falling." Lilyan gasped. "Nicholas got there in time. He caught him." She clutched Callum's arm. "He's bleeding."

A lance of fear struck its mark into her heart. *Laurel and Golden Fawn? Could they be hurt too? Please. No.*

Unable to wait a moment longer, she shoved the spyglass at Callum, grabbed up her skirts, and hurried across the yard. She'd traversed only a few yards when she spotted Nicholas sprinting toward her. She charged headlong down the hill so fast that when she reached him, she slammed into his body. He clasped her forearms and gently pushed her away. His broad chest heaved as he took a moment to catch his breath, and then he stared at her so intensely the muscles in her back grew rigid. His topaz eyes, always so full of warmth and a depth of love for her that touched her soul, were now filled with a strange emotion she had never seen in them before. It was fear—raw and bone chilling.

"What?" She almost gagged on the lump in her throat and clasped his arms.

"You must brace yourself, *aga'pi mou*." He gripped her arms and waited, never taking his eyes from hers. "It's Laurel. And Golden Fawn."

Oh, God. Oh, God. She dug her nails into his skin.

"They've been taken."

CHAPTER 2

ka'lanu ahkyeli'ski,
Fear the raven's cry and strong wind; someone will soon die.
Cherokee Mythology

Much had been done in the half hour since they had received the dreaded news. Andrew and Rider carried Smoke to their cabin and settled him in bed before saddling horses and packing a mule with supplies. Callum stayed with Smoke, binding the wound where a bullet had gone clean through his side.

Inside the cabin, Lilyan tried to calm her frantic thoughts enough to consider what supplies would be needed for their journey. She snatched a piece of gauze from the cupboard and folded it around a half-loaf of bread left over from the morning meal. She took a canteen hanging from a hook on the wall and filled it from the fresh water bucket, then sealed it with a cork. Leaning against the table, she searched the room for something else Nicholas might need.

Candles? She reached inside the taper box nailed to the wall beside the fireplace mantle, changed her mind, and secured the lid. *No. No need for candles. But a flint box? Yes.*

She found the palm-sized tin box on a wall shelf, lifted its lid, and took a quick inventory: flint, charcloth, and fiber.

What else? Cheese … and corn. Throwing open the larder door, she removed a small wheel of cheese, wrapped it in gauze, and threw it onto the trestle table beside the bread. She ladled corn into a pouch, then pushed all the food and the tinderbox into a leather bag and closed the string top.

Standing in the doorway to their bedroom, with the bag slung over one shoulder and the canteen over the other, she watched Nicholas throw open the top of his personal chest—the one possession of his she was not allowed to disturb. He retrieved a tomahawk and slid it into his belt. The black turkey feathers tied to the handle dangled across his thigh. He pushed the contents of the chest around and drew forth his sword. Lilyan hadn't seen it in years—not since he'd fought alongside Francis Marion's partisans and she was a camp follower.

As he strapped the sword around his waist, his jaw set as a slab of granite, a picture came to mind of her sitting at a campfire, studying her newlywed husband as he cleaned the blade. The weapons he now armed himself with once dripped with the blood of war. Would they be stained again, only this time with the blood of Laurel's kidnappers? For one horrible moment, she hoped so. Realizing the path of her thoughts, she blanched at her savage reaction. A goose ran over her grave, and she shivered.

Lord, You say vengeance is Yours. I submit to Your will, only … please … let me hold my Laurel in my arms once again.

Nicholas strode across the room and stood looking down at her, his golden eyes fraught with emotions. "My love, I must hurry. I can't wait for you and chance losing the trail."

She slid the canteen and bag from her shoulders and draped them across his arm. "We'll follow …" Her words caught in her throat. "… soon," she finished, her lips quivering and her eyes burning with tears.

He tilted her chin with his finger. "There's so much I want to say. I ... I ...."

She watched his Adam's apple bob as he swallowed hard.

"We *will* find her. I vow it." He gripped her forearms. "Give me your blessing?"

When he leaned down, she stood on tip-toe to meet him halfway and, cupping his face with her hands, she kissed his right eyelid. "May God bless you and keep you," she began. She moved to kiss his left eyelid, "while we are apart ...."

"One from the other," he spoke the last words with her.

He waited for her gentle kiss on his lips, then stepped around her, pulled his musket from over the fireplace, and secured it across his back. He draped a powder horn around his neck and strode out onto the porch. She didn't follow him but listened as he barked orders to the men gathering outside. At the sound of their horses' hooves galloping away, she ran to the door to wave, but Nicholas didn't look back.

Gathering her wits about her, she ran to Andrew's cabin and quickly changed into one of his shirts and a pair of his breeches. Back at her cabin, she scurried around stuffing whatever she could think of into saddlebags. She threw together a couple of bedrolls and scooped up her medicine kit and Nicholas's money pouch. It took several trips to haul everything out the door and across the porch. Standing in the doorway, she took another look around the cabin and spotted several stacks of deerskins in a corner. *Might need them for barter.* She dragged a sack of skins outside and closed the door behind her.

Rider toted everything she had gathered down the steps and secured them onto the back of a mule along with two extra muskets. Trembling from head to toe, she leaned against her horse and took comfort from the sturdy, warm mass of the mare's rippling shoulder. She twined the reins in and out of her fingers, barely paying attention to the frantic activity around her. *Hurry! Hurry!* Her mind screamed.

Pain, as if something predatory had slashed its claws across her chest, forced her to take in short, shallow breaths. She couldn't even manage to pray and hoped that God could read her pleas between the ragged beats emanating from her tattered heart.

Rider cinched the ropes one more time across the mule's back and then stood beside his unsaddled horse. He gripped its stringy black mane, sprang up from the ground, and mounted. "Time to go, Lilyan."

Silas, one of the vineyard workers, gave Lilyan a leg up. When she was settled, he climbed onto the mare next to hers. Rider secured the mule's tethers and took the lead. Lilyan started to follow but stopped when Callum limped out onto the porch and down the steps. He looked up at her with eyes so full of pain she had to glance away.

"Take this." His voice cracked as he held out a rag doll. "She'll want it when you find her. Tell my bonnie lass that her Lummy's waitin' for her."

Lilyan slipped the doll inside her saddlebag, leaned down, and kissed Callum's forehead.

Andrew joined them. "We should pray."

Lilyan bowed her head and clamped her eyelids shut as the reins dug into her palms.

"Father, we know You have a special place in Your heart for children. Protect our Laurel. Don't let her be afraid. Bring her back to us, we pray. And, Lord ..." He paused. "Please, take care of my wife. Give her strength, stamina, wisdom ... whatever she needs to survive and to care for Laurel. Please guard her, for she is my treasure. Whatever befalls us, give us the peace to accept that it is Your will. Thank You, and amen."

Andrew approached Lilyan and took her hand. "Sissy, you know I'd give anything to go with you. But ..." He looked away.

You would only slow us down. Lilyan finished his sentence in her head. Everyone was aware of Andrew's fragile health and the reason for it. The war had taken its toll. He had never been the same after hellish months aboard a British prison ship. Being wounded at the Battle of Camden, imprisonment, and a near-fatal bout with pneumonia had all matured him far beyond his seventeen years, etching deep crevices in his forehead and streaking his auburn hair with silver, making him seem the older sibling, though Lilyan was five years his senior.

Lilyan patted his hand. "I know."

She wanted to tell him how much she and Nicholas depended on him to keep the vineyard going and their home together and safe, but the anxiety that raged through her body held a stranglehold on her.

Andrew turned away, and Lilyan wiped her tears.

Take hold. No time to weep.

She scanned the fading horizon, where the gossamer mantle of twilight hovered over the mountains and turned them a smoky gray. *It will be dark soon*, she thought as she urged her horse into a canter.

Courage, my precious one. Ma and Da are coming for you.

A half hour later, after they had left the main road and taken the trail to the village, a chilling howl of grief whorled its way through the darkened forest, crept up Lilyan's arms, and blew a cold breath on the back of her neck. Her horse tossed up her head, and Lilyan spotted the moon reflected in the mare's wide-open eye.

She ran her hand down the mare's neck. "Steady, girl. Steady."

She wished she could steady herself, but questions kept bludgeoning her mind. *What's happening to my little girl? Is she hungry? Is she afraid?*

And worst of all, if they were slavers, wouldn't they value her little girl? Keep her alive?

They broke through a thick field of ripening corn and into the village. Campfires lit the front of the council house, a large structure built on a mound in the center of the clearing. Bunched around the council house was a collection of cabins and partially constructed summer homes—rectangular houses with upright poles for framework covered with woven siding coated with earth and clay.

A woman, her white hair sticking out from her head so that she resembled an ancient porcupine, sat cross-legged beside a fire, rocking to and fro. With tears spilling down her cheeks, she lifted her face to the full moon, raised her arms in supplication, and poured out her grief in groans and chants. Directly behind her, deep in conversation, stood a group of elderly men and women gathered in front of one of the cabins. A shaman circled the dwelling, puffing smoke from his pipe in several directions. When Lilyan spotted the black cloth wrapped around the pipe, she knew the cabin was a death house.

The shaman blew out a cloud of smoke and yelled, "Be gone Night-Goers, witches of the dark, come to worry our sick into the rim!"

Twirling his pipe in ever-widening circles, he moaned, closed his eyes, and bobbed his head back and forth. The cadence of his groans quickened, then transformed into a guttural whine that sent waves of gooseflesh up Lilyan's spine.

"I call upon you, oh Great Spirit, the Anointer; and you, the spirits of thunder and lightning. Take the wind from under the wings of Raven Mocker, our most feared enemy. Drown its fire as it flies across the skies. Rip the croak from its throat." The medicine man's mournful plea sliced through the night air, and the knots of frightened onlookers pulled together even closer. "Forbid him to consume the hearts of our dead."

Lilyan shivered at his last words and twined her arms around her waist.

The woman at the fire howled like a banshee. Lilyan watched in horror as Nicholas came out of the death house and skirted around the shaman. He looked up and, spotting her, sprinted across the clearing, pulled her from her horse, and gathered her into his arms.

"Please tell me they're not in there." She squeezed the words through her constricted throat.

"No. They're not."

Lilyan began to sob bone-wrenching cries from deep within. She had never known such pain, such fear. Wanting to scream her own banshee wails, Lilyan leaned into Nicholas, the thunder of her husband's heart in her ear. Drawing strength from his arms wrapped around her like bands of steel, she found safety from the pit that threatened to engulf her.

When Lilyan's weeping subsided, Nicholas, between murmured endearments spoken in Greek, pressed kisses across her forehead, on her cheeks and her lips.

"Cry now, my Lilyanista, and then purge the tears from your heart. You'll need all your strength for the time ahead."

Rider, who had been waiting patiently, stepped forward. "What news?"

"Before I tell you," Nicholas put his hand on Rider's shoulder, "how is Smoke?"

"Strong. The wound will heal fast."

"That's good to hear."

Nicholas put his arm around Lilyan's waist, and Silas joined them as they strode to the campfire farthest from the others.

Nicholas assisted her to sit on a rock and, with a weary groan, dropped onto the ground beside her. "I followed the trail as far as I could until the sun went down. They were headed south. And then, a couple of miles into the forest, they split into two groups."

Rider and Silas sat across from them, muskets balanced across their laps.

"Tell me what you know, Rider," Nicholas said.

"It was late afternoon. Smoke and I were at the river with others pushing a new dugout into the water. We heard gunshots, so we ran back. But by the time we reached the village, the white men had already killed or wounded our men and had tied the young women and older children together."

Nicholas clenched his fist. "How many men?"

"Twelve ... fourteen ... with many muskets and pistols. They fired at us all at once. When Smoke was shot, he landed against me so hard I fell. Hit my head against a stone." Rider ran his fingers across the slash in the skin above his right ear. "When I woke, they were gone. They took our horses, but not all. Some were hobbled near the river. I knew I could not fight them alone, so I got Smoke and we rode to your place."

Hannah, Golden Fawn's aunt, joined them and seated herself beside Lilyan, tucking her moccasinned feet underneath her.

Lilyan held the woman's gnarled hand and caressed her skin with her thumb. "Grandmother," she spoke the honorary title hesitantly, "can you tell me of my Laurel and Golden Fawn?"

Hannah groaned and clutched her chest. "It was time to go. Little Red Butterfly was very sleepy, so I get a shawl and wrap her up on my niece's back. Tucked in so tight only her little white cap peeped out of the top."

Lilyan had sewn the mobcap for Laurel's birthday, but she couldn't resist letting her wear it for her visit to Golden Fawn's family. She flinched against the vivid picture that entered her mind.

Hannah started to rock. "Then the demons came." She threw her hands up to her face. "So much killing. Aye-ee-ee!"

Demons. Lilyan dug her nails into her palms. She opened her fists, wrapped her arms around the grieving woman, and patted her back.

"They took the young women. My Golden Fawn." Hannah sobbed. "Little Red Butterfly and the older children. How could they do such a thing? Some of them were sick."

Lilyan cast a panicked look at Nicholas. "Sick? How were they sick?"

"Come. I show you."

Silas stood, clenching his musket at his side. "I'll see to the horses," he said, barely concealing his anger. "Fetch our bedrolls," he mumbled and then hurried away.

Nicholas and Rider jumped up to help Lilyan and Hannah, who led the way. Single file, they trailed her toward the death cabin, pausing long enough for her to pull a lighted stick from the fire. The deerskin flap that usually served as a door had been ripped away, and the stench of bodies, already decaying from the warm temperatures, tainted the air. Lilyan braced herself, clamped her hand over her nose, and entered.

Hannah held up her torch, lighting a scene so gruesome Lilyan knew it had branded itself into her mind and would never leave.

On one side of the cabin, about ten corpses—men, women, children—had been laid out on the dirt floor. Some faces were the color of ashes. Death beads glistened on the foreheads of others. She gagged at the sweet, cloying smell of blood, and her head swam with the buzzing of flies. On the opposite side of the cabin, five people lay on cots covered with cedar boughs. Some moaned and some, past moaning, teetered on the brink of death.

Hannah approached one of the cots that held a young boy. She lifted her torch and pointed to his forehead.

Lilyan gasped. "Dear God!"

She scrambled forward and frantically scanned the boy's palms and the soles of his feet. She seized Hannah's arm and pulled her from the cabin.

Outside, she stumbled into Nicholas, who held her close and asked, "What's wrong, dearest?"

Her throat muscles knotted against the dreaded word she was about to speak.

"Smallpox."

CHAPTER 3

To BRIGADIER GENERAL JAMES CLINTON
Dear Sir: I have reed your favs. of the 18th and 28th Decemr and
2d instant with their inclosures. I approve of your innocculating the
Soldiers of your Brigade upon the first appearance of the small pox
among them, and I would not have you confine that salutary operation
to them alone, but carry it thro' any of the other Corps which may not
have had the disorder.

General George Washington, Head Quarters, Philadelphia
January 19, 1779

Nicholas leaned down, his breath warm against Lilyan's cheek. "You're certain?"

She blew out the lungful of air she had been holding. "I know smallpox. We're old enemies."

Lilyan thought of Laurel's rosy cheeks and porcelain skin, but nightmarish memories she'd buried long ago thrust the loveliness aside. She stared into her husband's eyes. Spurred by the dread she saw in them, she asked, "When do we leave here?"

Nicholas chewed on his bottom lip. "We must wait till

morning."

"Why? Why can't we go now? The longer we delay …" She wrung her hands.

"Come." He took her by the arm and steered her toward the campfire where Silas awaited. They settled themselves on the blankets he had spread for them.

"How did you come to know about smallpox?" Silas asked.

Lilyan laced her fingers through Nicholas's. "Andrew and I were very young—I was only six—when we came down with the smallpox. I'll never forget the fear that reigned in our house as Ma nursed us."

Lilyan drew up her knees and rested her arms on them.

"I remember burning up with fever. Every muscle in my body ached. My back hurt so that I could hardly bear it. The nausea and vomiting were terrible, but not as terrible as the lesions that seemed to be everywhere—my face, my tongue, my throat."

Will my sweet Laurel get smallpox? Will Golden Fawn be there to care for her? Get her through it?

"We were fortunate, though. Neither of us bears the scars."

Rider furrowed his brow, his frown digging deep crevices into his cheeks. "I, too, was young when smallpox came to our village. It took a fourth of our number. Blinded others. Those it did not kill were left with scars, like our Golden Fawn. Some who could not bear the shame of those terrible marks took their own lives."

Rider turned his intense gaze on Lilyan. "Many would not have made it had it not been for you, Tsu la."

Nicholas shifted his weight and scanned her eyes for an explanation.

She curled her fingers around his again. "As you know—but Silas, you may not—I was born and grew up in Charlestown, South Carolina. My da was a trapper, a very successful one. I was ten when he decided to take me with him on a trading mission. Over a year's time, we traveled from the ocean to the mountains and back. It was such a magical adventure, I called it my *wonder time*."

Will our sweet girl experience such times with her da?

She mentally shook herself. "The things I learned saved my life, especially later when bounty hunters were after me."

Silas's eyebrows shot up. "You were a fugitive?"

Nicholas cleared his throat. "Another time, Silas."

Lilyan drew her legs underneath her and looked down at her trembling fingers as she fidgeted with the fringe on her leggings.

"Go on, dear." Nicholas reached over and laid his hand on hers.

Bless them both. They're trying to distract me.

"We were about six months into our journey when we came upon a Cherokee village—your village, Rider. Many people were already infected, and since Da and I were immune, we stayed and did what we could to ease the suffering."

The moment she said the word *immune*, Lilyan had a thought so alarming she dug her fingers into Nicholas's skin. "Nikki! You were in there. With them! And Silas? What about you?"

"Do not fear, my love," Nicholas answered, gently prying her loose from his arm. "Silas grew up on a farm and had the cowpox, so he's safe. As for myself, I've been inoculated."

"Inoculated?" she asked.

"Because we lived in Greece, we were exposed to many cultures, many diseases. When I was about eight, as I recall, someone explained the treatment to my father, and he insisted that our family be protected."

"But how?" Lilyan was stunned.

"The physician made a cross-cut in our skin. Then he smeared in scrapings from the sores of someone who had smallpox." He rolled up his sleeve, exposing two shiny streaks on his forearm. "See? This is the place."

Lilyan ran her finger across the familiar scars and then rubbed her hands up and down her arms to soothe the goose bumps that danced on her skin. "Ugh! Sounds ghastly. So, you got smallpox?"

"Yes. But not a bad case. Some got it worse than others. None of our family died, thank God."

Lilyan rolled her neck against the tension that gripped her muscles. At that moment, out of the corner of her eye, she spotted a young man about Rider's age preparing to mount his horse.

She whirled around and stared at him. "Who's that? Where's he going?"

"Do not be alarmed, Lilyan," Rider answered. "It is my friend, Sky. He will ride to the main village and bring men to help."

"No! He cannot," she shouted. "Stop him."

Rider jumped up and sprinted across the clearing. Lilyan watched anxiously as he ordered Sky to accompany him to the campfire. They both squatted beside Silas and waited for her explanation.

"No one must leave the village. At least not for a fortnight. The time it takes for the disease to come to an end." Lilyan sat up on her knees. "Sky, you must tell the others that they must burn the cabins with everything in them. They must gather the sick into one place, and only those who have had the disease before should tend to them."

She considered her next words carefully. "They must dispose of the dead quickly. It's best to burn them in the cabin, where they lay. Not to touch them."

Rider winced and glanced at Sky, whose grimace reflected his own.

"Rider," said Lilyan, "I know your people want to bury their dead, but you must explain to them that exposure to the bodies will only bring more death." She looked to Nicholas for confirmation.

He rose and walked over to the young men as they stood. "It has to be done this way. Otherwise, the disease may spread."

Sky shook himself as if to clear his head and murmured, "I will tell the others."

"Sky?" Lilyan said as he turned away. "Please ask Hannah to come and see me."

Without looking back, he trudged toward the people sitting around the other campfires.

Nicholas sat back down beside her. No one spoke as they waited for the old woman. It wasn't long before she joined them, carrying a basket laden with a meal she had prepared. She sat on a blanket and spread various items in front of her. Hannah handed Nicholas a slab of cornbread.

When he tried to pass it to Lilyan, she shook her head and pressed against her stomach to staunch the nausea that roiled inside.

Hannah frowned. "You must eat. There are long days ahead."

Lilyan took the cornhusk, still warm from lying next to hot coals, unfolded it, and scooped her fingers into the sweet-smelling bread. She forced herself to eat, inwardly repeating the words, *chew, swallow, chew, swallow.*

She ate enough to avoid a scolding from the woman who watched her every mouthful. "That was very good, Hannah. Thank you." She adjusted her legs that had almost fallen asleep and studied the survivors who now sat around their own campfires. "You will remember to use the leaves of blackberries on their sores? The astringent will dry them quickly."

Hannah nodded and pushed herself to stand. She groaned as her bones and joints popped and clicked. "Do not worry about my people. Though we are few now, we will care for each other." She spoke the last words with effort. Her sadness tugged on the wrinkles beside her red-rimmed eyes, etching deep curves into her cinnamon-colored face. She reached down to caress Lilyan's cheek. "Something tells me that our Little Red Butterfly will be back in your arms soon."

Lilyan's shoulder sagged. *Pray God that is so.*

As Hannah lumbered away, Nicholas launched into his plan. "We'll leave at dawn. There are two trails. Silas, you and Rider will take one. Lilyan and I will follow the other."

"But Nicholas, won't we need more men?" Lilyan asked.

"We will. I'm relying on Callum to spread the word."

She tugged at his sleeve. "But we won't wait on them, will we? We've not a moment to spare."

"If I thought we could follow the trail at night, I would. But I can't take the chance. Sitting here, waiting for the sun to come up while God knows what's happening to my darling girl ..." His voice became louder with each word.

He scrambled to his feet and, without another word, he turned on his heel and stomped away.

Lilyan jumped up and sped after him, finding him stopped a few yards into the forest.

"Nikki," was all she could say before he reached out and swept her into his arms.

His embrace became the grip of a drowning man clinging to a lifeline. His body shook so hard, she pulled her arm free to caress his face and discovered his cheeks wet with tears.

Suddenly she realized how insensitive she had been. Her strong husband, who had faced the horrors of war and who had spit in death's face many times, was hurting as much as she. Only once in their marriage had he shown her any vulnerability—the night he'd relinquished her to Callum's care to escape from bounty hunters.

"Shh, my love," she murmured between kisses she placed on his forehead and cheeks.

"I'm undone, Lilyanista." He raked his fingers through his hair and glanced away. "And it pains me for you to see."

"It only makes me love you more, dearest," she whispered.

She nuzzled her face into his neck and massaged his tense muscles. They stood quietly for some time until she drew back and gazed at the stars glistening like candles reflected in a thousand mirrors. "Look." She pointed. "There's Orion's belt."

She turned and leaned her back against him. "Do you remember the first time you pointed out Orion to me?"

"I do." He wrapped his arms around her waist and pulled her closer against his chest. "We were near General Marion's encampment in Wyboo Swamp. 'Twas the night I asked you to be my wife."

"Yes." She drew circles on his wrist with her forefinger. "I recall every word you spoke. How you said you had watched me during our escape from the bounty hunters. The way my body came slowly awake long before I opened my lovely green eyes, as you called them. How graceful my hands were when I braided my hair. Hair that looked like spun copper by firelight."

She closed her eyes as he twirled a tendril of her hair around his finger and rested his chin on her head. "How you lay down at night wondering what my hair would look like spread across your pillow."

He took a deep breath. "I longed for you, Lilyanista, with an ache beyond bearing. But it was such an uncertain time. Each time I left for battle, never knowing if I'd return. I didn't want to subject you to that. I agonized over asking you to be mine."

She turned around to face him again. "I told you then that I believe with all my heart God has given us the gift of each day—one day—and He expects us to live each hour, each moment, acknowledging and enjoying that gift."

He locked his eyes with hers. "It's a wonderful sentiment, my love, but difficult to live out." He clasped her hands. "Tell me. When will God allow us some peace? And how am I to enjoy the day our daughter was stolen from us?"

The vision of Laurel's laughing eyes stabbed Lilyan's heart with a pain so severe she pressed her fingers to the pulse at the base of her neck. "I can't answer that. I know only that we must try. We must pray without ceasing."

She searched his face, illumined by the full moon filtering through the canopy of branches overhead. "Would you pray for us, Nikki?"

He pressed her hands against his chest and curled his fingers around hers. In a steady voice, he lifted up their fears and emotions, beseeching the Lord for the lives of their precious daughter and sister-in-law. Afterward, they walked arm-in-arm to the campfire and lay down on the blanket. She scooted her back against his chest, and he tucked his knees under hers. Wrapped in the cocoon of her husband's protective embrace, mercifully, she gave herself up to sleep.

She awoke cold and foggy-headed. "Laurel?"

Reality splashed her face like freezing water from a high

mountain stream. Pushing away the blanket damp from the morning dew, she rolled onto her side and looked for Nicholas, but he was gone. She propped up on her elbows, and every muscle in her body protested. In the darkness, the ashes of the fire breathed their last breaths. She found a nearby stick and poked them back to life when she heard men's voices—many of them.

CHAPTER 4

Preparing Wool for Spinning
Soak husked rice in water for a day; change water and soak rice again until it can be squeezed into a flour; pour off water; rub with a stone until rice becomes flour; fuse picked wool into flour until it's clean; store in a covered earthen dish until ready for spinning.

Lilyan sprang up and spotted Nicholas standing next to the council-house fire surrounded by a handful of strangers. Not bothering to tuck in her shirttail that billowed around her knees, she hurried to her husband's side.

He held out his arm for her to slide in next to him. "Gentlemen, this is my wife."

The men, dressed in trappers' gear—fringed shirts, and trousers with buckskin leggings covering their boots—pulled their hats from their heads, except the youngest, who did so only after the man next to him prodded him with an elbow.

"Lilyan." Nicholas nodded toward the oldest of the five men. "This is Alexander Forbes, a friend of Callum's. And now a friend of ours."

Forbes bowed. "An honor, ma'am."

She bobbed a short curtsy, feeling awkward doing so in her male attire.

"I canna imagine a better introduction than to be dubbed a friend of Callum's," Forbes said, his words heavily flavored with a Scot's brogue. "'Tis sorry we are, dear lady, to have interrupted your slumber. And sorrier still to meet under sech circumstances."

Forbes swept his arm toward the others. "Permit me to introduce me sons. John, second oldest." He looked down at his feet. "Though, now, the oldest. Then there's William. Next is Duncan. And the youngest, Robbie."

The pale light of dawn filtered through the forest, revealing the handsome faces so like freshly burnished clay, imprinted with their father's image. Except Robbie. She studied his features. Gentleness lay in his dove-gray eyes. The lines of his nose and jaw were softer than his brothers', less chiseled.

He's his mother's child.

People often told Lilyan that Laurel was her spitting image. Maybe it was their coloring—the copper-red hair, light complexion, fern-green eyes. But her daughter's eyes mirrored Nicholas's, character, often sparkling with charm and good humor. The way she set her chin in determination was so like him, it was all Lilyan could do to remain firm with her. The ache for her child overwhelmed her.

Forbes cleared his throat, and his face contorted into a frown that Lilyan hoped would never be turned on her. "Make your bows, then, to the captain's good wife, you gomerals."

The young men swiftly obeyed.

"You're here to help?" she asked. Her spirits lifted with that thought.

"Aye. In whatever way we can, dear lady," Forbes said.

"In spite of the smallpox?"

"Dinna worry yerself, there. We're cattlemen, so we've all had the cowpox. Including young Robbie. He had it—"

"Two years ago, Da. Me and all four of the sisters. When I was thirteen," Robbie finished his father's sentence.

Forbes smiled at the mention of his girls. "Aye. Scared yer ma near to death, that did."

"So, you have four daughters?" Lilyan asked.

"That I do. And if anyone dared to harm a hair on their heads, I'd hound them to hell and back. That's why we're here. And," he said, sliding a haversack from John's shoulder, "to give you this. Callum said we were to hand it over to none but yerself."

Nicholas held the satchel while she rummaged through it.

"Paper, pencils ... charcoal?" *What must Callum have been thinking?* Then she withdrew several hand-sized pieces of paper. "Sketches of Laurel."

She spotted a picture she had done the day before their nightmare began. Laurel was looking directly at her, a mischievous grin on her face, leaving her ma in suspense as to how long she would keep on her new mobcap. Lilyan caressed the tiny dimple she had drawn on her daughter's cheek.

Nicholas took the sketches from her. "Wouldn't it be helpful to Forbes and his sons to see these? Take one with them, so they'll recognize Laurel when they see her?"

Callum's a wise man.

Forbes studied the portrait Nicholas handed him. "You did this?"

Before Lilyan could say anything, Nicholas answered, "My wife's an artist."

"'Tis as fine o' work as any I've ever seen." Forbes handed the paper to John, who passed it to his brothers.

Robbie adjusted the longbow slung across his shoulder, glanced at the charcoal rendering, then at Lilyan, and back. "She's bonnie. Looks just like you, ma'am."

The brothers stared at their sibling, their eyebrows bowed up like horseshoes. They poked each other with their elbows and grinned.

Forbes took one of the sketches, tucked it inside his sporran, and cleared his throat once more. "Right, then. Daylight'll be here soon. What's our plan, Captain?"

"There are two trails. One headed southwest, the other southeast. Silas, Rider, Lilyan, and I will go southeast. You and your boys, southwest."

"Agreed," said Forbes. "We're afoot, so we'll travel faster through the mountains. Your horses will fend better in the foothills."

Forbes looked over his shoulder at Sky, who leaned against a pine tree, ripping pieces of bark from the trunk with his fingernails. "What about the Cherokee? Aren't they coming?"

Nicholas shook his head. "We can't take a chance of them spreading the pox. They can join us in two weeks." He scrubbed a finger across his brow. "If we haven't found my daughter by then. Which—pray to God—we will."

Forbes slapped Nicholas on the shoulder.

Nicholas avoided eye contact. "We'd best be on our way."

"You heard him, lads. Let's be at it, then." Forbes made to walk away, but he turned back. "And if we find the wee bairn?"

Nicholas stiffened. "Take her straight to Callum. He'll get word to us. We'll do the same."

Assuming she's alive. The thought crept across Lilyan's mind like a bogle prowling in the night.

As they readied their horses, she scanned where she knew the mountains stood. A heavy mist obscured everything beyond a hundred yards, leaving her dull and melancholy as if trapped in the bottom of a giant gray soup bowl.

They left the village, Rider in the lead, followed by Nicholas, then Lilyan, and Silas leading the pack mule.

Lilyan glanced over her shoulder at the old men and women huddled together in mournful groups, blankets draped over their heads, shoulders drooped like abandoned, broken lances of corn in a fallow field. The handful of young men stood rigidly, hands balled into fists—their only outward signs of resistance to their orders to stay behind and wait.

"Nikki, do you think they will heed our warning about not

spreading the pox?"

"We can only hope. Though if given the same circumstances, I would choose not to."

She squirmed on the saddle, trying to find a good seat. "I thought as much."

Before entering the cornfield at the edge of the clearing, she twisted around and waved good-bye to the Forbeses.

Such generous men, she thought, *to put themselves in danger to help.*

"Nikki, what did Mr. Forbes mean about John now being his eldest?"

Nicholas didn't turn around and kept his eyes forward. "His firstborn, James, served with me under Marion. He was killed at Fort Motte."

So Forbes knows what it feels like to lose a child. How does one live with that? Please, God, spare us that feeling.

The farther they traveled, the more the sun burned away the haze, first revealing the edges of tree-topped ridges, then pulling back layer after layer of gossamer veils to expose the highest mountain peaks standing tall against a cerulean sky. From a distance echoed the *caw-caw* of a crow, the *fee-bee-fee* of chickadees, and the gloomy *coo-ooh* of a mourning dove.

Laurel always delighted in those sounds. Lilyan visualized her sitting in their yard, cocking her head to listen, her eyes dancing.

Her horse lifted her head and slowed her pace as if sensing her rider's tension.

Lilyan patted the mare's neck. "Sorry. I'll pay more attention." With her knees, she urged the horse to close the gap in their swift-moving column.

They had been riding at a steady pace for miles when Rider stopped and looked back at Nicholas, scowling.

Lilyan's heart sank. "Have we lost them?"

"No," said Rider. "But something as bad."

Nicholas nudged his horse forward. "What is it?"

Rider swept his arm in front of him. "Looks like they stopped here and divided again."

Lilyan noticed Nicholas's body sag momentarily before he straightened.

Pressing his knees into the horse's sides, Nicholas guided him back and forth, leaned down as far as he could, and studied the ground. "They're not worried about hiding their signs. They're traveling fast."

"How do you know that?" Lilyan fought against the thought of what the slavers might do to those who couldn't keep up.

"They didn't build a fire last night. Didn't cook. They're pushing hard to put ground between them and the Indians," he said as he traversed an ever-widening circle, still looking intently at the tracks and reaching out to touch the underbrush.

"One group goes west. One horse, one woman, and a child head east, downriver," Rider said, pointing toward a hammock of oaks.

Anxiety bubbled up in Lilyan's stomach. "A child? Could they be Laurel's footprints?"

Rider shrugged.

Like flooding water threatening to overflow its banks, Lilyan's apprehension rose with each breath. "Two trails. What will we do?"

"Split up again. Rider and Silas one way. You and I the other."

She leaned forward in the saddle and stared at the ground. "We cannot know if those prints are Laurel's or one of the other children from the village. So, which path do we take?"

He frowned, deep in concentration, and then looked her straight in the eyes. "You choose."

Dear Lord!

She squeezed shut her eyes and probed her deepest instincts. "Let's continue east," her words tumbled out.

Nicholas dismounted. "Rider. Silas. Same plan as before. But we must split the supplies. You take the mule."

They divvied up the provisions, securing sacks onto the backs of Lilyan's and Nicholas's mounts. Nicholas handed one of the extra muskets to Lilyan and helped her secure it across her back.

He approached each of the men and shook their hands. "Godspeed."

"And to you and the missus," Silas said before he and Rider turned away.

Lilyan and Nicholas wended their way through the forest and neared a dense patch of cane when she recognized the unmistakable gurgle of water rushing over rocks. She stood in the stirrups to listen when she caught another sound.

"Nikki, I hear a child crying!" Hope raced through her like quicksilver.

She strained her neck and turned her ear toward the cries. Frustrated, she gripped the reins. Still keeping her voice low, she said, "I can't tell if it's her. What's wrong with me? I'm her mother. Why can't I tell?"

He put up his hand to stop her.

"Dismount," he whispered. "We'll tie the horses here. Move as quietly as you can."

With muskets slung across their shoulders, they crouched and slinked from tree to tree until they came upon a cabin where they spied a young woman bending over a washtub. On the ground beside her, a golden-haired little girl wailed her unhappiness and tugged on the hem of her mama's dress.

Disappointment like freezing rain showered over Lilyan, leaving her shivering and bereft.

Nicholas leaned against a tree and looked down at her, his eyes full of regret. "I'm so sorry, my love." He took her hand. "You look exhausted. It'll be night soon, and we need shelter."

"But another night without her … I can go on. Truly, I can. What about the tracks? Shouldn't we follow them now, while they're fresh?"

He took her face in his hand and rubbed her chin with his thumb. "You need rest, dearest. We both do. And it's too difficult to follow tracks at night."

She nodded. Her shoulders drooped from fatigue.

He helped her slide the gun off her shoulder and took it from her. "You go first. Hail the family. The sight of a woman will be less alarming."

Lilyan stepped into the clearing and called out, "'Lo the cabin."

The young woman swept her daughter into her arms and took a step backward.

"Don't worry. We intend no harm to you." Lilyan signaled for Nicholas to join her. "My husband and I have traveled a long way. We're looking for our daughter, who was taken from us."

It hurts so much to say those words.

The woman eased her rigid stance and curved her lips into a timid smile. "Come on, then. We ain't got much. But you're welcome."

Lilyan stepped closer. "Thank you, Mrs.?"

"Greene. Miriam Greene. This is our daughter, Rebecca."

She studied the young mother as she nuzzled her cheek against her daughter's hair that matched her own, as golden and feathery as corn silk. Only, Rebecca's tendrils curled around her face while Miriam's hair was bound in a plait that draped over her shoulder. They both had intensely blue eyes—robin's-egg blue, if she were to paint them.

"My name is Lilyan Xanthakos, and this is my husband, Nicholas."

Nicholas bowed and tugged the brim of his hat.

Miriam curtsied, her bare feet striking a graceful pose.

Nicholas adjusted the muskets across his back. "I'll fetch the horses. Get them settled for the night."

"We ain't got no barn, but you can hitch them by the goat shelter yonder." Miriam pointed to a lean-to on the other side of a patch of deep-green grass where two goats and two kids chomped on the tops of dandelions. "There's hay and corn too, iffen you need 'em."

Rebecca squirmed in her mother's arms and started to whine.

"All right, little'n. Supper's ready." Miriam slid Rebecca onto her hip and stepped toward the cabin doorway. "Come on in, Miz Xanthakos."

"Please, call me Lilyan."

Inside the cabin, Miriam motioned for Lilyan to sit on the bench beside their table. "My man should be here anytime. He's been out choppin' firewood. We'll wait for him, but I'll go on and feed this hungry little bird."

"Can I help?" asked Lilyan.

"Thank you kindly, but it's all done. You just sit and rest a spell."

Lilyan surveyed the one-room cabin and its sparse furniture: a table and bench hewn out of oak, a rocking chair and ladder-back chair both facing a surprisingly well-crafted stone fireplace, with a rag rug spread on the dirt floor at the foot of the hearth. Beside the fireplace, L-turned stairs led up to a loft. A spinning wheel and loom stood to the side of the room tucked underneath the loft. Bulky loops of spun goat hair hung from pegs lined across the wall behind the loom. Paddle combs full of thick tufts lay on the floor beside the rocking chair that was draped with the whitest knit blanket she had ever seen.

After darting glances several times at the door, Lilyan walked over to take a closer look at the blanket. "This is very fine work."

"Thank you kindly."

With Rebecca resting on her hip, Miriam ladled mush from a cast-iron pot on the hearth into a wooden bowl and sprinkled it with strawberries she had cut into bite-sized pieces. She put the bowl and a small whittled spoon on the table and sat on the bench with Rebecca on her lap. Her daughter clasped the spoon in her chubby fingers, stuck it in the oatmeal, and poked it into her mouth.

Lilyan observed the child who, with dainty fingers, picked up a bit of strawberry and slid it onto her tongue. Watching Rebecca intensified the pain in her heart. Grasping at something, anything, to attract her thoughts elsewhere, she asked, "How did you get the yarn so white?"

Miriam used the spoon to scrape the oatmeal dribbling from

the side of Rebecca's mouth. "I washed the goat hair in rice starch."

Lilyan scrunched up the material. "It's so soft."

Miriam smiled, pointing to a terra-cotta pot underneath the deerskin-covered window.

Lilyan crossed the room and examined the plant inside the container, running her fingers across the spiky gray-green leaves. "Aloe."

"Just a tiny bit." Miriam dipped her fingers into the oatmeal, brought out a morsel of strawberry, and fed it to Rebecca.

The sound of men's voices came from outside, and Miriam and she exchanged a glance. They jumped up at the same time, Miriam slung Rebecca onto her hip, and they hurried out the door.

A lanky, dark-haired young man, who could not have been more than sixteen, stood with an axe leaning on his shoulder, talking to Nicholas. He buried the axe into a stump beside his bare feet. When he saw Lilyan, he removed his hat.

"Ma'am," he said. A friendly welcome lit blue eyes the same color as his wife's and child's.

"They's lookin' for their little girl, Jedediah," said Miriam. "I didn't ask her none of the particulars. Figured she'd tell me iffen she had a mind to."

"Yes. The mister was telling me about it."

Lilyan caught the foreboding look that passed between husband and wife and shot a glance at Nicholas. He stared back at her with bleak eyes. She pressed her hand to the base of her neck, where her racing pulse threatened to burst through the veins. He stepped close until his hip pressed against hers.

Jedediah avoided their eyes and stubbed a toe into the dirt. "Got some right bad news, though."

Nicholas slipped his arm around Lilyan's waist, and she balled up her fists, bracing herself for the onslaught.

Jedediah tucked his thumb under the strap of his overalls. "I found two bodies in the woods. An Indian woman and a little girl. Came back here to get my shovel. Wanta give them a proper burial."

CHAPTER 5

After fireflies led the Cherokee father to his lost daughter, he watched them grow brighter and larger, floating higher and higher in the darkness, until they became stars in the night sky.
Cherokee Legend

Lilyan's legs buckled. Panic invaded every pore of her body as Nicholas swept her up, carried her inside, and set her down in the rocker.

"I'll go with him. See if it's ..." He covered her hands with his and rubbed them, warming her numb fingers. "Courage, Lilyanista."

When the men left, Miriam finished feeding Rebecca and then trod back and forth across the cabin until the child drooped in slumber.

Lilyan slumped in the chair and closed her eyes. *Dear God, please, please, please.* She heard the woman at her side and looked up.

"What's your little'n's name?" Miriam asked, her eyes filled with concern.

"Laurel. It's Laurel."

"That's a nice name." She took hold of Rebecca's fist that rested on her breast and kissed it. "Would you like to hold her?"

Lilyan held open her arms. Her body grew warm where the sweet-smelling child molded into her, tapping her heels against Lilyan's thigh, the way Laurel did. Tiny fingers curled around one of hers, and she yearned to hold Laurel again. She stared into the fire and pressed her feet against the rug, rocking back and forth.

It seemed like an eternity before the men finally returned and entered the cabin.

Miriam reclaimed her daughter, cuddled her up on her shoulder, and motioned for Jedediah to follow her upstairs.

Lilyan gripped the arms of the rocker until her knuckles ached.

Nicholas knelt on the rug beside her. "It was not them. It was not them." His voice shook.

Nicholas slumped onto the rug, and she fell from the chair into his lap, sobbing from blessed relief. *Yet another futile trail. Where next?* Guilt overcame her bemoaning, and she grieved for the woman and child so callously treated and abandoned in the woods.

After crying herself out, Lilyan realized that the Greenes had edged their way out of the darkened cabin. Jedediah cradled Rebecca in his arms, and Miriam stood in the doorway holding a lantern, a quilt draped around her shoulders.

"Where are you going?" Lilyan's question came out so hoarse she cleared her throat several times.

"Figured we'd let you have the cabin. We'll sleep outside," Jedediah answered.

"We can't let you do that." Nicholas stood, helped her to her feet, and rested his hand on the small of her back

Miriam waved. "It's a fine night out. Besides, iffen it was left up to him, Jedediah would sleep outside every night. I had him fetch a bucket of water and put it on the hearth. There's cloths and some soap I made from goat's milk, so's you can clean up a bit. And I made the bed up nice for you. We'll see you in the mornin'."

Lilyan hurried to the doorway and watched them walk away.

"Thank you, Miriam," she called out and closed the door behind them. "Such kind and generous people."

She turned to find Nicholas at the fireplace, rummaging through the pile of cloths. "Bathing would be nice, don't you think?"

He held a bar of soap to his nose and sniffed. "Smells like lemons."

"I don't care what it smells like. I'm going to bathe."

It took her seconds to slip out of her boots and pull her shirt over her head. She flung the shirt across the rocker and started to untie her chemise when she looked up to find him staring at her. "You go stand watch at the door, please."

She slithered out of her breeches and kicked them away. Standing naked in front of the fireplace, she lathered a cloth with soap and began to wash.

"Are you watching?" she asked as she ran the warm, sudsy cloth down her arm.

He cleared his throat. "Yes, madam. I am."

She glanced at him and caught the crooked grin on his face as he took her in from head to toe. "I meant the door," she said as she smiled back.

When she had finished, she donned her shirt again. "Now you."

It took him less time to undress than it had taken her. Standing beside him, she opened the lid of the candle box nailed on the wall next to the fireplace, pulled out a taper, and lit it from the fire. She threw her clothes over her arm and started up the stairs, stopping halfway to watch her husband as he washed and then dried off and put on his shirt.

We've been married two years, and my heart still trips over itself at the sight of him.

The last time she saw him bathe, he had been sitting in the bathtub in front of the fire in their cabin with Laurel balanced on his chest. Laurel slapped her hands against the water and splashed it into his eyes. His comical faces sent their little girl into a fit of giggles.

How she longed for those special family times. And to look

upon her husband again with a desire free from the burden of grief and loss and guilt.

Reluctantly, she turned and finished her ascent.

Upstairs, she peeled back the medallion-patterned quilt of azure blues and maroons and admired the tiny, even stitches. Guessing it must be a treasured wedding present, it moved her to think that Miriam had offered her guests the best of her belongings. She dripped some of the hot wax onto a mound of dried wax on the corner of the nightstand and secured the candle to it. She slipped under the covers and placed a pillow at the foot of the bed for Nicholas. During the war, he had become so accustomed to sleeping on the ground, often without even a blanket, that he didn't like sleeping on a pillow. Instead, he preferred to rest his feet on it to keep his legs, too long for most beds, from dangling over the edge. When he came upstairs, she lifted the cover for him to slide in beside her.

She stretched her legs as far as she could. "Delicious. I only wish we had clean clothes to change into. But at least we bathed."

"Yes." He sniffed his armpit. "We used to smell like dirt. Now we smell like lemon dirt."

She leaned over and cupped her hand around the candle and blew it out. Laughter bubbled up inside her. "You sound so cross," she managed to say through her giggles.

Soon they both laughed so hard they shook the bed.

How can I be laughing when my daughter is out there, somewhere, experiencing God knows what? Her jubilance ceased as quickly as it had begun.

Nicholas pulled her close, tucked his knees up under hers, and draped his arm across her. His breath fanned the hair on the back of her neck. "It nettles you to laugh when our daughter is in danger?"

She nodded.

"Me too."

She lay still a few moments and listened to a mourning dove outside their window, its call in tune with her own deep melancholy. "Will we ever be truly merry again?"

As soon as she murmured the words, she regretted saying them aloud. But Nicholas's breathing had slowed to a steady, even pace. *He's asleep. Maybe he didn't hear me.*

Sometime later, lying on her side with her back pressed against her husband's, she stared out of the tiny window that provided a welcome breeze across the room. Stars sparkled like burnished sterling coins against the black velvet sky. She rolled onto her back, pushed up on her elbows, and glanced over her shoulder. Nicholas had fallen asleep almost the moment his head touched the mattress. But she was not so fortunate. Her thoughts simply would not still. She had succumbed to a fitful sleep several times during the night, only to awaken again with her shirt twisted into a knot around her hips.

She flipped over and watched her husband's chest rise and fall in his slumber, observing him as he lay in a partial shadow cast from the moonlight. His hands that could wield a knife with deadly accuracy—and yet gently rock a cradle. His arms that could sling an axe for hours—but also encircle his child and wife in a tender embrace. His broad shoulders that could bear the weight of a felled tree, and yet they provided a nestling place for his wife's head. His firm chin that jutted out in moments of white-hot anger—but also nuzzled into his daughter's feathery curls. Lips that shouted orders so harshly grown men cringed also whispered endearments to his wife in their most intimate moments. She regretted the furrow that creased his brow, the only outward sign of how much he missed his *koukla*—his little doll.

She lay on her back again and stared at the ceiling. If they failed to find their daughter, they would have to make a new life, learn to laugh again. If so, would there ever come a night when she didn't cry herself to sleep? A day when she woke without heartache? Somehow she doubted it. Yes, there probably would be other children—they had shared their hopes of having many—but no one could ever take Laurel's place.

This is too much.

Lilyan inched off the bed. Deciding not to dress and take the chance of waking Nicholas, she clutched her haversack to her chest and crept down the stairs. Kneeling on the rug in front of the smoldering fire, she prodded the embers with a piece of wood, then placed it on the resurrected flames. She searched inside the bag and found paper and charcoal and was soon immersed in her sketching. A couple of hours later, she finished just as she heard Nicholas moving about. The cabin had grown lighter.

He joined her downstairs and sat beside her. "You were up all night?"

She stretched her arms up over her head before she picked up the paper in front of her. "I worked on this."

Taking it from her, he leaned toward the fire to better see the images of the Greenes and their daughter. "They'll treasure it, I'm certain."

He stood, helped her up, and then cradled the side of her face to his chest and rested his chin on her head. "I love you. More than I could ever say. I can't take a breath that you're not a part of. No matter what happens, please, remember that."

She tightened her arms around his waist until they heard Rebecca chattering outside.

"Hurry and dress, Lilyanista."

Downstairs again, Lilyan sat next to Nicholas at the table. A few minutes after they downed the biscuits and ham Miriam had prepared, Nicholas led the horses into the yard. While Lilyan gave Miriam a hug, she pressed the drawing she had done—of the family who had become so precious to her—into her hand.

Miriam hugged her again and ran into the house. She returned with the white cover Lilyan had admired. "Here." She handed the blanket to Lilyan. "To wrap Laurel in when you take her home."

With tears burning the backs of her eyes, Lilyan clutched the blanket to her chest. "I ... Thank you," was all she could manage.

As they rode away, Lilyan twisted around to wave one last good-bye. Her heart resembled an abandoned canvas compared to the perfect picture of the Greenes.

Would her family ever be perfect again?

"Where do we go now?" she asked as she turned back around in the saddle.

"We backtrack. To pick up the trail Rider and Silas are following."

Hours later, Lilyan gritted her teeth, determined not to protest, but her back and neck muscles throbbed as if they had been ground underneath a grist stone. She wanted to cry—for many reasons. They had traveled the entire day without dismounting, except for the two times they stopped to care for the horses and once when Nicholas shot a rabbit. Their noon meal, eaten in the saddle, consisted of deer jerky and biscuits Miriam had packed for them, washed down with tepid canteen water. At least they had found the path they sought.

Lilyan noticed fewer and fewer birdcalls as the diurnal animals turned their territory over to the night watch, a depressing signal that yet another sun would set without her little one.

Is she well? Is she afraid? And what of Golden Fawn? Andrew must be nearly out of his mind.

The sound of a waterfall—not the powerful rush of a high mountain fall, but the murmur of cascades dancing over rocks—lifted her from her melancholy.

They came upon a pool at the base of a ledge where the water spilled over and lingered before it flowed downstream. Finally, her husband spoke the words she longed to hear. "We'll camp here for the night."

He dismounted, came to her side, and stood looking up at her. "You've done well this day. Not many of Marion's men could have fared better."

She'd done right to stifle her complaints.

When he lifted her down from her horse, her legs wobbled, and she wilted against him.

He tipped up her chin and brushed his thumb under her eye. "You're exhausted, yes? But if you could start a fire, I'll tend to the horses and prepare the rabbit."

She cupped his cheek in her hand and caressed his beard, now thick with several days' growth.

He turned his face and kissed her palm and then stepped back and smiled, a hint of regret in his eyes. "We must hurry, before night falls."

She followed his every step with her eyes as he hobbled the horses, realizing how fortunate she was to have won his love—this man, so confident, so steadfast.

He will find her. I know it.

They cooked and ate the rabbit, and both agreed it was the best-tasting meal they had eaten in a while. Stretched out on the bedroll she had placed next to the campfire, she gazed at the shadows of their bodies as they flickered across the trees around them.

"Nikki?"

"Hmm?" He used a stick to toy with a glowing pinecone that had escaped the flames.

"Do you know what I was thinking?"

He shoved the pinecone back into the coals and shook his head.

"I was thinking about how fortunate I am to have someone like you to love me."

"I'm the fortunate one."

She sat up. "I want to tell you—to assure you—I'm confident that if anyone can restore my daughter to me, it would be you."

"You do not fault me for failing to keep her safe?"

"Oh, Nikki." She jumped up, dove onto the blanket beside him, and ran her fingers across the deep furrow in his brow. "There is no fault, except that which lies at the feet of the men who did this evil. You're an excellent husband and father. Please, drive those thoughts from your mind." She pressed harder on his forehead as if to displace the thoughts herself and then kissed the small scar at the corner of his mouth.

Once Nicholas's muscles relaxed, Lilyan curled her body into his. They had been lying quietly when an itch crept up and down her arms and legs. She scrubbed her hands across her skin, but to no avail.

"Nikki?"

"Yes?" Drowsiness slurred his question.

"I must wash my clothes."

He snorted, awakened. "Most definitely."

"What?" She sputtered and sat up, looking down at his grinning face.

He leaned across her, hauled a saddlebag toward him, and searched through it. "Ah-ha!" He held up a slab of soap Miriam had packed for them.

He stood and held out his hand. "Come."

Ignoring his hand, she jumped up and ran for the pond, where she plopped down on the bank to tug off her leggings and boots.

"How wonderful to get those things off." She stood and dug her toes into the cool, damp moss. She looked down at her shirt. "And these clothes. I truly feel that if I took the breeches off, they could stand up by themselves."

Nicholas chuckled and tossed his boots beside hers. "I say we jump in as we are."

He took a running leap and dove in, showering her with droplets of water that sparkled from the light cast by the half-moon suspended in the clear night sky.

"Lilyan," he shouted as he broke back through the surface, "be careful—"

She dove into the water after him and came up sputtering, barely able to catch her breath from the shock.

"It's very cold," Nicholas finished his warning.

"Oh, my. It is that."

While her skin bristled from the frigid water, she paddled over to him. "Here, let me loosen your braid."

He turned around, and she untied the strip of rawhide, wrapped it around her wrist, and pushed her fingers through the plait until his hair flowed around his shoulders. "Where's the soap?"

He handed it to her over his shoulder. As they bobbed in the water, their bodies acclimated to the cold temperature. She lathered his hair, working in the lemon-scented froth, and then moved around in front of him to wash his beard. When she finished, he dipped his head back and rinsed off.

He took the bar from her. "Now you."

Soon her hair was free to float out over the rippling water, and she moaned with pleasure as Nicholas massaged her scalp. After he doused her hair until it squeaked between his fingertips, he rubbed soap over his shirt and breeches, pulled them off, and threw them onto a limb that draped out from the shore. She followed suit while he treaded water, waiting for her to hand him her clothes, which he folded across an overhanging branch. When she struggled with her chemise, he swam close and slipped it from her body.

Free from the restraints of her clothing, she swirled her arms at her sides and kicked her feet to stay afloat. "Oo-oo, the water feels like satin."

Nicholas, his broad shoulders gleaming in the moonlight, turned his back to the falls. "Come here, Lilyanista."

She obeyed, and as she drew near, she noticed a strange glow reflected in his eyes.

"Now, put your arms around my neck and close your eyes."

She did as he said, and he whirled them around until they faced away from the falls. He kept moving until their feet touched the ground and then he stood behind her, resting his hands on her shoulders.

"Look now, aga'pi mou."

She opened her eyes and caught her breath as one firefly after the next floated toward them across the water. The trail of lights, like miniature lanterns bobbing in the air, appeared to go on for miles. The tiny creatures hovered everywhere—near the ground, in bushes, in trees, and overhead—rivaling the stars.

"There must be thousands of them," she whispered. "Do you think Laurel is somewhere close, watching this too?" The thought pressed another mark into her already bruised heart, and she wrapped her arms around his neck again.

"It is my prayer."

"Nikki, love me. Make me forget this pain. Make us both forget. If only for a little while."

CHAPTER 6

Hriso mou—my golden one, my treasure

Two more days passed, and they still hadn't caught up with Silas and Rider, though Nicholas assured Lilyan they were closing in.

Late the second evening, they stopped at a trading post to refurbish their supplies and purchase some much-needed clothing. She stepped across the threshold, and it took a moment for her eyes to adjust to the dim interior. On one side of the rough-hewn walls, a row of wooden bins held sundries—shirts, breeches, moccasins, seal-skin hats, and bolts of cloth. A stone fireplace took up another side of the one-room establishment and was flanked with a variety of pots, pans, and utensils hanging from hooks. She wrinkled her nose at the cookware that looked as if it hadn't seen a brush in months.

On the opposite side from the fireplace, a couple of trappers slouched in chairs pulled close to a table. Cigar smoke clouded around their heads. Lilyan nearly choked as she inhaled the stench mixed with their sweat. In stark contrast to the blackened fringe on their oil and blood-stained jackets, one of them sported a brilliant white egret feather in his hat.

While Nicholas dropped a pack of deerskins and their saddlebags onto the counter, she sorted through a stack of homespun shirts, straining to listen as he questioned the proprietor.

"Any strangers, any … suspicious-looking men pass this way lately?"

The owner grinned, exposing a gold front tooth. "Hell, mister. Most people stopping in here are strangers. And a lot of them," he cocked his head toward the men sitting at the table, "are suspicious lookin'."

Nicholas leaned in closer. "Slavers?"

The man frowned and stroked his beard. "Don't hold with messin' in other people's business. But, there was a group of men. Passed by here a coupla' days back. Had a passel of Indian women and children with them."

Lilyan perked. She steadied herself against the counter and clutched the shirt in her hands.

Nicholas caught her glance. "Did you happen to see a white girl among them? About a year old? Red hair?"

The owner shrugged. "Sorry. They never really got close enough for me to see."

The air left Lilyan's chest so fast she dizzied.

Nicholas approached the trappers sitting at the table gulping down ale. With his back turned to her, she couldn't hear all that he said, but she noticed he stiffened when one of them reared back in his chair.

"Ain't none of your business, I said." The man's voice was loud and his words slurred. "Another," he yelled as he held up his empty mug.

"Better mind your p's and q's," the proprietor bellowed back. He struck a piece of chalk across a wooden plank mounted on the wall behind the counter. "One more and your tab's up."

"Shut your trap, old man," the other man shouted from beneath the hat he wore pulled down to shield his face. "Long as I'm payin', you bring 'em."

Nicholas turned on his heel and stood beside Lilyan.

She clasped his sleeve. "Should we leave?"

"We came here for supplies, so we'll get supplies." He gripped the handle of the knife strapped to his waist. "Take your time."

Despite his instruction, she hurriedly chose what she needed and put everything on the counter.

Nicholas untied his pack of buckskins. "How much?"

The proprietor brushed his hand across one of the skins, dug his fingers into the fur, and draped it across his arm. "Good quality. Good weight. A pound and three quarters each."

He put down the skin and spread out the blue blanket Lilyan wanted to purchase. One by one, he placed their other items on the blanket. "Two skins for the blanket. One for the four measures of powder and one for the box of flints. Two for the shirts. That's six."

Nicholas nodded. "We'll need a sack of flour, a sack of corn, a half-pound of sugar, a measure of salt, a half-pound of coffee, and a slab each of bacon and jerky."

"I'll throw all that in for another four. Ten altogether."

Nicholas pushed the skins toward him. "Deal then. That's the lot."

While the owner moved around behind the counter as he filled their order, Lilyan felt like she was being watched. She glanced over her shoulder to find the man with the white feather peering at her from under the brim of his hat. A bead of sweat trickled down her back, and her shoulder muscles bunched. She quickly stuffed the twine-wrapped packets inside her saddlebags.

Their purchase complete, Nicholas rolled up the shirts inside the blanket and took another look at the trappers. "I get the feeling they know more than they're telling."

The owner frowned. "They're a mean bunch. People say before the war, Regulators cleaned out all the outlaws from the backcountry. But taint' so. Them two is proof. Best you and the missus het out of here."

The trapper who had stared at Lilyan sat up in his chair and sneered. "Yeah. You'd best het on out."

Nicholas turned around slowly and rested his hand on the tomahawk tucked in his belt. "I didn't spend six years of my life fighting tyranny to be told when and where I can go." His voice got louder with the last words.

Lilyan's body tensed.

The man with the white feather held up his hand. "Don't get riled up. Josh here didn't mean nothin'."

Josh drooped back in his chair, held up his hands, and guffawed.

Nicholas, his jaw set and his body taut, slung the blanket and one of the saddlebags over his arm. "Got any fresh water?"

The owner nodded toward the door. "Rain barrel. Outside to the right."

Lilyan picked up the remaining saddlebag and led the way out the door. While Nicholas repacked the horses, she filled their canteens, keeping a wary eye on the tavern door. Finally, to her relief, they left, but she didn't relax until they were several miles away.

✳ ✳ ✳

The following days of their journey passed in a blur of repetition—waking before dawn, swilling down hardtack with tepid canteen water, hours in the saddle broken only to rest and water the horses, more riding, a hastily prepared and eaten supper, then collapsing bone weary onto bedrolls, and falling into a fitful sleep. By the fifth day, though Nicholas seemed to know where he was going, Lilyan empathized with the Israelites who had wandered in the desert. But the rigors of travel could not compare with the cruelty of her heartache and the wearing of her spirits as she struggled to remain optimistic about holding her darling girl again.

Mid-morning of the sixth day of their search, Nicholas stopped abruptly and leaned forward in his saddle. Cupping his hands around his mouth, he gave out a shrill whistle.

Lilyan jumped in the saddle and covered her ears. She hadn't heard that soul-piercing sound in a long time. Francis Marion had taught his partisans to signal each other with it in the swamps along the South Carolina coast. The first time she experienced it, Nicholas was escorting her and her dearest friend, Elizabeth, to safety among a group of camp followers and away from men seeking the reward for their capture. She and Nicholas had not yet married. *My sweet Elizabeth was still alive.* She sighed. It seemed a lifetime ago.

Nicholas whistled again. And then it came—the responding signal. He guided them toward the sound on a beeline through the forest, over a creek, up an embankment—whistle, response, whistle, response, until, finally, they spotted him.

"Samuel!" Nicholas shouted and drove his horse toward the Indian sitting astride a red-brown bay.

"Nicholas. Good to see you." The men clasped each other by the forearm.

"And you, Lilyan," he greeted as she drew near.

She smiled. "Samuel. We've missed you."

She loved her husband's best friend, who had fought at his side through so many battles that they often argued about who had saved whose life most often. A handsome man with a wide, square jaw and full lips, he wore moccasins, buckskin leggings, a breech cloth, and a drop-shoulder shirt. Over his shoulder he'd strapped a powder horn engraved with a carving of a black snake, identifying him as a Catawba, some of the fiercest and most feared warriors in the Carolinas.

"Callum sent someone to my village. Told me what happened." He glanced away and gripped the reins until his knuckles turned white. "I traveled three days to find you. The Cherokee were not happy to see a son of the flatheads in their camp. Still, they sent me your way. I doubled back from the cabin of the young people. Came across your trail sign and knew I was close."

"Thank you, my friend." Nicholas turned his horse in the direction from which they had come, and Lilyan followed.

"Which way?" Samuel moved his horse to the rear of their column.

"As you know, one party of men move southwest, the others—the ones we follow—move southeast. But, the ones we follow have split their course three times. We're following the trail Rider and Silas took. We're not far from them."

They rode farther in silence until Lilyan remembered something Samuel had said. "Nikki, what trail sign was Samuel talking about?"

He stopped and reached into the tree limb above him, bending a slender branch and twisting it in an *L* shape. "It's one of many signs we used when fighting with Marion."

Puzzled, she stared at the *sign*. "I recall—that terrible time when I was running from bounty hunters—we were in the middle of the backcountry, much as we are right now, and Andrew pointed out the two notches Indians had carved in trees to mark their path. I admit, it took a while for me to recognize them on my own. But this—" She looked up. "It doesn't look much different than any other branch hanging from the tree."

Samuel shifted his weight and cocked his head, exposing the shell woven into a braid behind his ear. "You have to know what to look for." He crossed one wrist over the other and leaned on his horse's neck. "Speakin' of which. Was somebody else followin' you besides me?"

"I hadn't picked up on it." Nicholas moved his horse forward. "Come. Let's press on."

As they entered a span of woods with sparse vegetation and trees, a wider trail opened, and Samuel guided his horse next to Lilyan's. "You're holding up?"

"I waver from wanting to sob, wanting to scream, and wanting to kill someone. Thank God I have Nicholas to keep me steady."

He splayed a hand across his chest. "My heart's sad for you."

She glanced away and pulled a breath through her nose. "My heart's broken."

"Know that I will stay until your daughter's found."

Though her lips trembled, she smiled at him. "I know, and I can't thank you enough."

Samuel was a good man. Even so, watching him with Nicholas brought back memories of their times with General Marion and his men. And of Elizabeth. Though Samuel had never spoken the words, Lilyan knew he had loved her beloved Cherokee friend. Elizabeth, in turn, glowed like a candle in his presence. But cruel, vile men had snuffed out her young life. At first, Lilyan's wretched grief had prevented her from seeing past her own loss. Later, Nicholas had advised her to avoid any mention of Elizabeth around Samuel. She followed his wise counsel, and Samuel had never broached the subject.

They had traveled about a mile when Nicholas motioned for Samuel to join him.

"What do you make of this?" He pointed toward his horse's hooves and the ground covered with a thick layer of leaves.

As Samuel glanced down, the sun lit the tips of the turkey feathers that adorned the crown of his hair. He studied the surrounding terrain and looked again at the forest floor.

She angled her horse beside them. "What?"

"The trail we follow continues. Looks like Silas and Rider veered west—sudden like," Samuel said, sweeping his arm out.

Nicholas ran his fingers through his beard. "They've got to be close. I say we hail them."

Curious, she watched Samuel sling his musket around in front of him. "Hail them?"

"Two shots. Reload, then one shot. That means, 'Where are you?' If we get the same signal back, that means, 'I'm here. What do you want?'" Samuel explained. "We sound back one shot to say we want to know where they are. Three shots means we're in trouble."

Nicholas readied his musket. "I'll fire the first round and reload. Then Samuel. Then you, Lilyan. You understand?"

"Yes." She swung her musket from her shoulder and pointed it toward the sky.

They executed the signal and waited, but not for long, as a response soon echoed through the woods.

"That way." Samuel pulled a pistol from his belt and discharged it.

They returned their firearms and headed due west.

Please, Lord, let this be good news.

They broached a clearing, and right away Lilyan saw the Forbses, Silas, and Rider. Her spirits soared when she spotted a cluster of Indian women and children, then plummeted when she realized Laurel was not among them.

Rider was the first to reach them as they dismounted. "I'm happy you found us."

Nicholas waved to the Forbes men headed their way. Robbie walked beside one of the girls who looked to be about five or six and who clutched his hand with both of hers.

"Samuel," Nicholas said, "meet Alexander Forbes and his sons. Gentlemen, this is my friend, Samuel Harris."

Samuel nodded to the men who looked him over.

Rider swept his arm toward the encampment. "Forbes and his sons rescued these here, the largest party. Seven women, eight children."

The brothers stood by as their father tipped his hat to Lilyan and slapped Nicholas on the back. "They dinna put up much of a fight. Some ran off like the mongrels they are."

"Cowards from start to finish." A chorus of *ayes* from Robbie's brothers followed his statement.

Forbes frowned and glanced over his shoulder. "Left them in a terrible way."

"Everyone is accounted for, except for Aponi, Salali and ..." Rider glanced toward Lilyan. "Golden Fawn and Laurel. We still don't know where they are."

Nicholas frowned and curled his fingers around Lilyan's. "Aponi and Salali?"

"Mother and child." Rider pointed to a woman sitting with the others, half her face swollen and covered in purplish bruises. "Chenoa's sister and niece."

Mother and child. Sister and niece. Two people who loved and were loved. Is there no end to this sadness? Lord, please draw near.

"I'm afraid I must tell you news that I truly don't want to speak." Nicholas tightened his grip. "Days ago, we found two bodies. I'm pretty sure they were Aponi and her child."

"How did they die?" Rider asked in a low voice.

"We couldn't tell." Nicholas glanced away to stare at the sky. "The animals had gotten to them."

Lilyan gasped. Until now, she had been spared that detail, and, by the look in her husband's eyes, he would have liked for it to stay that way.

He freed Lilyan's hand, reached into his haversack, and pulled out a fist-sized pouch tied onto a rawhide string. "The woman's medicine bag."

Lilyan caught a glimpse of a tiny beaded butterfly worked into the leather. Nicholas was right about the dead woman—Aponi meant butterfly.

Rider took it and crouched beside Chenoa, resting his hand on her shoulder. He spoke with her, and when he gave her the pouch she began to wail, clasping the last remnant of her sister and beating it against her breast. He returned, his teeth clenched.

"Do you know what this means?" Nicholas straightened. "The trail we were following, the one we left to join you here? It has to be Laurel and Golden Fawn."

Rider nodded. "Makes sense. The women said they were separated early on."

Nicholas gripped Lilyan by the shoulders. "They're very near. I know it."

Newfound hope rushed through her body. "Then let's go."

"But Da?" Robbie motioned to the girl beside him, stopping everyone as they made to leave. "Who will tend to them? Some won't make it if they're not cared for."

All eyes turned to Nicholas, who still held Lilyan. He returned their stares and then searched her eyes for an answer to Robbie's question. "What say you? 'Tis a decision I'll not make."

She pictured her baby girl, her face smiling, her arms reaching. And then she considered the little girl holding Robbie's hand, her forlorn face a sad testament to her ordeal. Someone had to stay and care for the ones who had stared evil in the face and been so horribly damaged. Someone with a gentle hand, sympathy, and care. A woman's touch was needed here. Looking again at the little girl and at the others huddled close by, she said, "I'll stay."

Nicholas enfolded her in his arms. "Hriso mou," he murmured.

He stood back, and Lilyan furrowed her brow at the unfamiliar endearment.

"My golden one, my treasure," he interpreted and then kissed her temple before turning and shouting his orders. "Robbie. You, Rider, and Silas stay. They will need your protection. The rest of you men, come with me. Take as few rations as possible. We travel fast."

Samuel and Nicholas mounted their horses and waited while the others made their good-byes.

"Robbie." Forbes clasped his son's shoulder. "'Tis a mighty task you've been given. The captain entrusts his wife to your care. His wife, lad," he emphasized. "And these poor unfortunates ..." He looked toward the Indians. "You show them what we Forbeses are made of. Aye?"

They circled together, the father and the older brothers laid their hands on Robbie, and they prayed for safety and the grace to be together again as a family.

The men departed quickly, leaving Lilyan listening to their fading hoof beats and lifting up her own prayer. *That's what I ask, too, Lord. To be together again with my family.*

CHAPTER 7

The medicine bag is sacred, guarded, and very personal. Some may include sage, sweetgrass, and tobacco, along with other items of pleasant memories or meaning gathered over time, prayed over, and blessed. No one else must touch it or see its contents. It brings Peace and Balance, and when one walks on to the Rim, the medicine bag goes with them.
Cherokee Saying

"Three days and still no word." Chenoa wrapped a cloth around the handle of a kettle sitting on a rock next to the fire. She filled a tin cup and handed it to Lilyan.

"Yes." *I have counted every minute of them.* Lilyan blew on the dark brown coffee and took a sip. The brew was strong, just what she needed.

Chenoa sat beside her by the fire, the damaged side of her face exposed.

Lilyan gingerly touched the woman's jaw. "You're healing well."

"On the outside. But not here." She pressed her hands to her heart and then dropped them to her sides.

Lilyan covered Chenoa's hand with hers, and they sat quietly and watched the boys and girls play stickball. Some laughed out loud and some giggled. Two of the girls remained wary, though, often scanning the woods, listening for the men who had invaded their lives and destroyed their innocence to return. One of them, who clutched a rag doll under her arm, darted glances at Silas, who stood watch, his ever-ready musket laid across his arm.

Chenoa picked up a small sack of corn and poured the kernels onto a flat rock. Using another rock, she began to grind the corn into meal.

Another woman, Dyami, came to the fire and greeted them with a smile. "Mausi is much better today." She bent down to examine the trout roasting on Y-shaped sticks next to the coals. She poked their shiny pink underbellies that crackled and split, and an enticing aroma wafted throughout the encampment. "Your medicines are working, Lilyan. She is ready to travel."

Lilyan studied Mausi, who laid on her side and watched the children, a faraway look on her face. In her mid-thirties, she had been the one who, at first, had fought the hardest. For her punishment, she was brutally beaten and nearly starved to death as a lesson to the others. If the women didn't move fast enough, if they displayed the smallest sign of rebellion, if they were heard whispering, Mausi paid the consequences. As a single consolation to them all, one of their captors would bear to his grave a slash across his face from his ear to his chin, ripped open by a bear claw Mausi kept in her medicine pouch.

How ironic, Lilyan mused, that someone so fierce, so courageous, would have a name that meant *plucks flowers*.

She heard a burst of laughter and turned to see one of the boys pointing to Robbie, who struggled to blow into the end of a six-foot-long section of green river cane.

Robbie's cheeks grew bloody red from his efforts. "Try as I might, I canno' get the gist of this bloody instrument."

Rider grinned as he leveled the blow gun and repeated his instructions. "Once more, my friend, and you will have it."

Robbie sucked in a deep breath, pressed his mouth to the end of the gun, and blew. The ten-inch dart fletched with bull thistledown didn't go very far. But it went far enough to bring a smile to his face.

Rider slapped him on his shoulder. "It was no harder for you to learn this than for me to master your longbow. We will hunt together soon. You with my blow gun. I with your longbow. Yes?"

Robbie retrieved his arrows, Rider gathered his darts, and they joined the women by the fire.

"When do we eat?" Robbie pulled his longbow and quiver from his shoulder.

Dyami snickered. "So like young men. Ready to gobble everything in sight save a deer's tail."

They looked so sheepish, Lilyan took pity on them. "Almost ready."

Silas approached. "Your watch, Rider." He accepted a cup of coffee from Chenoa and sat down with a groan.

"Save me something." Rider secured his musket across his chest and loped away to the other side of the clearing.

"Robbie, I watched you show Rider how to use your longbow. How did you come to choose such a weapon?" Lilyan asked.

"My mother is English. Her great-great-grandfather was a forest ranger for the king. The men in her family have passed the longbow on to each generation."

Lilyan positioned a tin plate underneath the spit, pulled off one of the fish, and handed it to Robbie. "You're quite good at it."

Robbie's face flushed. "Kindly spoken, Mrs. Xanthakos. But it is you I wonder about."

"How so?" She licked her fingers and watched him pull a chunk of fish from its bones and pop it into his mouth. He ate with the abandon of a growing young man, and she wondered if God would bless her with sons. She pictured an older Laurel walking among the grapevines, holding her little brother's hand ... or running about the yard with a passel of brothers playing ninepins. Chills of despair shot through her body, and she shivered.

Robbie swallowed and washed down the fish with a cup of water. "You seem to understand so much about getting along out here."

"My father was a trapper and took me with him when I was a young girl." She fixed her gaze on bits of fish smoldering on the white coals of the fire. "And then there was a time when I had to use those skills to stay alive."

Silas leaned closer. "You said something like that. Once before. Back at the Cherokee village. About you being a fugitive?"

"What!" Chenoa exclaimed.

Lilyan wiped her hands down her skirt and pondered a moment, hesitant to relive the memories she'd struggled two years to suppress.

"I grew up in Charlestown. And when the British took over the city, I joined a group of patriots doing whatever I could for our cause."

She picked up a stick and scribbled in the dirt near her foot. "Elizabeth—my most cherished friend—and I accepted a mission at the plantation of a loyalist."

The memory of Mrs. Melborne's face makes me ill.

"She hosted parties for high-ranking British officers. I was to paint a mural for her. But it was a ruse for gathering information. One night, one of the officers—a vile man—attacked Elizabeth. He tried to harm her in the most degrading way a man can injure a woman."

Chenoa glanced at Mausi and scowled.

"I came upon them but wasn't strong enough to make him stop. He slung me away, and I fell down some steps. I grabbed the closest thing to me—a statuette—and ..." She snapped the twig in half. "I hit him with it. I killed him."

"You did what you had to do, Lilyan," said Chenoa, who took hold of Mausi's hand. "If only I could have had the courage to do the same for my friend."

Lilyan appreciated Chenoa's words. Others, including herself, had voiced the same sentiments. Nevertheless, the burden of guilt remained.

Lilyan shifted her attention back to her audience. "Turns out, he was the son of an earl. From a very rich and prominent family, who put a bounty on our heads. A huge bounty. A king's ransom, someone called it."

She threw the stick pieces into the fire and brushed the dirt from her hands. "Nicholas and Samuel helped us get away and under the protection of Francis Marion. But the bounty hunters found us." She chewed on her bottom lip. "They killed Elizabeth."

The dreaded memory surfaced once again—Samuel carrying her friend, her lifeless body covered in blood. A tide of pain washed over her and threatened to tow her under.

"I grieve with you," said Chenoa, clasping the medicine bag around her neck.

Lilyan nodded in acknowledgment, then glanced down at her wedding band. "By that time, Nicholas and I had married. Because he was so concerned for my safety, he sent me away. To a Cherokee village—Elizabeth's and Golden Fawn's home in the mountains. It was on that journey through the backcountry that I learned to survive."

"Did the bounty hunters give up then?" Robbie asked.

"No. One caught up with us—Andrew and Callum were with me—and he captured me. But I got away."

"Huzzah, Mrs. Xanthakos!" Robbie said.

"It was then that Callum and Golden Fawn hatched a plan to feign my death and let it be known in Charlestown that I had died."

Robbie snorted, his dark auburn eyebrows arching toward his hairline. "And here I thought you were someone who needed our protection, when you have lived more adventures than I could ever imagine."

Painful, tortuous adventures that still disturb my sleep.

Rider slung his musket up onto his shoulder and took aim. "Someone's coming," he yelled.

Everyone jumped up, and Chenoa and Dyami called out for them to gather around Mausi's pallet. Chenoa clasped a rock in each hand. Dyami wielded a stick. Lilyan ran to her bedroll, picked up her musket, and stood with them.

"'Lo the camp," came a shout from the woods.

"It's Nicholas!" Lilyan exclaimed and dropped her weapon.

And Laurel?

Her husband was the first to enter their camp, staring straight ahead, his shoulders set.

Why won't he look at me?

She spotted the woman mounted behind him, her arms clasped around his waist. "Golden Fawn!" she shouted and took off running. At first she looked at Nicholas, then at Golden Fawn, then from one rider to the next in the column, searching for her daughter. She reached them as Nicholas pulled Golden Fawn from his horse and set her on the ground.

She clasped her sister-in-law by the shoulders. "Where's Laurel? Where's my baby?"

Golden Fawn looked hesitantly at Lilyan and whispered, "Do I know you?"

CHAPTER 8

When he thunders, the waters in the heavens roar;
he makes clouds rise from the ends of the earth.
He sends lightning with the rain
and brings out the wind from his storehouses.
Jeremiah 10:13

Lilyan, Nicholas, and Rider watched the women gather Golden Fawn into their midst as each tried to cajole her into remembering them and their families waiting at home.

"She does not know me," Rider spoke in a barely controlled whisper. "Her own brother!"

He leaned closer. "Nu-da?"

Nicholas looked to his wife for an explanation.

"Insane," she interpreted.

"No, not insane." Nicholas rubbed the back of his fingers across his jaw. "I saw this during the war when men took a blow to the head. They could not recall anything from their past. Not even their own names. Amnesia, the doctor called it."

"There *is* a large purplish lump at the base of her neck," Lilyan noted, still trying to overcome her bitter disappointment. Where was her daughter? Who was caring for her? Was she afraid or even aware of what was happening to her?

"Will she remember again?" Rider asked.

Nicholas held his hands out, palms up, and shrugged. "I believe so, from what I witnessed during the war. But I can't say for sure. I don't think anyone can."

She must.

Lilyan clinched her fists at her sides. "But when? The longer we wait … How will we find Laurel now?"

She looked over her shoulder at her sister-in-law and turned back around. "Nikki, I love her. You know I do. And I don't want to seem callous. But …" She noticed how much her hands trembled. "I want my little girl back. What if she never …?"

She could barely see his face through the tears that swam in her eyes. She scrubbed them away with the back of her hand.

"Come." Nicholas took her by the elbow and guided her away from the campsite.

He sat with her on a fallen tree trunk. "We have a plan. You must go back home—"

"But—"

"Hear me out," he said, his voice raised.

Lilyan blanched. Already she did not like the sound of the plan.

"Please." He spoke more softly.

"All right."

"We found Golden Fawn at a tavern in a small settlement not far from here. The keeper said someone chanced upon her wandering in the woods. That is where we will begin."

"There's no more trail to follow, is there?"

"No. But a settlement means more people, more witnesses who may have seen Laurel."

Lilyan's heart lay like a rock in her chest. *My child is slipping away from me.*

He searched her eyes. "You cannot … you must not … give up.

You hold the key to our quest."

"Golden Fawn."

"Take her home. Be gentle. Be patient. You and Andrew and Callum make her feel safe again. Maybe she'll remember."

"And if she does?"

"Send someone to the tavern. We'll use it as our base. Silas, Rider, and Robbie will accompany you. When you reach home, they'll continue on and return the women and children to their village. They'll stay with you and be at the ready to bring us news. The rest of us will continue fanning farther and farther out from the tavern." He dropped down on one knee. "You will do this?"

Another crossroads, another gut-wrenching decision. Continue on or abandon the search? *Fulfill my own needs or care for Golden Fawn?* Who else knew her well enough, loved her enough, to nurse her back to health? She was their only source of knowledge. Like reeds caught in a raging river current, her thoughts swayed back and forth until she looked into Nicholas's eyes and realized what she must do.

"I will." She gently massaged the line across his brow.

"Pray for us?" she asked as she slid to her knees beside him.

Afterward, they returned to the campsite, and Lilyan's spirit ached. But her courage was girded for the task ahead.

* * *

The journey home proved arduous, necessitating frequent stops for rest, especially for Mausi. Near starvation and mistreatment by their captors had worn down the children, and the trek taxed their endurance. Their constant pleas for food kept the men busy hunting and foraging. Screaming nightmares often disturbed the camp.

Would the children's lives ever be normal again? Lilyan's prayers contained many petitions for healing.

She alternated riding her horse and walking alongside Golden Fawn as she rode. Lilyan seized every opportunity to relate tidbits of information about her background, her husband, where she lived, and she even showed her some of the sketches of Laurel.

But to no avail. Her sister-in-law grew more morose with each passing day, constantly apologized for her inability to remember, and voiced the notion that Laurel's disappearance was her fault.

Even the weather reflected her gloom. Mid-afternoon, black clouds rolled in, throwing the already dense forest into an eerie darkness. The women and children bunched closer together and stared over their shoulders, ready to run.

Silas approached Lilyan. "A storm's coming. No sense in trying to make it any farther today. We'd best make some shelter and ride it out."

"Whatever you think best, Silas."

She helped Golden Fawn dismount and passed the word to gather firewood and branches for a lean-to. Silas strung a tarp between two trees for a roof. Working together quickly, within a few minutes they had built a shelter with a thick, pine needle floor. They'd secured it on three sides and left an opening for the smoke from the fire to escape. Silas and Robbie fashioned a shelter for the horses and put cloths over the horses' eyes. No one wanted to deal with a frantic animal in the imminent storm.

At the first rumble of thunder, the children scurried into the shelter. There was a flash of lightning followed by a boom of thunder and a rush of rain. One of the girls tucked her body next to Lilyan, who wrapped her arm around her and rubbed the gooseflesh from her arms.

Is someone consoling my baby through this storm? Is Nicholas somewhere safe and dry? Lord, please protect my dear ones.

Chenoa shooed a couple of the boys farther away from the flames. Silas joined them, followed by Rider, who tossed three rabbits on the ground near the fire.

Lilyan scanned the woods. "Where's Robbie?"

Silas shuffled to the side of the shelter. "He's on the lookout." He pulled the rim of his hat down over his eyes. "I'm going to rest a bit."

How anyone could sleep through the storm that raged around

them was beyond Lilyan.

For a while, everyone remained still and quiet. The only sounds inside came from Golden Fawn and Dyami's knives as they dressed the rabbits and from Rider's axe as he fashioned a spit over the flames.

Golden Fawn broke the silence. "Why is it I can't remember my own name, but I do remember how to prepare a rabbit?"

Lilyan patted her sister-in-law's shoulder. "Be patient. Your memory will return soon."

When it does, will she be able to lead us to Laurel?

A bolt of lightning cracked, and the children screamed and clasped their hands over their ears. Lilyan had to force her own hands to remain in her lap.

From the back of the shelter came the sweetest singing voice Lilyan had ever heard. She turned to see that it was Mausi, and though Lilyan couldn't understand many of the words, she knew it had to be a lullaby. The other women and a few of the children joined in, breaking the tension. Within a few minutes, the thunder and lightning abated, but the rain continued to pour. Chenoa, a mischievous smile lighting her face, jumped up and pulled a couple of the children outside of the lean-to, and they danced and played in the downpour. Enticed by the giggles, everyone except Rider and Silas joined them in their merry celebration.

Glad for a chance to wash her clothes, Lilyan pulled the tail of her shirt from her breeches, rubbed up and down the sleeves, and ran her fingers through her tangled hair. She laughed and blinked up at the sky through soaked eyelashes, then stuck out her tongue to catch the raindrops. One of the girls pointed at her and laughed.

What a wonderful sound. Thank you, Lord.

Later, after eating a meal of corncakes and rabbit, Lilyan and Golden Fawn decided to fetch firewood.

"Don't go far," Rider warned as they left the encampment.

Lilyan looked up at the pine branches drooping with the weight of the rain. "Everything is so green after the storm. So clean."

Golden Fawn nodded and continued on in silence. When their path narrowed, she stepped in front of Lilyan.

Lilyan spotted a fox peeping out at them from under a mountain laurel. They both jumped when a deer crashed through the trees and bounded across their path. Her nerves now on edge, she wanted to turn back, but she heard the rushing waters of a stream.

Golden Fawn dodged an overhanging branch, pushed it out of the way, and it showered raindrops down on her shoulders. "I saw some blackberries earlier. Near the banks. Why don't we pick some for the children?"

They had already gone farther from the camp than Lilyan had intended. But this was the first time her sister-in-law had shown any enthusiasm about anything. Against her better judgment, she agreed. They came upon a swollen stream. Its water roared from the recent deluge.

"There." Golden Fawn pointed toward the bank of the stream. "Under the ferns."

Lilyan took a step forward but was stopped short by an iron grip around her waist and the blade of a knife pressed against her neck.

"Lookie what we got here," the stranger said as he pulled her against his chest. A foul odor enveloped her.

Her eyes wide with fright, Golden Fawn started to run away, but another man ran to her at lightning speed and threw her face down in the mud. She struggled, but he ground his moccasin into the small of her back.

He took hold of her by the elbows and hauled her up to face him.

With the wild-eyed stare of a trapped animal, Golden Fawn twisted and turned, kicked at the man's shins, and clawed her fingers as if to rake her nails across his face.

"If it ain't my sweet little Cherokee maiden. The one I told you about, Josh. The one that got away from me." The words slithered from his mouth. He yanked his captive's hands behind her back. "Settle down, or I'll have to club you," he growled.

Josh? Lilyan stiffened. *The white egret feather. The men from the store.*

"You was right, Jasper. Nice figure of a woman. But them scars. I'd have to turn out the lights to bed that one." Josh snorted, and Lilyan's stomach quivered at the stench of his fetid breath. "This one, though, is right fine. We're gonna have us a time."

Dear Lord, save us.

Lilyan thrashed and kicked back against Josh's shins, but he only cinched his vise-like arm around her ribcage—so tight she had trouble breathing.

Josh chuckled. "Calm down, missy. Won't do you no good to fight me."

Golden Fawn breathed in huge gulps and searched Jasper's face. She looked at Lilyan and back at him, her face blank.

"Come on. It ain't been that long." Jasper sneered. "You had that mewling little baby with you."

Laurel! Lilyan's heart pounded louder than the stream bounding over the rocks. "The little girl? Where is she?"

"I gave her away. Last time I saw her she was ridin' off in a wagon." Jasper lifted an eyebrow. "What's it to you?"

"She's my daughter."

"Well, now. Makes things interesting, don't it?"

Lilyan couldn't stop trembling. "Please, sir. Please. Who did you give her to?"

Jasper clasped Golden Fawn's forearms and shook her. "How come you didn't tell her?"

Golden Fawn continued to stare quizzically at him while her eyes swam in unshed tears.

"She didn't tell me because she can't remember. She lost all memory of what happened."

Jasper chortled. "Well, I did hit her hard enough to knock the sense out of her. Would've hung onto her too, if some people

hadn't happened by. Shame too. Cause I had some plans for her."
He rocked his hips back and forth. "O-o-o, it hurts just thinking
about it."

Lilyan shuddered at his vile gesture.

"You think I can knock the sense back in?" Jasper shook Golden
Fawn with such force, her head bobbled back and forth.

"Leave her be," Lilyan shouted. Her neck stung where the knife
dug in and broke the skin.

"Do what she says!" Robbie yelled at them from across the
stream, his long bow stretched taut, aimed at Golden Fawn's
captor, ready to fire.

Josh slid his knife closer to Lilyan's ear. "I'll kill her. Won't think
twice about it neither."

Lilyan rose up on her toes, stretching away from the knife.

"Release her." Robbie swiveled his body and re-aimed. "If you
don't, I'll put this arrow straight through your eye."

Lilyan gasped as Robbie's arrow whistled past her head. The
crack of Josh's skull followed a squishing sound as the arrow
ripped into his cheek. He screamed and fell backward, spinning her
around to face the gruesome sight of an arrow protruding through
his eye socket and out the back of his head. Her stomach heaved,
and she retched, gripping a bush to keep her balance. She looked
up in time to see her sister-in-law stomp on her captor's shin and
push him away. He bellowed out his anger but took off running
when an arrow flew at him from another direction. Too stunned to
move, Lilyan watched as the woods swarmed with fierce Indians
intent on catching Jasper.

She staggered toward Golden Fawn, and they both crumpled to
the ground and hugged each other as they watched Robbie sprint
across a fallen log, fording the river. Lilyan pushed herself up, and
on wobbly legs she ran to him with her arms open. He threw down
his bow and they embraced.

"Robbie. Thank you, dear Robbie," she muttered and buried
her face in his neck.

Robbie stepped back and surprised her with a face as angry as a thundercloud. "You are hurt." He brushed at the blood streaking down her neck.

She touched her collar and examined her bloody fingertips. "It's a scratch."

Golden Fawn joined them, and they huddled together until they heard the whoops of the Indians rise to a crescendo.

Lilyan hunched her shoulders at the gruesome sound. "The men from the village?"

"Yes. And they have him." Robbie clinched his fist. "They will do what I should have done."

Lilyan panicked. "But he has information about Laurel!"

She turned to head toward the sounds in the distance, but Robbie clasped her elbow. "No, Lilyan. It is not a place for you. They're out for blood vengeance and will not listen to reason."

Defeated, she put her arm around her sister-in-law. They returned to camp, where news of the slavers' deaths was greeted with cheers.

Later that evening, with the demeanor of a highland chieftain, Robbie paced in front of the subdued band of survivors that he had designated into groups of three. "From now on, you will watch out for each other. You will go nowhere without the other two."

"But what about … times of privacy?" Embarrassed for asking such a question, Golden Fawn stared at the toes of her moccasins.

Several of the women tittered.

Robbie jabbed his fists into his hips. "Nowhere," he reiterated, a frown knitting his brow, his face beet red.

The look he gave Lilyan was intense. "No one will be injured again on my watch. God willing."

At that moment, Lilyan caught a glimpse of the man Robbie would grow to be—a man of spirit, of courage and integrity. A leader and a man of God.

Over the next two weeks, with Robbie as their recognized "chief" coupled with the deaths of their tormentors, the children broke free of their fears, often dancing and singing, eager to reach home.

Lilyan held out hope that once her sister-in-law was wrapped in her husband's arms, once she sat in her own rocker by her own fireplace, her memory would return.

That did not happen.

CHAPTER 9

anhdadia, I remember
Cherokee

Golden Fawn's condition shocked Andrew into a stoic silence. The tale of what happened and what had almost happened was difficult for Lilyan to relate, but she was certain he and Callum would want to know. Her old protector reacted as she expected, slamming doors and stomping up and down the porch, finally swinging up an axe and heading toward the woodpile. In two days he cut enough firewood to last them half a winter.

Two nights later, Andrew saw Golden Fawn to bed before he joined Lilyan and Callum on the porch. "She still does not know me. I've been praying with all my might, but I need to do something. What are we to do, Sissy?"

"Nicholas suggested we be gentle and patient. Do what we can to make her feel safe again."

Callum leaned forward in his rocker. "Sound advice. I agree."

Andrew sat on the top step of the porch and rubbed the back of his neck. "How do we go about that?"

"I know your frustration, Andrew. On our journey here, I strived to talk to her about things I thought would help her remember. But the more I tried, the more unsettled she became."

She left the rocker, sat beside her brother, and draped her arm over his shoulder. "Let us limit our conversations to everyday concerns. Allow her to go about her daily routine and do what she did before the kidnapping." She leaned back against a post. "Pray God that I glean some peace from the same."

Andrew held her hand as his eyes roamed the mountain peaks and scoured the valley below. He ground his teeth so hard that a muscle in his jaw bulged.

* * *

Lilyan hated to witness her brother's torment, which only increased with each passing day. He adored his young wife. But they were newlyweds, not yet married a year, and they still danced around each other's feelings. Knowing what to say and do became a challenge for him. He made one decision that gave Lilyan misgivings; he had chosen to sleep on a pallet on the floor in front of their fireplace rather than with his wife, who looked at him as if he were a stranger. But, she determined, it was his choice to make and really none of her business.

The homecoming had proven difficult for Lilyan, too, entering their cabin, empty without her husband and child. Remembrances of Laurel were scattered about in every room—her tiny red velvet shoes by the hearth, a wooden rabbit Callum had whittled for her, and a pile of folded diapers on a chair. She had intended to put the diapers away, since Laurel didn't need them anymore; although, on that terrible day, she had sent a couple of them along with Golden Fawn.

One morning, feeling particularly tearful, she picked up the padded pudding cap from her rocking chair and sat, burying her face into the material in hopes of catching a whiff of Laurel's scent. It *was* an odd-looking garment—a quilted pink velvet hat lined with a thick layer of horse hair and ties for under the chin. It would cushion Laurel's head if she fell while learning to walk. She recalled the first time she secured it on her daughter's head.

Callum had had a fit. "Such mollycoddling. Never heard of such a thing. The lassie needs to learn how to come back from a fall. But she can't do that unless she bangs her head once in a while."

The first time Laurel stumbled and hit her head, she had held up her arms to Callum, her bottom lip quivering. He had avoided Lilyan's eyes as the unhappy little girl fell asleep cuddled against his chest. And that was the last complaint she heard from him about the pudding cap.

Lilyan slumped back in the rocker. In her short life, their darling child had already left her imprint on their lives. *Please, Lord, let her come back to us.*

* * *

Two weeks passed without news from Nicholas or any promising sign from Golden Fawn. Lilyan struggled for patience, but it was like waiting for the first drop of syrup to bubble up and slide down the side of a maple tree and into a bucket. Ever so slowly … drip by drip by drip. Finally, one morning she asked Rider to fetch his mother in hopes that she might help restore Golden Fawn's memory.

Days later, standing at the bottom of the cabin steps, Lilyan warmly greeted the woman with a hug. "Robin, welcome to my home."

Lilyan admired Robin's wrinkle-free skin and her eyes the color of cattails in the fall. "Goodness, you could be Golden Fawn's sister, instead of her mother."

Robin's cheeks turned pink. "Thank you for inviting me, Lilyan." A frown etched her flawless skin. "Where is my daughter? May I see her?"

Lilyan heard a gasp behind her and turned to find Golden Fawn hovering in the doorway, poised to flee like her namesake.

"S-te-si!" Robin called out and ran up the steps, arms open wide.

Upon reaching her daughter, she clutched her to her breast and murmured in Cherokee. After finally realizing that her embrace was

73

not returned, Robin stepped back and cupped her hand around Golden Fawn's cheek and caught a tear with her thumb. She ran her hands up and down her daughter's forearms and looked deep into her eyes. Tears spilling down her face, Golden Fawn traced her fingers across Robin's forehead, across her eyebrows, and down her cheeks.

Robin dropped her chin to her chest and then pressed her cheek to Golden Fawn's, where their tears mingled.

The bittersweet reunion chilled Lilyan, who scrubbed the hairs standing up on her arms. *Will my Laurel know me after so much time has passed?*

"I was told my mother was coming to see me. Are you ... are you her?" Golden Fawn choked on the words.

Robin sighed and pressed her forehead to her daughter's. "You truly do not know me, little one?"

Golden Fawn's shoulders began to shake with her sobs.

Robin fondled the plait of hair that draped across Golden Fawn's shoulder. "Shhh. Don't cry. It will come to you in time."

That evening, after Andrew and Golden Fawn had retired, Robin joined Lilyan at the table and handed her a package. "Thank you for loving my daughter. Please accept this as a small token to give you hope and to raise your spirits."

"What a lovely surprise." Lilyan turned the gift over and over. "Robin, before I open this, I must ask something I've often wondered. Why do you and your children speak with British accents?"

Robin cocked her head and shrugged. "Your question surprises me. It's not something I've been asked before. But, our people were always close allies with the British, who, despite the war, are still welcome in our homes." She smiled. "Also, we were taught to speak English by a missionary from London."

"That does explain it." Lilyan untied the twine and rolled open the cloth wrapping, exposing a pair of child-sized moccasins. She caught her breath, and her vision blurred.

"A gift. From one mother to another whose daughters are lost to us, though only for a little while, I am certain."

"They're perfect." She cradled the tiny shoes in her lap. "Excuse me a moment." She went to her bedroom, where she gathered a pair of Nicholas's moccasins and a pair of hers and placed them side by side next to the bed. After rubbing her fingers across the intricate bead work on Laurel's new moccasins, she wiggled them into the space between the other shoes.

One day they would all be home again. They would slip off their shoes and place them just as they were now. One day.

When she returned to Robin, the woman rested her elbows on the table and leaned forward. "Now. If you would be so kind. Please, tell me what happened to my daughter. Everything. I know Andrew left some things out."

Lilyan spent the next hour relaying the gruesome story. In that telling, once again she refreshed the details of the nightmare that haunted her sleep and found her waking at dawn, sobbing into her pillow.

Two days later, Robin returned to her village, still bewildered that her only daughter did not know her and wishing hot coals upon the heads of the men who had harmed her.

The following day, Lilyan and Golden Fawn boiled bayberries in a huge cast-iron pot in the courtyard of their compound. Golden Fawn stirred the berries while Lilyan skimmed the surface of the mixture and poured the waxy green scum into candle molds fixed with wicks.

Golden Fawn stopped stirring and breathed in through her nose. "It smells so sweet."

Lilyan took in another gulp of air and pressed her hand to her stomach. "Almost too sweet. It's making me ill."

Panic crossed Golden Fawn's face, and she dropped the paddle. "Can I do anything for you?"

"No. It'll pass."

"Why don't you go inside? I can finish this. Truly, you look as pale as when we faked your death."

They both jumped at the same time.

"You remember!"

"I do!"

They hugged each other, but Golden Fawn pulled back, frowning. "But only that. Is that how it will happen? Coming in bits and pieces?"

Later that night, as Lilyan lay in bed, she considered that question. There wasn't a doctor within miles, and her limited medicine kit contained nothing in it—no herbs, no special remedies—to revive one's memory, to fight amnesia. Should she send for a doctor? As she blew out the candle on her nightstand, she decided she would check into it.

After tucking the covers under her chin, she closed her eyes. But the sleep she longed for evaded her as visions of Laurel filled her mind.

My darling girl, where are you? Are you safe? Are you hungry? Has another tooth broken through your gums and Ma isn't there to rub them with chamomile tea?

Nikki, I need you so.

A desperate yearning struck her, and she shook as hot tears streamed down her cheeks and neck until they soaked her pillow. Half an hour later, her body spent, she drifted into a fitful sleep.

Someone screamed. Lilyan jerked up from her pillow, fuzzy-headed. She threw off the covers and sat on the side of the bed. There it was again. She jumped up and ran into the front room, where she heard more shrieking coming from the direction of Andrew's cabin.

"Laurel," came an anxious shout. "Laurel!"

She took off running and met Rider and Robbie, knives in hand, racing across the courtyard. She shoved open the cabin door to find Andrew trying to console his wife, who spoke and cried at the same time.

Golden Fawn stared at Lilyan, her eyes wide with fright, her face pale. "I remember. Dear God, I remember what happened."

CHAPTER 10

Two hundred seventy miles from the Xanthakos vineyard to Charlestown, SC.
If we press hard, we can make it in two weeks.

Andrew sat in a chair and pulled his badly shaken wife onto his lap. Lilyan knelt beside them, her heart hammering. Rider and Robbie stood nearby.

"Tell us, sweeting," Andrew cajoled.

"We were traveling east toward the main road to Camden when we happened on a large house. We were in the woods, and Holden ..." Golden Fawn furrowed her brow. "That was the man's name who took us. Holden signaled for me to stay down. Laurel was asleep, tied onto my back with my scarf."

She looked down at Lilyan, her eyes wide. "Laurel was so brave, so sweet. I tried to protect her. But she sensed how wrong everything was. And she was hungry. That evil man barely fed us enough to keep us alive."

The words stabbed Lilyan's gut. Her fingers curled into claws, and she knew if the man suddenly appeared in front of her, she would rip out his eyes.

"The people were packing their belongings onto a wagon. A white couple and two Negro slaves." She twisted her gown in her fingers. "I couldn't make out everything, but I did hear the woman say she was glad to be rid of the backcountry. They were going first to Charlestown and then north to family in Baltimore."

She clenched her fists. "And then Holden took Laurel from me, gagged me, and tied me to a tree. Laurel started crying, and he snatched her up. Headed toward the house."

Golden Fawn clasped Andrew's hand. "I heard him tell the woman that he had saved Laurel from some Cherokee, who killed her family. Wanted to know if they would take her since he was a 'poor bachelor, not much used to caring for children.' Told them how he'd been providing for her the past few weeks. That he had grown attached to her. How hard it would be to let her go."

Rider sneered.

Golden Fawn nodded at Rider. "I squirmed around as best I could to see what was going on. He had to speak loud because Laurel was squalling, arching her back, and beating him with her fists."

Robbie slapped his knee and grinned. "Huzzah for our brave little bonnie miss."

The vision of Laurel in such distress tortured Lilyan.

Golden Fawn clasped Andrew's hand so tightly her knuckles turned white. "Then the woman took Laurel. Finally, our girl was quiet. Holden hightailed it back to me. Showed me the bank note the man had given him—shoved it in my face, so proud he was of it. Bragged about the money he was going to get for me when he sold me as a camp wife."

She shuddered, and Andrew pulled her closer. "He waited for the people to leave before he untied me. That's when I tripped him and ran as fast as I could. I yelled and screamed, but they were too far away. Next thing I know, something hit me on the back of the head."

Lilyan inched closer. "What was the couple's name?"

Golden Fawn scrubbed at her forehead. She slid from Andrew's lap to pace the floor.

"I know. I do. Somehow I know the name." She scrunched up her face and closed her eyes. "Why can't I remember? Everything else came back."

Lilyan stood. "Where would you have heard it? At the house? When Holden was speaking to them?"

"No. Not at the house." She held out her arms. "I'm trying, Andy. I really am."

He crossed the room and wrapped her in his arms. "My brave darling. Look what you've been through, and so well. Calm yourself. It'll return to you."

Lilyan watched Golden Fawn nuzzle her face into his shoulder. *How sweet they look. How precious they are to me.* They had been restored to each other, and she enjoyed this moment of calm in the ocean of despair that swirled around her.

Robbie leaned his arm on the fireplace mantel. "Could it have been at the tavern?"

Golden Fawn let go of Andrew and pointed at Robbie. "Yes. Yes. Someone was talking about a family pulling up stakes." Her face beamed. "Jonathan Bramble! That's it, Jonathan Bramble."

Lilyan hugged her sister-in-law, kissed her on her forehead, kissed her brother on his, and rushed out the door.

Beloved,

I pray this missive finds you well and safe. I have news of such import I cannot contain myself.

Golden Fawn's memory was restored to her. She named her captor. Holden. By happenstance one of the unseemly men you and I met at a tavern and whom our little band of survivors chanced upon on our journey home. He met his fate at the hands of the men of the village he plundered. He no longer lives to terrorize innocents and has stood before his Maker at the judgment seat. But my account must wait for another time, though Rider may share with you some of the particulars.

The family in whose care our darling daughter now resides are Mr. and Mrs. Jonathan Bramble. They left their farm near Camden three to four weeks past to board a ship in Charlestown destined for Baltimore.

Be as encouraged, my love, as I am from Golden Fawn's account of the Brambles. They were tricked into thinking that Laurel's parents were the victims of savages, leaving her alone in the world. Surely, they must be kind, Christian people to make a place for a child in their family.

My prayers are filled with thanksgiving for this most encouraging turn of events.

I miss you, Nikki. My heart yearns to behold your beloved face and to witness you embrace our Laurel and to see you smile once again at your koukla. It is a picture I cherish in my heart.

Your most obedient and adoring,
Lilyan

Before dawn, Lilyan waved good-bye to Rider as he headed out with a mission to find Nicholas and place her letter in his hands.

Later, over breakfast with Robbie, Callum, Andrew, and Golden Fawn, Lilyan detailed her plan. "Robbie, you and I will go to Charlestown— "

"Not without me." "Only you and Robbie?" "No!" Callum, Andrew, and Golden Fawn spoke at once.

"But Robbie and I can travel so much faster by ourselves." Lilyan stopped as a frown as deep as a snow-plowed gorge furrowed Callum's forehead. Her sister-in-law set her lips into a thin line, and Andrew crossed his arms across his chest.

In the face of such resistance, Lilyan took a moment to rethink and to come at the problem from another direction. "But, Andrew, what if you grow tired and start coughing? And, Callum, you know you can't drive the wagon or ride a horse with your arthritis the way it is." She held her hands out, palms upward. "I won't have either of you sick or hurting."

The two men turned to each other with blank stares until Golden Fawn spoke up. "We could rig the wagon with a cot for

Andrew should he grow tired. And we could put a chair in the wagon bed and cushion it with quilts for Callum."

Callum nodded. "Smart thinking."

The usually obstinate old man's acquiescence to Golden Fawn's suggestion astounded Lilyan, breaking up the log jam of doubts crowding her mind. "Well, Charlestown *is* a big city, and it might help to have more of us searching for Laurel."

"What about the vineyard?" asked Andrew. "Harvest time's a month away."

"I've spoken with Silas. He's agreed to act in our stead and tend to the vineyard."

Andrew shifted in his chair. "I ain't certain how to say this, so I'll come out with it. What will we do for money to buy information?"

Lilyan tented her fingertips on the table top and tapped them together. "I raided our coffers. Took the last penny we had. There's still a large amount of my bequest from Da with our solicitor in Charlestown." She swallowed the lump in her throat. "And there's always my wallpaper business. I can sell that."

"But, Sissy—"

"No arguments. I'll do whatever needs to be done."

That night in bed, Lilyan spent a restless hour wondering if she'd decided rightly to take the family along. But she'd rather face the hardships of the trail than the disappointment of the people she loved.

* * *

It took them a day to load and rig a wagon. On the morning of their departure, Callum broached a question Lilyan had been avoiding. "What will you do when someone recognizes you? Someone who is aware of the price on your head and the very obvious fact that you are not dead after all?"

"A while back, I wrote everyone I care about to let them know I was fine. You never collected the bounty, so we broke no laws."

"But what about the murder?"

Lilyan's stomach burned. Bradenton ... creeping into my life again.

"It's been two years, and many things have happened in Charlestown. And besides, he was a British officer. Surely no one would still want to prosecute me?" Niggling doubts plagued her mind.

"Even so, we should be prepared," Callum grumbled.

She cupped his cheek in her hand. "You're always looking after me. And I love you for it."

His eyelids dropped over his watery blue eyes. "It's time we get going, lassie."

With her heart near bursting with hope, she packed a haversack with Laurel's rag doll and the cover Miriam had given her and climbed onto the wagon seat.

Next time I come home, it will be with my child and my husband.

CHAPTER 11

A South Carolina act of 1770 established a separate fish market in Charlestown explicitly acknowledging the preeminent role of slaves called "Fishing Negroes."

Twelve days later, sitting on the wagon seat with Golden Fawn and Robbie as he guided the horses through the crowded Charlestown streets, Lilyan craned her neck left and right, taking in the sights.

A breeze played with wisps of hair that strayed from the mobcap Lilyan wore underneath a straw bonnet. "Things don't seem to have changed much in two years."

Callum grumbled from the back of the wagon. "Then let that be a warnin' to ye, lassie. Could be someone out there has a long memory and is still aiming to claim the bounty on yer head. Take care, I said. But there you sit, bold as brass, in front of the wagon for all to see."

Lilyan cast a furtive glance at some of the passersby and tugged her bonnet closer around her face.

The wind, sweltering and moist, wafted scents of the salty ocean, oysters, clams, and sulfur from the pungent loamy soil. The heady, familiar aromas of home.

Seagulls drifted around them, landing on a pile of garbage. Fat brown pelicans, their rubbery gullets flapping in the wind, winged their way to the sea in a lazy *V*.

Vendors ambled down the cobblestone lanes, calling out their wares:

"Beeswax candles! Sweeter than honey!"

"Pralines! Sugared almonds, brown sugar pe-e-e-cans."

"Eggs. Brown, white, chicken, duck, turtle!"

A fishing Negro slave strolled past them balancing on his head a wooden tub filled with freshwater blue catfish and black and striped bass caught in nearby rivers and channels. "Catch o' de day. Catch o' de day," he shouted in a thick Gullah accent.

A female slave stood in a yard, arms crossed, keeping her eye on the cutler sharpening the household scissors and carving knives. Next door, a broomdasher strode up the steps toting a long, slender wicker basket full of sorghum and sweetgrass brooms.

Callum and Andrew moved forward in the wagon bed to kneel behind the seat, and Andrew rested his hands on his wife's shoulders.

Golden Fawn looked back at him, her face alight with wonder. "The sounds, Andrew."

"Aye. Things I've never heard nor dreamt of before." Robbie bobbed his head as if unsure of which way to look.

Lilyan had forgotten about the noise—a cacophony compared to the mountain cabin, where she could linger on her porch and listen to crickets dueling with cicadas. The sounds were invigorating, but not as much as the thought that Laurel might be somewhere near.

"Here we are." Lilyan pointed, and her body tingled with the urge to jump down and sprint to the door.

Robbie stopped the wagon in front of her house, situated on one of the busiest streets in town, three blocks from the Cooper River, which flowed down the east side of the city. The Ashley River bordered the west. The two rivers met at the tip of the peninsula, meandered around marsh-lined inlets and tiny islands that hosted a myriad of marine animals, waterfowl, and wildlife, before they finally mingled with the sea, forming estuaries and playgrounds for dolphins.

Golden Fawn, her eyes darting from one thing to the next, took in the pedestrians ambling toward shops on the thoroughfares that led to the wharfs. "So many people."

"There were more than fifteen thousand when I left two years ago. But there are probably many less since the British left in December."

Is my darling girl among them?

Golden Fawn reached down and rested her hands on Andrew's shoulders as he lifted her down from the wagon. "Fifteen thousand? It is a number I do not understand."

Robbie jumped down and assisted Lilyan, ran around to the back to help Callum, and then stood with the others looking up at the two-story brick house, its beauty marred by barricades nailed to the door and windows.

Standing on the stoop, Lilyan tried to read a piece of paper attached to the door behind the crisscrossed boards. "Robbie, see if you can find something to pry these loose."

"Someone has thrown mud at the door." Puzzled, she stood back to give Robbie room.

After a couple of tugs with a hook, he threw the wooden slats to the side of the steps and headed to uncover the windows.

Andrew reached through the barrier, freed the paper, and angled it so Lilyan could read it with him. "Looks like some kind of official document."

She squinted at the writing. "I can make out, 'By order of Commandant ...' And 'protected.'" She scratched her nail across the surface. "Everything else is covered in mud."

It was then she noticed a handful of people across the street huddled together and pointing at them. One woman shot her a look of disgust.

Ducking her head close to Andrew's, she whispered, "Why are they looking at us like that?"

Andrew glanced at them and raised his eyebrows.

Callum lumbered close and ducked his head. "Don't like the looks of it." He kept his voice low. "Let's get off the street."

Though the door hinges squeaked in protest as they entered, once inside Lilyan could not believe how undisturbed everything looked except for a thick layer of dust and spider webs that clung to the ceiling and draped like scalloped, gossamer lace between the candlesticks on the mantel. They threw open all the windows while Andrew trudged upstairs and opened the door to the widow's walk. A torrent of air rushed in and pushed out the musty odor.

The fatigue etched into Callum's face worried Lilyan. She beat the dust out of the camel-hair settee cushions and bade him to sit. With his legs propped on a footstool, he directed them as they made the house livable before they unloaded the wagon and hauled in their clothes and supplies. Lilyan knew what they were doing was necessary, but she resented every moment their tasks kept her from initiating inquiries about Laurel. Though everyone hurried, her instructions became more and more waspish. Several times, as she paused on the front stoop, she had a niggling feeling that something was awry—that the city wasn't quite the same after all. If that wasn't enough, each time she trekked to the wagon and back, she kept her head down, avoiding eye contact with the knot of onlookers who seemed intent on watching her family's every move.

Are there enemies among them?

When all was accomplished, they slumped down on the parlor chairs.

Standing at the doorway, Lilyan tucked a tendril of hair behind her ear. "Well done, everyone. I say we tidy ourselves up a bit and go to Mrs. Snead's. It'll be a good place to start our search."

"Who is Mrs. Snead?" asked Golden Fawn.

Andrew stood, arching his back and stretching his arms over

his head, and then held out his hand to help Golden Fawn from her chair. "She's the mother of Lilyan's apprentice and the proprietress of a tavern."

Groaning, Callum planted his feet on the floor and stood, his bones loudly cracking their protests. "Fine woman. Has her thumb in many pies." He chuckled at his own joke.

Lilyan nodded. "During the war, she was one of my main contacts for passing along information for the patriots."

"Yep." Callum winked. "What she don't know ain't worth knowing." With his back bent, he took a few hesitant steps. "Fine cook, too. She could make the sole of a shoe taste good."

It didn't take them long to pile into the wagon. Flanked by Lilyan and Golden Fawn, Robbie took the reins and, at Andrew's instruction, headed north toward the tavern.

Robbie craned his neck right and left, once again enthralled with the unfamiliar sights that surrounded them. "How far?"

"About a half-mile or so," Andrew answered from the back of the wagon.

They hadn't traveled far when Robbie turned to Lilyan, his eyes twinkling. "Could we go by way of the water? I've never seen the ocean before. 'Cept what I could peek at through your house windows."

Golden Fawn's face lit. "Yes, please, dear sister. May we see the ocean?"

"Of course. I'm so sorry I didn't think of it sooner. I've lived in Charlestown all my life, and the ocean is a part of me. I forget others might not have seen it." She pointed to the next intersection. "That way, Robbie, down two blocks. We'll go by my shop. It's right on the water. We can pick up some paper for notices, and I've got a bit of money stashed there."

At the end of the first block, she told Robbie to hand over the reins and ordered him and Golden Fawn to cover their eyes. Arriving at her business, she steered the horses into a wide turn, positioning the wagon at just the right angle.

"Now." Lilyan pulled back the wheel brake, locking it into position. "Open your eyes."

Golden Fawn sucked in a breath. "I cannot believe it."

Robbie sat speechless, his wide eyes scanning the horizon and the vast waters laid out before him.

"Rolls of blue and green. Reminds me of our mountains at home, Andrew." Golden Fawn's voice trembled in awe.

Not taking his eyes off the harbor, Robbie climbed down from the wagon. "Only this seems endless." As if drawn by a magnet, he walked to the water's edge.

A hand covered Lilyan's and she turned to Callum, his eyes gleaming.

"The lad's awestruck," he said. "Can't take his eyes off it. I've seen that look afore. Poor Forbes might be losing his youngest to the sea."

She cupped his cheek in her palm. "I think you're right."

She stepped down from the wagon, walked to the entrance of her business, and ran her hand behind a rock beside the door. "Still here." She held up the key.

She unlocked the door and stepped inside, breathing in the familiar smells of paint and newly shaved wood. Wandering past the counter and a small sitting area with a dormant Franklin stove, she headed to the back storage area. There she found stacks of wallpaper samples, clay jugs of pigment, brushes, blocks of wood, and a bin full of carving utensils.

Callum and the others, who had followed her inside, gathered in the barn-like room and stood before the sample mural she had painted on the wall covered with a layer of gesso.

"Did you do that?" Golden Fawn asked.

"I did." Lilyan ran her fingers across the sinopia drawing of a Japanese woman standing in a garden amid cherry blossoms. "It seems so very long ago," she said, walking toward the back door. She opened the door and paused on the deck that ran across the back of the building.

Robbie came and stood beside her.

She leaned against the railing. "It was from here that I would keep my eye on the prison ship where Andrew and his friend, Herald, were. I used to pray with everything I had that God would protect them. Keep them safe. Here and the widow's walk at our house were my favorite places to be. There's something about the rolling sea, the sun, and the wind ..." She breathed in deeply. "... the smells that calmed me. Made me feel that everything would be fine."

She gazed across the dark green, rolling waves, but they offered her no peace, no calm. Her pain ran too deep.

Robbie looked at her, his eyes bright. "I could never have imagined such a thing as the ocean. What it must feel like to have it underneath your feet."

Callum is right. The young lad's been snared by the sirens of the sea.

Back inside the shop, Lilyan gathered a pile of leaflets and shook the dust from them. As she stuffed them into a satchel, she wondered where the stacks of paper were that used to fill the shelves. She took a ceramic jar from another shelf and wiped the thick layer of dust from the cork stopper. Sneezing, she opened the jar and pulled out a thick roll of sterling notes and slipped them through the slit in the side of her skirt, into the apron underneath.

"Come, Robbie." She handed him the satchel. "I'm anxious to speak to Mrs. Snead. And, we're all hungry. You can come back tomorrow and spend as much time as you want."

Reluctantly, the young man followed her and took his place on the wagon seat. He guided the horses along Bay Street, but from the way he kept fixing his gaze on the water, Lilyan knew that something very striking had happened to her young friend. When they arrived at the Snead's tavern, Lilyan noticed a new sign on the post: *The Bells*.

The moment they entered, the proprietress spotted them and came running from around the counter. "I'll be! What a sight for sore eyes!"

Almost as big around as she was tall, Annabelle Snead clasped her arms around Lilyan, and the comforting aromas of whortleberries, apple flummery, and cinnamon wafted around them.

Unexpected tears welled up as Lilyan stood back. "It's so good to see you."

"It is that." Making little clucking sounds, Mrs. Snead wiped Lilyan's eyes with the corner of her apron.

"Callum." Mrs. Snead kissed the old man's cheek. "Haven't died of orneriness yet, I see." Despite her teasing, her eyes held special warmth for her friend.

"And you, young man." She curled her hands around Andrew's cheeks. "It does my heart good to see you so well."

She turned to Golden Fawn. "Who do we have here?"

Andrew placed his hand on the small of his wife's back. "This is Golden Fawn. My wife."

Mrs. Snead smiled. "Lilyan wrote that Andrew had gotten married, but she did not tell me how lovely you are."

Lilyan was pleased to see the cloudy look in her sister-in-law's eyes transform into delight. She was always so terribly self-conscious of the pockmarks on her face.

"This is Robbie Forbes, a family friend." Lilyan motioned the young man forward, though she grew increasingly impatient to get to the heart of why they had come.

"That makes you a friend of the Sneads, too, Robbie." Mrs. Snead draped her arm through the crook of his elbow and motioned them toward the back of the tavern. "Come with me to the private room. I cannot wait to hear your news."

As they passed the counter, she called out to a woman pouring a draft from the beer keg. "Sally, bring supper and plenty of ale."

When they were all settled around a table, Mrs. Snead shut the door and scraped a chair close to Lilyan. "So tell me, dear. What's the matter? 'Twould take something dire indeed to bring you back to Charlestown. Does it have something to do with your husband and little one not being here with you?"

Lilyan plucked at the fabric of her skirt and struggled with the fear that twisted her insides. "Laurel was taken by outlaws. Slavers."

Mrs. Snead gasped. "What! How? When?"

"About a month back, Golden Fawn took Laurel to visit family in a nearby village. The village was attacked by outlaws and patriot renegades, who kidnapped them along with about twenty others. Nicholas and I trailed them and found our sister-in-law in a terrible state. She had been separated from Laurel, and her memory had abandoned her. She and I returned home while Nicholas continued the search."

Mrs. Snead glanced at Golden Fawn, who had lowered her head.

Mirroring her sister-in-law, Lilyan gazed down at her hands resting on the table. "When her memory returned, she was able to tell me that the man who took Laurel gave her to a couple, Jonathan Bramble and his wife. They lived near Camden but were leaving to come here and then sail for Baltimore."

Mrs. Snead furrowed her brow. "Bramble. That's a familiar name, somehow."

Lilyan leaned forward. "I sent word to Nicholas and hope he's on his way. Could you help us find our daughter? Get word out through the people we worked with when the British were here?"

"Of course. I'll do anything you ask." Mrs. Snead stood. "Matter of fact, there're two men having supper right now I can count on to help us. I'll be back shortly."

Having Mrs. Snead on their side meant a lot. The long trek to Charlestown, unloading the wagons and getting the house in order, the seeming inaction—all burdened Lilyan with a level of agitation she had never experienced before. Every pore of her skin chafed from it. Finally, something was being set in motion, and she allowed herself to feel a flicker of hope. While the others spoke together in low tones, she kept her eyes trained on the door.

When Mrs. Snead returned, everyone stopped talking and waited for her to sit beside Lilyan again. "It's started. I can't make any promises, but we've thrown the nets, and we'll wait and see what we catch."

Though *wait and see* were dreaded words, they brought Lilyan another measure of relief.

Andrew smiled and sank back into his chair. "We can't thank you enough."

An awkward silence fell over the group until Andrew coughed. "You changed the name of the tavern, Mrs. Snead. Why *The Bells?*"

"For our lost bells of St. Michael's," the woman responded with a frown.

"Lost?" Lilyan asked.

"You don't know, then?"

Lilyan shook her head. Andrew and Callum sat up in their chairs.

"Well, maybe you don't know, Golden Fawn, or you, Robbie. St. Michael's took much abuse during the war. At first, the patriots painted the steeple black to keep it from being a beacon to the British fleet—"

Callum harrumphed. "Stupid idea. Made it a better landmark than before."

"Well," Mrs. Snead continued, "during the occupation, the British stabled their horses in the church and stripped the lead roof and melted it down to make bullets."

"I remember." Lilyan thought back to the Christmas Eve she had stood at the window of her house and wondered if other worshippers, deprived of their meeting places, were holding their own services as she and her family were.

"You wouldn't've thought things could get any worse, but they did. When the British hightailed it out of Charlestown, hauling with them everything that wasn't nailed down, they stole the bells from the tower."

"No!" Lilyan gasped.

"But, that's an outrage," shouted Andrew.

"I'm surprised you didn't notice them not ringing out the

time," said Mrs. Snead.

"We were so occupied, trying to settle in." Lilyan sighed. "But ... there was something bothering me all day. A feeling that something was missing."

Mrs. Snead glanced at her guests. "'Tis sad I am to bring you such news, what with all you've had to think about."

"You said the British ransacked the city." Lilyan paused, thinking of the half-empty shelves in her business storage room. "I noticed that a large supply of my paper is missing."

"Don't surprise me none," said Mrs. Snead. "What with the value they put on paper these days."

"But my house was untouched."

Mrs. Snead shifted in her chair. "You can thank Captain McKenzie for that. He had a protection order posted on it. Got your neighbors all riled up, that did. And, I've got to warn you— that's something that don't bode well for you."

"Who is Captain McKenzie?" asked Robbie.

"A British officer billeted with us," said Andrew. "Became a friend of sorts—"

"A friend? But he was a Brit!" Robbie exclaimed.

Andrew shrugged. "I know. But we saw him every day and got to know him. He was a gentleman. A kind man who helped me get well from the wound I got at Camden. He often expressed his regrets that we were forced to provide him lodging."

Just then, Sally opened the door, carrying a tray with pewter mugs and a pitcher of ale. Behind her, a young man struggled with another tray loaded with meat pies, loaves of bread, and a platter of sweet potatoes. While Callum said grace, Sally hurried away and returned with plates and utensils, and soon they were all tucking into the meal.

"Mmm," Robbie said, "sweet potatoes with nutmeg and molasses. Reminds me of Ma's."

"Well, then, dearie, have some more." Mrs. Snead ladled a pile of potatoes onto his plate. She folded her arms across her stomach and grinned as he dived into the food. "I do appreciate a good appetite."

Lilyan envied her friend, so content to sit back and watch them enjoy the supper she had prepared. *How I long to cook for my family again.* Having difficulty swallowing, she laid down her fork and took a sip of ale. "What news of your family, Annabelle?"

"I wrote to you about my husband's death. Did you get the letter?"

"I did. Such sad news."

"Yes. I miss him sorely. It was especially hard on the twins."

"How are the boys?"

Mrs. Snead beamed. "Herald was married this past month."

"Did you hear that, Andrew?" Lilyan asked. "Herald is married."

"Huzzah!" Andrew exclaimed, holding up his mug in a toast.

"Do I know her?" Lilyan asked.

"I suspect not. She's from over Haddrell Point way. That's where they're living."

Haddrell Point ... Violet Plantation ... the ugly memory surfaced. "And Gerald?"

"As you know, he's kept your business going, mostly by painting signs for businesses, but ..." Mrs. Snead clapped like an excited child. "He's about to be married."

"Good fellow!" said Andrew. "To Lisa, I suspect."

"Lisa?" Golden Fawn asked.

Andrew put down his fork. "She and her family sheltered Lilyan, Elizabeth, Callum, and Gerald after they escaped from the British."

He held Lilyan's gaze. "Seems like an eternity has passed since that time—since you helped Herald and me escape from the prison ship."

"Hoots!" exclaimed Robbie. "Escape from a prison ship? Mrs. Xanthakos, you continue to bumbaze. I must know the gist of it."

Andrew scooted forward and leaned his wrists on the table. "After the Battle of Camden, I received a parole by taking an oath not to fight for the patriots again. But since the oath was forced on me, I felt no honor to heed it. I began working with Captain Xanthakos and other spies in Charlestown, including"—he nodded at the proprietress—"Mrs. Snead and her sons."

Mrs. Snead folded her hands in her lap and sat quietly.

Andrew grimaced. "Herald and I were captured and put aboard the *Brixham*. A more hellish place I cannot imagine."

Picturing the prisoners, walking skeletons, their eyes filled with despair—the wounded, the sick and dying—was painful for Lilyan.

"My brave, dear—shall I say it?—headstrong sister joined the spies and hatched a plan to rescue us."

Lilyan blushed at her brother's lavish praise.

"That's how she first met her husband, you know," Mrs. Snead interrupted. "It happened right here in my tavern. Downstairs in the cellar."

They had actually first met on the street in a short encounter when Lilyan, in a fit of temper—the reason for which she could not recall—had kicked a stone that skipped across the lane and struck Nicholas on his shin. She warmed at the vision of the first time he smiled at her. A *coup de foudre* was how the French said it. A thunderbolt.

I miss him so much. How long until he joins me? Till we're reunited with our baby girl?

Andrew continued. "The ladies of the city had gathered food, clothing, blankets, and all manner of things to comfort the prisoners and planned to deliver them to our ship on Christmas Eve. Lilyan talked them into letting her escort the supplies and to help the doctor who would attend the wounded. One of the ladies held a ball that evening and invited all of the prison ship's officers, leaving only a skeleton crew. But ..." He lifted his eyebrows. "Captain McKenzie made a last-minute decision to accompany her."

Lilyan pressed her fingers to the base of her throat. "I remember how terrified I was when he joined Dr. Cheek and me on our way to the ship."

The others sat still, spellbound. Except for Callum, who was dozing, his head drooped back against the chair.

"It all moved swiftly once the plan was set in motion," said Andrew. "Nicholas and his men boarded the ship and overcame the guards. When one of the prisoners tried to attack Captain McKenzie, Lilyan shielded his body with hers and took a knife wound to her arm."

Robbie looked thunderstruck. "You shielded the enemy?"

Lilyan rubbed the material of her sleeve that covered the scar. "As Andrew explained, he had befriended us. And the poor man had been knocked unconscious during the fray. I couldn't allow him to be harmed."

Robbie bobbed his head as if weighing the sides of the story. "Aye. I ken."

"Turns out, that helped Lilyan avoid any suspicions about her part in the rescue. The loyalists called her *the heroine of Charlestown*," said Mrs. Snead.

Callum snorted so loud he woke himself up and, disoriented, glanced around the room.

"We'd best be getting home," said Andrew, who stood and pulled out Golden Fawn's chair for her.

"I agree." It pleased Lilyan to see Robbie assist Callum from his chair, though the old man mumbled under his breath that he didn't need no help. "We've much to do tomorrow. I want to wake early and go to the sheriff's office and the bill poster's. Someone must visit the wharves and talk to the boarding officers."

"What about the bumboatmen? They always know what's going on at the docks and the ships," Andrew said.

Lilyan's muscles complained as she rose from her chair. She was more tired than she realized. "Good idea."

As the others filed through the doorway, Mrs. Snead took Lilyan aside and whispered, "I must warn you. The city is not as it used to be. There is turmoil about the loyalists still living among us. Trouble which may make its way to you."

CHAPTER 12

*The Marine Anti-Britannic Society, founded in 1783 in Charlestown,
opposed the easing of restrictions on British merchants and the liberties
granted by the General Assembly to returning Loyalists and fueled
anti-British sentiment and unrest during the summer of 1783.*

As Lilyan strolled down the street with Golden Fawn, her every
pore tingled with anticipation of seeing Laurel. At each turn of
a corner, scenarios played out in her mind: Laurel tottering around
in a yard, coming toward her carried in someone's arms, sitting on
a counter in a store, riding in an open carriage.

The laughter of children enticed her to step closer to an iron
fence that separated the house's side garden from the street.
Searching the happy little group, she spotted a toddler with a mop
of red-gold ringlets. But it wasn't her Laurel. Anguish weighed
down her heart like ballast in the hull of an empty ship. Even so,
she lingered to watch them play, the girls with their dollies, the
boys trying to solve metal puzzles, taking the iron rings and squares
apart and putting them together again.

How much longer could she function with her emotions in
such a raw state? One minute her hopes rode high only to be

dashed against disappointment, like waves cresting on the winds of a storm, tumbling onto the shore, succumbing to the undertow, roiling around in deep waters, only to rise again. God knew she had cried an ocean of tears, her wretched heart tossed about like a piece of flotsam.

Frustrated, Lilyan kicked a rock across the street. "Time is racing away. I'm barely able to hold on, when all I want to do is run around screaming at the top of my lungs, 'Please help me. My precious baby has been taken.' I want to shove her picture at their faces and shout, 'Have you seen my little one?'"

"We will find her," Golden Fawn declared, gently pulling Lilyan's arm, guiding them back down the street.

At the bill printer's, they placed an order for fifty handbills with a drawing of Laurel and instructions on how to contact the family with information of her daughter's or the Brambles' whereabouts. Half of the broadsides would be posted on notice boards and in taverns and public houses around the city. The other half would be delivered to Lilyan and her family to use as they inquired door to door.

Next, they visited the office of *The South Carolina Gazette* at 94 Church Street. There they spoke to John Miller, the public printer, who kept apologizing about the irregularity of his publication. He seemed deeply moved by Laurel's kidnapping and followed them to the door, promising to include the reward notice in the next issue.

As they walked down Bedon's Alley to the sheriff's office, several passersby glared at Golden Fawn, some grumbling epithets under their breaths. When one of them threw out a vile remark about Cherokees, Lilyan turned and defiantly stared at him until her sister-in-law tugged her elbow. She was aware of the bad feelings some patriots had toward the Cherokee, many of whom had fought alongside the British. Passions ran so high that for two years, groups—mostly former militia—had attacked Cherokee villages, burning them out. According to Nicholas, that was why the men who kidnapped Laurel felt confident no one would come after them. But they were in for a surprise if ever they crossed paths with her husband.

Golden Fawn pulled her cloak tight around her. "Maybe I should go home, Lilyan. I fear for our safety."

"No. All will be well. Besides, we're almost there."

They walked another block, passing more and more people with grim faces and striding with purpose toward the center of town. Several women carried brooms and rakes. Something sinister pervaded the air. Lilyan anxiously glanced over her shoulder and quickened their pace.

When she finally spotted the sheriff's signpost, No. 7, she opened the door and hurried in. "Here we are. Thank goodness."

She approached a man sitting at a pinewood desk in the center of the room. "Sheriff Stevens?"

He jumped up, ran his hands down the sides of his wrinkled, dark green jerkin, and bowed. "Sheriff's out for a while, ma'am. I am his assistant, George Martin."

Lilyan returned his bow. "Mr. Martin, I'm Mrs. Xanthakos, and this is my sister-in-law, Mrs. Cameron. We're here to report a kidnapping." She slipped her hand into the slit at the side of her skirt and withdrew a picture of Laurel from her apron pocket. "It's Laurel, my one-year-old daughter." She couldn't stop her lip from trembling.

The street door opened and closed, and Lilyan looked over her shoulder at the well-dressed gentleman who took a place in line behind her. His first glance was cursory, but then, as he studied her face, his eyebrows formed a *V*. Lilyan quickly turned around as unease creeped across the back of her neck.

Mr. Martin waved to the man. "Be with you in a moment, Chambers."

Chambers? The barrister for the family of the British officer she had killed?

Mr. Martin turned his attention back to Lilyan, took the

drawing from her, and walked back around the desk. He indicated the two chairs facing him. "Won't you have a seat, ladies?"

Lilyan shook her head. "No, thank you, we are fine standing. Laurel was taken—"

The front door flew open, and a cooper, hammer in hand, his untied apron swinging from his neck, shouted, "Best to come, Martin. Something ugly's about to happen!"

Mr. Martin grabbed a stave, shoved it into his belt, and ran outside on the heels of the cooper. Lilyan and Golden Fawn hurried out, followed closely by Chambers.

"Traitor! Loyalist! Dirty Tory!" She heard the angry shouts from a distance before coming upon a mob gathered in front of a two-story stucco house. Several people waved signs that read *Marine Anti-Britannic Society*. Many brandished brooms, clubs, sticks, and pitchforks at the rotund man staggering at the top of the steps as he struggled to pull away from men who gripped his arms. His powdered wig had slipped off his head, and his shirttail straggled halfway out of his breeches. Someone ripped off the man's shirt, exposing the creamy white rolls of flesh on his torso. Others kicked his legs out from under him and tied his feet and arms to a long, thick pole, which they lifted onto their shoulders. Trussed up like a pig ready for the spit, the man cried for mercy, craning his neck back, seeking his sobbing wife, who clutched the door brace.

Mr. Martin tried to shoulder his way through the crowd but kept getting bounced back like a rock skipping across a pond. "Cease and desist!"

He yelled his orders again, but to Lilyan's shock, a handful of burly men picked him up like a cord of wood and shoved him to the ground.

"Dear Lord, what's happening?" Golden Fawn lowered her head and clutched Lilyan's arm.

A woman in front of them spun around. "Damned king's lackey! He was warned to leave South Carolina but refused. Too thick-skinned. Now he'll have a new layer of skin." She cackled at her own joke, and loud guffaws swelled through the crowd.

Golden Fawn drew nearer to Lilyan and whispered, "What does she mean?"

A breeze wafted overhead, carrying with it the cloying smell of melting tar. Nauseated, Lilyan had difficulty breathing. "Come." She covered her nose and tugged on Golden Fawn's arm. "We must get away."

They tried to skirt around the crowd but got caught up in the tangle of people pressing closer. Then Lilyan heard a mewling sound that rippled the skin up and down her arms. The whimpering grew into sobbing and crescendoed into screaming, and she looked up to see thick, black liquid dripping from a long-handled ladle held high above their heads. The odor of burning flesh assaulted her nose and she gagged. Suddenly the air was filled with feathers showering down on them like snow, and the crowd began to squeal like a pack of wild hogs.

She clasped Golden Fawn's wrist and stepped back, pushing against several onlookers, not caring that she had trodden on their toes, when she realized that the stranger from the sheriff's office was trying to make a path for them. Suddenly the mob parted, allowing the men to cart their prey down the steps and across the street, near enough for Lilyan to observe that he had, mercifully, passed out. She quickly averted her eyes, but not before catching a glimpse of blisters forming on fiery red skin. Vomitus burned the back of her throat, and she took off, dragging her sister-in-law behind her. Glancing over her shoulder, she watched the crowd close in behind them, laughing, jeering, and gesturing their fists at the man's poor wife as she crumpled on the stoop. With Golden Fawn in tow, she didn't stop running until they reached her house, where she tossed up the contents of her stomach in the yard.

Golden Fawn took gulps of air. "I have seen what enemies can do to one another ... but that was ... terrible."

Lilyan's eyes watered, and she withdrew a handkerchief from her apron pocket and wiped her mouth. "I think this is what Mrs.

Snead was trying to warn me about."

They trudged inside, where Golden Fawn proceeded to tell Andrew and Callum what she had witnessed. Lilyan begged leave to lie down and announced she would not join them for supper. Upstairs, she lay on the bed and burrowed underneath the covers, pulling them completely over her head. She fell into a fitful sleep, only to awaken to the sound of someone banging on the front door.

News of Laurel?

She leapt from the bed, slipped on her shoes, shoved her unruly hair under a mobcap, and hurried downstairs to find Andrew talking to a stranger who practically filled the doorway. Mr. Martin and Mr. Chambers stood behind him.

Andrew whirled around as she descended the last step, a deep worry line furrowing his brow. "Lilyan—"

"Mrs. Lilyan Cameron Xanthakos …" The tall man elbowed his way past Andrew and towered over her, clasping a piece of paper. "I am the sheriff, and I hold here a writ for your arrest for the murder of Captain Remington Bradenton."

CHAPTER 13

Remember them that are in bonds, as bound with them; and them
which suffer adversity, as being yourselves also in the body.
Hebrews 13:3 KJV

The wooden doors of the Exchange Building closed behind Lilyan, plunging her spirits into an abyss. With her hands chained in front of her, she preceded the jail keeper down a narrow, uneven stairwell, the punched tin lantern bobbing in his hand barely lighting their way. At the bottom of the stairs, they stepped into the Provost Dungeon, where a solitary torch on the wall cast eerie shadows across the vaulted ceilings and huge brick columns. Cold, dank air wafted gooseflesh up and down her arms, and she couldn't stop shaking.

After the jailor freed her hands, she moved forward hesitantly onto the hay-covered floor. A cloud of dust rose up, and she sneezed. She listened to the man's retreating footsteps and waited as the cavernous room dimmed and the echo of banging doors and rattling keys swirled around her. Keeping her back to the stairs as her eyes adjusted to the dark, she began to distinguish her cellmates. Some stretched out on cots, some huddled together on pallets, and several curled up on bales and piles of hay. She guessed their number to be about twenty, all of whom seemed asleep, judging from the variety of snores and snorts. She eased down onto a vacant bale, drew her feet up under her skirt, and wrapped her arms close to her body. When she laid her head back, the stench of unwashed bodies, decayed food, and urine filled her nostrils.

"Ugh," she gasped, her stomach protesting.

"Take deep breaths from your throat," someone whispered from behind her. "Don't breathe through your nose. You won't even notice the stink after a time."

Lilyan swung around to discover a woman sitting beside her on a pallet, her dark hair thick and stringy with oil and sticking out from a dingy mobcap.

"My name's Mildred."

"Mine's Lilyan."

Someone coughed a loud crackling sound from deep in the chest, and Lilyan cringed.

"It's easy to get sick down here," said Mildred. "But I hear tell this ain't as bad as the District Jail where we was supposed to be put."

Lilyan nodded. "I was told there's malaria at the jail."

Mildred tugged a blanket out from underneath her rail-thin body. "Here. Until you get your own."

"Are you certain you don't need it?"

"Naw. I got two." Mildred pulled her other blanket around her shoulders and lay back down. "Best to get some rest. They wake us up early."

Convinced she would never be able to sleep, and trying not to think about the vermin that might be crawling around in the filth, Lilyan glanced around before loosening her stays. She draped the wool blanket, still warm from Mildred's body, up under her neck and rested her chin on her knees. Feeling very much alone, she prayed, asking for Laurel to be returned to her, for protection for her family, for Nicholas to come soon, and for her freedom. She had long ago sought forgiveness for killing another human being. Now she asked for justice, for understanding. She ended the prayer the way it began, with a plea for her daughter.

She wasn't sure how long she had been asleep when she woke with the feeling of being watched.

"Right perty miss, ain't she?" came a man's voice from nearby.

Too nearby, Lilyan thought, and she opened her eyes to find four men leaning over her. All were dressed for an evening on the town, except their rumpled waistcoats were unfastened, their cravats were askew, and their stockings sagged. They had tucked their hats underneath their arms.

Lilyan jerked up, planted her feet on the floor, and clutched the blanket to her chest. Fingers of nausea clawed her stomach, and she jumped up, ran to the corner of the cell, and vomited. Choking, eyes watering, utterly humiliated, she leaned against the clammy wall.

"I say! Never had that effect on a woman before," one of the men grumbled.

Another responded with a hiccup.

"Away with you, you louts," said Mildred, who hurried to Lilyan and wiped her face with a handkerchief. "Come, now. Let's have a seat and see what's going on here."

As they walked back to her makeshift bed, Lilyan took note of the other occupants. To her horror, several of the men were relieving themselves in various corners of the cell. The women took turns holding up a blanket to shield one another as they used the chamber pots. Her insides threatened to heave again, and she sucked in deep, gulping breaths.

Mildred ladled water from a bucket onto her handkerchief and pressed it to the back of Lilyan's neck. "It ain't none of my business, but—"

"Breakfast!" the jailor yelled as he descended the steps.

A couple of women carrying buckets and pitchers trailed behind him.

"Gentlemen," the jailor addressed the men who had been staring at Lilyan, "you're free to go." He snickered. "'Til the next time you get tippled."

"What ho!" one of them shouted as they stumbled out, doffing their hats.

"Drunkards," Mildred mumbled, taking two cups and plates from a serving woman.

The jailor filled his own cup and drank heartily. "Someone's got a benefactor this morning, folks. We have ale and cider." He swirled a ladle in one of the buckets. "But same ole fare."

Hunger cramping her innards, Lilyan downed a cup of cider and asked for another before making swift work of eating the salty concoction that passed for porridge.

Mildred finished her mush, wiped her hands with her kerchief, and offered it to Lilyan, who cleaned her hands as well. "It's good. Eating, that is. You need to keep your strength up. No telling how long they'll make you wait for a hearing."

Lilyan didn't like the sound of that. "How long have you been here?"

"Me?" Mildred frowned. "A week. A very long week. And should you be too mannerly to ask, I was arrested for pilfering. Which, upon my oath, I did not do. But I have no way to prove it."

"Surely there's a way."

"I'm an indentured servant with three—now two—weeks to go on my contract. I was apprenticed to a hairdresser and was getting along right well when this happened. Truth be told, my bondholder more 'an likely did it."

Mildred grew quiet, and Lilyan sensed she was waiting for the particulars of her own arrest. "I've been charged with murder."

The others in the cell paused and stared at Lilyan.

"Blimey. Did you hear that?" said one of the men. "That makes three."

Curious, Lilyan cast a glance over her shoulder. "Three?"

"Murderers. Two are locked up in them cells. Over there." The man pointed toward nearby alcoves and to a set of wooden doors secured with chains and padlocks. "Who'd you do in?"

"A British officer."

"A Brit!" The man's bushy eyebrows shot up, and he gawked at her. "They orta give you a bloody medal, not coop ye up in 'ere."

"Breakfast is done," the jailor announced from the steps.

The prisoners lined up and walked toward a half-barrel washtub at the front of the room where they dropped their plates and cups. Lilyan, last in line, followed suit and then returned to the bales to watch a serving woman tote the tub to the far side of the dungeon and rinse the dishes over a drain in the floor.

The jail keeper moved to the side to make way for a woman who stood in front of him, hands on hips.

"Chambers!" yelled the necessary woman, her face puckered as unpleasantly as the chore she was about to perform.

Some of the prisoners gathered the chamber pots scattered about the room and laid them at her feet. She picked up the pots, emptied them into the drain, and lined them up underneath a bench. Once she and the jailor left, the prisoners clustered into small groups. Several conversed in low tones, two began a cribbage game, and some went back to sleep.

A couple of women sat with Lilyan and Mildred. One, stocky and smelling of ale, sported a black eye and a split lip. Her loosely tied scooped-neck shift exposed bruises of many hues on her shoulders and across the tops of her breasts. The other, younger woman wore a coarse linen blouse and skirt and kept wringing her hands marred by swollen knuckles and chilblain scars. Lilyan sensed that she had met her somewhere before.

The bruised woman twirled the ties of her shift around her finger. "I'm Constance. Barmaid at the Boar's Head." She curved her thumb toward the other woman. "And this here is Sally. She works at *The Bells* and at old Blackstock's laundry."

As soon as Constance mentioned Mrs. Snead's tavern, Lilyan

remembered that was where she had seen Sally.

"I'm Lilyan. Do you remember me from last night?"

The tiny woman, whose frizzed hair stuck out from the edges of her mobcap, stared at Lilyan with anxious eyes the color of aged hazelnuts. "Yes, ma'am. I do."

"Hauled in for assault, we was. A couple of louts tried to nab my fifteen bob. Would've beat me to a bloody pulp if Sally hadn't stepped in." Constance grinned at her companion, who looked even more nervous. "Gave one of them a clout on his jolly nob, she did. Neither of us thought to ever see the inside of a gaol, but here we sit."

Lilyan heard a noise at the stairs. She glanced up, and her heart tumbled over itself. Mr. Martin was walking toward them, followed by Andrew, Callum, and a gentleman whose white wig, severely cut black coat, and tabbed cravat identified him as a barrister.

Lilyan stood and hurried to them. "You work here, Mr. Martin?"

"The sheriff and I take turns on jail duty, Mrs. Xanthakos. 'Twas my turn today." He scanned the cell and grimaced. "'Tis an awful thing to see you in these circumstances."

She looked back and forth between Mr. Martin and Andrew, who stood directly behind him. She yearned to throw her arms around her brother, but, not at all sure of the rules, she held her wrists forward, waiting for the shackles.

Mr. Martin's face flushed. "No need, ma'am."

The stranger behind Andrew straightened to his considerable height. "Good thinking, Mr. Martin. I am the lady's representative, and this is her family. We will not breach the law, sir."

With a nod, Mr. Martin indicated benches on the far end of the cellar. "You can sit over there. I'll be at the top of the stairs when you're ready."

Before the jailor turned to leave, Lilyan ran forward and hugged Andrew so tightly she feared she might break his ribs.

He wrapped his spindly arms around her. "Sissy."

He stood back, kissed her cheeks, and then stepped aside for

Callum, who caught her up in a big bear hug. He smelled of pinewood campfires and pipe tobacco—aromas so familiar and comforting, she realized how terribly frightened she would be if she never saw her family again.

"Any news of Laurel?" she asked, but she read in Callum's eyes that there was none—another stab to her already battered heart. "And Nicholas?"

Andrew shook his head. "Not yet, Sissy."

The stranger cleared his throat.

Andrew turned. "Sorry, sir. May I introduce you to my sister, Mrs. Lilyan Cameron Xanthakos. Lilyan, this is James McCord, Esquire."

Lilyan bowed, and he responded very formally, bending low from his waist. When he straightened, his eyes bored into hers as if he were trying to read her mind. At first she thought his irises were black, but after returning his stare, she realized they were midnight blue. His soot-black eyebrows contrasted starkly with his pristine white wig with its three rows of curls above each ear. His face, though pleasantly formed, was so closed she could almost feel the wall he used to separate himself from others. *He would make a difficult subject for a portrait.*

"Come." He motioned toward the benches. "Time is of the essence, and we must proceed quickly."

Callum and Andrew sat on either side of her, and Mr. McCord dragged another bench across from them.

Andrew scanned the room. "Last time I was here, *I* was the prisoner."

Lilyan had barely arranged her skirt around her on the seat when Mr. McCord asked bluntly, "Did you kill Captain Remington Bradenton?"

"I did," she answered with similar bluntness. "And if the circumstances repeated themselves, I would do it again."

"Plainly spoken, Mrs. Xanthakos."

Lilyan thought she caught a glimmer of admiration in his eyes.

He looked down at the lapdesk resting on his knee. "Now, if you would be so kind as to explain those circumstances."

"I'm not sure how far back I should go." She looked to Andrew for guidance.

Her brother shrugged. "When you joined the patriot spies to rescue us from the prison ship?"

Mr. McCord raised an eyebrow. "You had a part in the rescue from the *Brixham*?"

"I did."

Andrew leaned toward her. "Mr. McCord's brother, Wilson, was aboard the ship but was too ill to go with us." He knit his brow. "He died a few weeks after we got away. On the way to the prison at St. Augustine."

Struck by the news, Lilyan patted the hem of Mr. McCord's sleeve. "I'm so very sorry. Please accept my condolences."

The momentary lapse of his guard surprised her, for she was certain he was someone who hardly, if ever, revealed his feelings. "My husband, Captain Xanthakos—we were not married at the time—was under orders to take only the able-bodied prisoners with him."

"Understood." Mr. McCord's countenance shut down again. "Explain, if you would, how you managed to avoid being arrested for your part in the rescue."

"I was part of an escort for supplies and food that was taken to the ship on Christmas Eve—"

"The origin of these supplies?"

"Ladies of compassion, Tory and Whig." She reached for Andrew's hand. "There was a British officer, Captain McKenzie, who had been billeted with us. He was very kind. Helped Andrew recover from a gunshot wound he received at the Battle of Camden. The evening of the rescue, he insisted upon accompanying us. But during the scuffle, he was knocked unconscious."

Andrew, curling his fingers around hers, blurted, "One of the prisoners tried to stab Captain McKenzie, but Lilyan thwarted him. Took a knife wound to her own arm."

The barrister furrowed his forehead. "Sir, I must hear Mrs. Xanthakos's account."

She glanced askance at her brother. "It is as Andrew described."

"And the wound?"

She pulled up the sleeve of her dress to expose the long, jagged scar.

"Who attended to you?"

"Dr. Cheek. A physician at the British hospital who accompanied me on board the *Brixham*. But, if you're considering questioning him, I don't know if he and his wife remained in Charlestown or left when the troops did."

Mr. McCord opened his lapdesk and pulled out a sheaf of papers and a pencil and scribbled a few notes. "You were interrogated about the incident?"

"No. The next day word had spread that I had saved the life of a British officer. They called me the heroine of Charlestown. I assume that because of that, and because I was recuperating, I was spared the inquisition."

"Go on."

"After that, the patriots asked me to accept a commission—"

"A commission?"

"To paint a mural. I'm an artist, Mr. McCord."

He regarded her with speculation and then returned his attention to his notes, rotating his hand to spur her on.

"As I was saying, I was to paint a mural at Violet Plantation."

"The scene of the crime?"

Callum, who had remained uncustomarily quiet, groused under his breath. "An act of courage. Of heroism. Not a crime."

"The plantation was sequestrated from its owner by a loyalist. A Mrs. Felicity Melborne." She cocked her head to see what Mr. McCord was writing. "Her husband served under Cornwallis, and she was a cousin to Tarleton."

Felicity Melborne and Tarleton—both names left a sour taste

in her mouth.

"Mrs. Melborne was quite the hostess, opening up her home to high-ranking British officers. My mission was to pass along any information I came across while I was painting."

She dropped her hands into her lap and studied her fingernails. It had been quite a while since she had painted. Turning her hands over, she realized how empty they seemed. But not from the absence of paintbrushes. *How long it's been since I tucked my daughter's hair underneath her mobcap. The weeks gone by since I caressed my husband's face.*

"Mrs. Xanthakos?"

She glanced up and met Mr. McCord's discerning eyes.

"Right." She straightened her spine. "Captain Bradenton came to dinner one evening, and Mrs. Melborne insisted that Elizabeth and I dine with them."

"Who is Elizabeth?"

"Elizabeth was my dearest friend. She was Cherokee. Someone who acted as a nanny to Andrew and me when our mother died, but who became a part of our family."

For the next half hour, the attorney compelled her to walk him through, step by painful step, the events of that evening. After probing into the minute details, he concluded that there had been no witnesses to the event except Poseidon, a freed slave and servant to the former owner of Violet Plantation. But even he had not actually seen the crime, coming upon Lilyan and Elizabeth only after the fact.

Overwhelmed, Lilyan pressed her fingers to her temples.

Mr. McCord leaned forward. "You are tired, madam. We have gone over much. I will come back another time," he said, rising from the bench.

"No, wait, please. There are three women …" She looked at the prisoners. "Over there … who need your help. I don't know them well, but I do believe them when they say they're innocent. And I'm certain they can't afford representation. My family will pay if necessary." She held her hands out to him. "Can we help?"

"I will see what I can do." He made to leave but turned back. "Do you know if this is their first offense?"

Lilyan shook her head.

"Can they read?" he asked.

"I don't know that either."

"It's important you find out. And now I will leave you to your family."

After he departed, Lilyan spent some time huddled between Andrew and Callum, drawing much-needed strength and reassurance from them, until Mr. Martin announced that visitors must go. They stood while Andrew prayed, and then they hugged each other one more time.

"Mr. Martin? Is it permissible for my brother to bring me a few things?"

"Such as?"

"A blanket. Some clean clothes ... my medicine chest?"

"Yes. I'll allow that."

Andrew left with Callum and returned an hour later with the items she had requested as well as some extra blankets, which she gave to other prisoners. As he was leaving again, he turned around at the bottom of the stairs. His forlorn expression almost crushed her, and she had to dig into her reserve of courage to smile and wave good-bye.

She joined the others and sat on the bale that had become her settee and bed. She opened her medicine chest and pulled out a tin of salve. After unscrewing the top, she beckoned Constance to sit beside her. Taking the utmost care, she bathed the crusted blood from the woman's swollen lip and spread a layer of ointment on the cut.

Lilyan was surprised to see tears in her eyes. "Am I hurting you?"

"No. It's just that ... well." Constance touched the corner of her mouth. "No one has treated me so gen'le in a long time."

The woman's soulful eyes tugged at Lilyan's heart, and she raised a silent prayer that her new friend would be treated more kindly in the future.

"You must keep this clean, Constance." Lilyan took the tin cup she kept in the chest and filled it from their drinking water bucket and then stirred in a pinch of chamomile leaves. "If allowed to heal, I don't think it is deep enough to scar."

She poured a bit of the mixture on a cloth and gingerly pressed it into the abrasions on the woman's shoulders. "This should relieve the soreness and help the bruises fade faster. Apply this two to three times a day, and I think you'll heal quickly." She handed the cup and the cloth to Constance.

"Now, Sally, let me see your hands."

Hesitantly, Sally rested her gnarled hands palms up on Lilyan's knees. "Can't hardly feel my thumbs no more."

Lilyan traced the tendons that stretched across her wrists. "There's a deal of damage here. The tendons are very thick. From all the twisting and wringing of clothes, I imagine."

Dejected, Sally dropped her hands into her lap. "Can you make it better? I gotta work. Else I'll be on the streets."

"I'm not a doctor, and I'm sorry I can't help with numbness, but I can give you something that will give you relief from the chilblains."

"Hey, missy," one of the men yelled, peering through the barred windows of his cell. "Got me a rash. You know. In me privates. Think you could give *me* some relief?"

Lilyan bristled. *Foul-mouthed clod.*

Several of the male prisoners snickered, but Constance jumped up and pumped her fist. "Keep talkin' like that, you bloke, and you'd best not sleep heavy. You might wake up missin' part of them privates."

Pursing her quivering lips, Lilyan could not suppress the giggle that built up inside. She glanced at Sally, who had her hands clamped over her mouth, and then she caught the merriment in Mildred's eyes. Mildred was the first to give in with a loud *whoop*. Soon all four of them were laughing, until Constance begged them to stop to avoid cracking open her lip again.

Still chuckling, Lilyan delved into her medicine kit and pulled out the items she needed. "Sally, I'm combining a little bit of turmeric and ginger into an ointment that I have, but you can use lard. When you are back home, rub it onto your fingers before bedtime each night and cover them with gloves. That should help the inflammation."

"My. My." Sally flexed her fingers as Lilyan massaged the salve into her skin. "Feels better already."

Lilyan wiped her hands on a piece of cloth. "Now, I want to tell you something, but I don't want to get your hopes up."

The women leaned in.

"Mr. McCord has agreed to try to help you—"

"Help *me*?" Sally yelped, clasping her hand to her heart.

"Yes, all of you. But he needs some information. Is this your first offense?"

They nodded.

"Yes, I promise." Mildred held up her hand in a swearing motion. "And I pray it's the last."

"And can you read?"

Mildred stared at her. "Can't think where this is headed, but yes."

Constance nodded again, but Sally ducked her head and whimpered, "Does that matter?"

"I don't know. Don't you worry, though. We'll sort it out."

Lilyan snapped the latch on the medicine chest and was putting it next to the things Andrew had brought when she noticed a piece of paper that had been folded into her clean dress. Taking a furtive look around, she lifted the material and found a sketch of Laurel. Seeing her daughter's face pierced her like a knife, and she clutched the picture to her breast.

"What's wrong?" Mildred scooted next to her.

Lilyan showed her the paper. "It's my daughter, Laurel. She was kidnapped. Six weeks ago."

Mildred took the sketch and turned it so the others could see.

Sally ran her gnarled knuckles across the paper. "She's beautiful."

"Like an angel," said Constance. "Who'd do such a terrible thing?"

Lilyan took back the picture. "Slavers. They attacked the Cherokee village where my sister-in-law's family lives. She was visiting and had taken Laurel with her."

Mildred crossed her arms in front of her. "Losing a little one ... it's a pain like no other."

"You lost a child?" Lilyan asked.

"She'd be four years old now. Died of measles. She and my husband both. Thought I'd lose my mind. So I indentured myself and came to America. But ..." She glanced away. "You can't never get away from something like that."

Lilyan sorely wanted to express her empathy, but she couldn't form the words.

Mildred tutted. "You got enough to worry about without taking on my troubles."

The remains of the day passed slowly for Lilyan, whose melancholy grew almost unbearable after sharing with her new friends about Laurel. By suppertime, her emotions were so ragged, the women had to cajole her into eating, which she promptly lost a half hour later. Preparing for bed, they pulled several piles of hay together to form one large mattress, not only for comfort and security, but, Lilyan thought, also to assuage their desperate loneliness.

Lying on her side, Lilyan rubbed her fingers across the picture tucked into her chemise. *Do not forget me, dear one. Please, do not forget your ma, who loves you more than life.* It took a while, but her body finally gave in to sleep, only to be partially roused sometime during the night by the arrival of more prisoners.

She awoke before the others with a painful cramp in her calf. She slid from the bed and hopped around, struggling to loosen the knotted muscle. Trying not to wake anyone, she hobbled back and forth when suddenly a hand clamped over her mouth and an arm snaked around her middle, slamming her against a chest as hard as stone.

"Don't scream," the man ordered.

CHAPTER 14

For he shall give his angels charge over thee, to keep thee in all thy ways.
They shall bear thee up in their hands, lest thou dash
thy foot against a stone.
Psalm 91:11-12 KJV

Lilyan wrapped her hands around her assailant's thick wrist and pulled with all her might, but she couldn't budge his viselike grip.

"Easy, Mrs. Xanthakos." The man's mouth almost touched her ear. "Callum sent us."

Relief shot through her body and she wilted, her knees no longer able to support her.

"Here, now." He removed his hand from her mouth and helped her to a seat.

She slumped onto the hard wooden plank, leaned her head against the wall, and waited for the tremors in her arms and legs to subside.

"Sorry, Mrs. Xanthakos. But I had to take my moment when I could, you know. Didn't mean to give you such a scare. Callum would chew my ears off if he thought I'd brought you harm."

She opened her eyes and took a good look at him. Tall and sinewy, his features could have been carved out of granite. Skin the color of one of Lilyan's clay pots, a badly set broken nose, and a day-old beard added to his rugged appearance. He glanced around the room, his hawk-like eyes wary, his body coiled as tightly as a freshly baited wolf trap, reminding her of the men who fought with General Marion—hardened, seasoned, and dangerous.

"Callum sent you?"

He jerked his head, and two men appeared like ghosts from behind a brick column and stood beside him.

"Sent *us*. I'm Gilbert." He looked to one and then the other. "This here is Thompson and Bell."

The men, cut from the same swath as Gilbert, nodded.

Thompson chuckled. "Never had to bribe my way *into* a jail before."

Gilbert jerked his head again, and his companions returned to the shadows.

"Puttin' it as quick as I can … there's rumors brewing about you being a loyalist. People are gettin' all fired up. There's some talk about takin' you from the jail and—"

"T-tar and feathers," she stammered, horrible visions from the day before looming in her head.

"Yes, ma'am. But, don't you fear none. There's only three of us in here. Sent to get you out, if needs be. But there's many more outside." He grinned. "One in particular who might interest you."

She stared, not sure of his meaning.

"Captain Xanthakos hisself."

"Nikki!"

His furtive eyes scanned the dungeon. "Not so loud, ma'am."

She hunched her shoulders and lowered her voice. "My husband? In Charlestown?"

"Got here a coupla hours afore we hatched this plan. Said he'd see you first thing in the morning, when visitors are allowed."

Her heart soared. *Thank you, God. Thank you.*

"Mr. Gilbert?"

"Ma'am?"

"Was there any mention of our daughter, Laurel?"

"No news. But, there's people out there lookin' hard." His face muscles set, he stood and held out his hand. "You'd best try an' get some rest. There's still some time left to the night. Though how a body can tell in this hellish pit, I ain't sure."

She returned to her pallet where she kept repeating to herself, "I'll see my Nikki soon," and fell into a fitful sleep intermittently disturbed by the snoring duel between Constance and Sally.

Her news the next morning sent her friends scurrying. Somehow, among the prisoners, they managed to scrounge a brush and a splinter of soap. They held up a blanket while Lilyan sponged off and donned a clean dress. She let Mildred wash and dry her hair and then braid it, fluffing out tendrils from her mobcap to frame her face. Using a cloth from her medicine kit, she scrubbed her teeth. She uncorked a bottle of dried mint, put a pinch of the leaves on her tongue, and swirled it around in her mouth. Her stomach in turmoil, she refused breakfast and sat facing the stairs until she caught the sound of keys and heard footsteps coming down the stairwell. Tension whirled through her body, and when she spotted someone standing in the entrance, she sprang up. But as she took a step, the world went hazy.

Semiconscious, she felt herself being picked up and carried, cradled in a pair of strong arms and pressed against a solid chest. Struggling through a fog, she came to, expecting to see her husband's golden eyes. Instead, she found a mixture of indigo purple and woad.

Mildred and Constance hovered over her.

Sally bounced around on her tiptoes and kept saying, "My. Oh. My. Oh. My."

Lilyan blinked, trying to make sense of what was happening, and found herself looking up at Mr. McCord's face very close to her own.

He tightened his hold. "I have you."

"Lilyan?" a wonderfully familiar voice called out.

She eased up and turned to discover her husband, wide-eyed and incredulous. Without a word, she held her arms open wide, and Nicholas strode forward and swept her up.

"*I* have her now," he said gruffly, before carrying her to the farthest corner of the room.

He dropped onto a bench, and without either of them saying a word, they clung to each other, unable to hold on tight enough. After a time, he pushed off her cap and rained kisses over her face, then leaned back and searched her eyes.

"Ei agapomene mou. My beloved," he whispered and then drew her lips into a kiss that warmed her down to her soul, leaving her breathless.

"You're here. You're really here," she murmured, fighting back tears.

He hugged her again, pressing his face into her neck and breathing deeply. "Kardia mou. My heart."

She tucked her face into the opening of his shirt and sighed from pure happiness.

Taking her by the forearms, he gently pushed her away. "You are well?"

Regretting the worry lines on his face, she caressed his cheek. "As well as can be expected."

"When I reached the city, I could not believe my ears when they said you had been arrested." He perused the dungeon. "That you should be in this terrible place. Diavolo!"

"What about our little girl?" she asked, sliding her hands onto his shoulders.

"No word, my love. But. Know this. We will find her."

Lilyan's lip quivered. "I miss her so."

"As do I."

Lilyan heard someone clear his throat and turned to find Mr. Gilbert and his men standing nearby, respectfully looking the other way. Behind him she noticed Mr. McCord conversing with Constance, handing her a book. He caught her eye, and when he started walking toward her, she slipped from Nicholas's lap.

"Nicholas." She put her hand on his shoulder. "This is Mr. McCord, my representative."

Nicholas stood and clasped the barrister's hand, tension crackling between them as they took stock of each other. After a few moments, he relaxed his shoulders, a telltale sign of his unspoken approval.

"What are your plans?" Nicholas asked, sitting back down with Lilyan and motioning for him to take a seat.

"Thankfully, time is on our side," Mr. McCord began. "The grand jury has already been called for three cases—two murders and a burglary arson. The jury will hear arguments from the attorney general and members of the bar this Saturday, and we plan to make sure our case is added to the docket."

"But I thought you said time is on our side." Nicholas frowned and worked his jaw. "Can you prepare arguments that quickly?"

Mr. McCord raised an eyebrow. "I have prepared them already. The reason I said that time is on our side is, if Lil—your wife's—case is not heard this week, she would have to stay here for three more months until the grand jury reconvenes again in October."

Lilyan looked over Nicholas's shoulder at one of the women plucking lice from another's hair. Feeling queasy, she squeezed his hand. "I'm not sure I could bear that."

He threaded his fingers through hers. "Don't worry. I assure you, I would not have allowed that. I have the means to get you out of here, if need be."

Mr. McCord seemed to consider Nicholas's proclamation.

"What I would like to know, Mr. McCord, is who brought the charges against my wife?"

"Daniel Chambers, Esquire."

Lilyan gasped. "I knew it."

"Who is this Chambers?" Nicholas spoke in a tone usually

reserved for his soldiers.

"The Bradenton family's attorney. The one who put the bounty on my head. I saw him in the sheriff's office. Though we've never met, I was familiar with his name, and I could see that he knew who I was. From the wanted posters, I'm sure. But it's been over two years."

Nicholas turned to Mr. McCord. "Would the governor allow a British sympathizer to continue practicing law?"

"No, I'm certain he would not. But Chambers comes from a family that supported the American cause with everything it had. One would find it a difficult task to disbar him."

Nicholas raised an eyebrow. "But if he is a patriot, why would he want to continue representing the family of a man who fought against us?"

"Excellent question," said Mr. McCord. "Chambers has a reputation—he is a zealot for justice, and he is tenacious when it comes to the law. A veritable stickler for following it to the letter." He smirked. "That is why he aims to be chief justice."

Nicholas looked at the barrister as if taking his measure. "And you are not a stickler for following the letter of the law?"

"I? My ambitions lie elsewhere. I desire to irritate the men who make the laws." Mr. McCord put his hand to his heart and bowed from the waist. "That is why *I* plan to be the next governor."

Nicholas chuckled, and Lilyan was relieved by the dissipating tension between them.

Mr. McCord removed a piece of paper from his pocket. "Speaking of the governor. Mr. Xanthakos, do you or does someone close to you know him? Or anyone else of consequence who could write a letter to the associate justices presiding over the hearing? Judges have been known to dismiss even the most serious of charges if a recommendation carries enough weight."

Lilyan waited for Nicholas to speak, but he seemed deep in thought, so she forged ahead. "My husband was a captain in General Marion's militia. I had the honor, upon occasion, to share the general's company. He is a quiet … shy … man, and thus our conversations were limited, but my husband knows him well." She put her hand on her husband's knee. "Do you recall, Nikki, how gallant he was? Though he could not attend our wedding, he provided an orchid for my bouquet."

He nodded slowly, a corner of his mouth curled into a melancholy smile. "I remember."

"Could we prevail upon him to help us?"

"I know we can. I remember the general's exact words on the day we disbanded. He promised he would be happy to render every service in his power should any of us at any time need such help."

"Excellent!" Mr. McCord slipped the paper back into his pocket. "Governor Guerard has convened the legislature for next week. So it's very likely Marion, who is a senator now, is already here in Charlestown. I will seek him out."

Mr. McCord stood, his face unreadable once again as he turned to Lilyan. "I probably will not see you until Saturday. I will attempt to send word if I am able to enlist the senator's help."

He bowed. "Madam. Sir."

He had reached the stairs when Nicholas sprang up and called out, "One moment."

Lilyan studied them as they stood together, guarding their conversation. They were exactly the same height with similar frames, Nicholas's soot-black hair contrasting with Mr. McCord's white wig. They were handsome, each in his own way. Nicholas wore the coarse linen shirt and buckskin breeches of a woodsman, his boots scuffed from weeks of travel. There wasn't a piece of lint to be found on Mr. McCord's severely cut black suit. His white, starched collar was as pristine as his highly-polished buckled shoes. Similar in many ways, both were honest men of strong character, ready to serve when needed. But there was a vast difference. Simply put, she adored one of them with all her being and admired the other.

After talking with the barrister, Nicholas spoke briefly with Mr.

Gilbert before returning to her.

Lilyan waited for him to settle beside her before she spoke. "Nikki?"

"Yes, my love?"

"You asked me earlier if I am well."

He slumped onto the bench and lifted her hands from her lap.

She clasped his warm fingers. "You have been under such strain. So many responsibilities and worries. I struggled with this decision to tell you—"

"Lilyanista, you are driving me insane. What is it?" The gold in his irises intensified.

She cupped his face in her hand, caressing his smoothly shaven cheek with her thumb. "It is something quite wonderful compared to all else." She leaned close, kissed him on the corner of his mouth, and whispered in his ear, "I am with child."

CHAPTER 15

Have mercy on me, O God, according to your unfailing love; according to your great compassion blot out my transgressions. Wash away all my iniquity and cleanse me from my sin.
Psalm 51:1

The following morning, Lilyan shared her news with her friends.

Mildred slapped her knee. "I knew it. The way you kept casting up your accounts after eating."

"Ah! That's what you told your husband that made him act so," said Constance. "First he looked perplexed. And then, when he dropped to his knee and put his head in your lap ... 'twas enough to make me cry. And I haven't cried in a long time."

Dreamy-eyed, Sally pressed her hand on her heart. "Such a handsome man, your husband."

Mildred snorted. "Do forgive us for snooping."

"Not snooping. Sharing good news, I'd call it." Constance looked over her shoulder. "Besides, there's scarce privacy here."

Sally scrutinized the people clustered into groups, all within earshot, though most seemed to be minding their own business. "You got that aright."

"We have news of our own," said Mildred. "Mr. McCord said, since each of us is charged for the first time, we can claim benefit of clergy. Depending on the judge, it could lessen our sentence or do away with it lock, stock, and barrel."

"Benefit of clergy?" asked Lilyan.

"Some kind of way—I don't understand why—we have to prove we can read," Mildred answered. "Most often it happens by reading Psalm 51."

"Them two can read, but ..." Sally's chin quivered. "Since I can't, Mr. McCord says I gotta memorize it and hope and pray that's the one they pick to test me."

Mildred hurrumphed. "I might be able to read, Sally, but the brooch I'm accused of stealing cost three pounds, so I'm charged with larceny. If the judge doesn't want to grant me benefit, he can give me five lashes. And where would I get the kind of money it'll take to pay a solicitor?"

"Five lashes!" Sally screeched and jumped up, her eyes darting toward the stairway. "I heard we could be branded, too. Lord, save us."

"Get a hold to yerself." Constance gripped Sally's arm and sat her back down. "Remember what Mr. McCord said? We go before the justice of the peace where the benefit should get us off safe. Our crimes ain't bad enough for general sessions. There'll be no lashes. No branding."

"My bondholder's the only one I can borrow from if I get shackled with lawyer costs." Mildred sighed. "There's something even worse. Because I ain't been working, she can lengthen my contract six weeks for every one I'm gone. My contract woulda been over in two weeks. No telling how much longer I'll have to work."

"We'll find a way." Lilyan took the Bible from Constance. "In the meantime, let's start memorizing."

Sally, despite her timid demeanor, proved she had a lively mind by learning the passage much faster than Lilyan expected, which turned out to be fortunate, for after lunch, the jailor entered the dungeon carrying two sets of shackles.

"Prisoners Hastings and Franklin, you're being summoned before Justice Carleton this afternoon."

Sally balled up her skirt in her fists. "But I ain't ready," she wailed.

Lilyan stood with the women, forming a circle around their friend.

"You're ready. Trust me." Lilyan handed the Bible to Sally. "Would it make you feel better if we prayed?"

"Y-yes. It would."

They held hands while Lilyan lifted up their friend to the Lord, beseeching Him for mercy and a good outcome. Feeling Sally trembling beside her, she added a silent prayer of her own for courage.

"Can't wait here all day," the jailor interrupted, taunting them by jangling the chains. "The hangman awaits."

Lilyan glowered at him. "Why would you say such a thing? Can't you see these women are afraid?"

The man sniffed. "A little jailhouse humor, ladies. Don't take it so serious." He pointed to Mildred. "Your time's coming. Most likely tomorrow."

The jailor fastened the cuffs on Sally and Constance and stepped back to allow them another round of hugs. Sally's eyes were so wide, Lilyan could see the whites all around the irises. Sally kept whispering under her breath, saying over and over the verses she might have to recite in front of a judge. Constance, though tense, seemed more confident.

As Sally disappeared up the stairwell, clutching the Bible, she hollered, "Pray for us."

Dear Lord, life hasn't been easy for these women. Let there be a good outcome to all of this.

"Have mercy on me, O God, according to your unfailing love," Lilyan called out one of the lines from Psalm 51.

"According to your great compassion blot out my transgressions," Sally shouted back the rest of the verse before the dungeon doors shut.

Lilyan and Mildred sat quietly until they heard the opening of the dungeon door followed by footsteps on the stairs. A small group of people huddled at the entrance, peering into the dimness, adjusting their eyes to the torch-lit cavern. A handful of prisoners rushed forward to greet their visitors, each group separating itself from the rest, seeking as much seclusion as possible.

Lilyan heard a familiar voice call out "Mrs. Xanthakos" and looked up to see Robbie striding toward her. Delighted, she jumped up and threw her arms around him, not realizing until that moment how lonely she had been for a familiar face.

"Ach." Robbie gently untangled her arms from around his neck. "'Tis a gruesome place we find ourselves in."

Lilyan smiled. "It took me a while to accustom myself to the smell."

His derisive snort told her he wondered how she could have managed that. But he didn't say the words out loud. *His mother raised him well.*

Lilyan motioned for Mildred to join them away from the others.

"Mildred, this is Robbie Forbes. He and his father and brothers have been helping us search for my daughter. Robbie, this is Mrs. Mildred Lewis, my friend."

Robbie bowed. "Pleased to make your acquaintance, Mrs. Lewis."

Mildred bobbed a curtsy before they sat on a bench that had been pushed against the wall near one of the torches.

Lilyan leaned forward and glanced at the entrance. "You're alone?"

"Aye. Feelings are riding high in this city, ma'am. Andrew doesn't think it safe for Golden Fawn to leave the house, so Callum bides his time standing guard."

"All are well?"

"Aye. Golden Fawn spends hours up on the widow's walk. Callum is … well … Callum. Ye ken?"

Lilyan clearly pictured a very worried Golden Fawn pacing the house and a frustrated Callum downstairs, growling like a bear with a thorn in its paw. She nodded. "I ken."

"Me and Andrew, we've been combing the docks trying our best to find your bairn."

"And my husband?"

"He's chasing down some clues with Samuel. I dinna know where or when they sleep."

"Robbie, there's something I need for you to do. Concerning Mildred."

He looked at her with a steady gaze.

"Her trial's tomorrow. If all goes well, she'll be released. You must go there. If she's charged with any costs, you'll pay them for her—"

"But—" Mildred began.

Lilyan stopped Mildred with her hand. "Ask Callum for the monies. Then accompany Mildred to the person who owns her contract." She turned to Mildred. "What's her name?"

"Collins. Mrs. Collins."

"You must go with her to Mrs. Collins and offer to purchase her remaining indentured time. If she refuses, tell her that our representative, Mr. James McCord, Esquire, will begin inquiries into who really pilfered the brooch Mildred is accused of stealing."

Mildred wiped a tear away with her knuckle. "You would do this for me?"

"Most assuredly." She thought it humorous to be using the phrase Nicholas was in the habit of saying. "We're friends. I would do anything for you."

Lilyan glanced at the entrance once more, and her heart almost jumped out of her chest when she saw Nicholas sprinting toward her, his eyes brilliant with hope.

"It's Laurel," he shouted. "I know where she is!"

CHAPTER 16

The chamomile is the rebel flower, a symbol of the patriots because the more it's trod upon, the stronger it comes back.
Anna Elliott, Charlestown, SC

"Where?" Lilyan screeched, throwing herself into his arms.

"She and the Brambles sailed for Baltimore yesterday."

Joy rushed through her body, and she clasped his forearms. "To think she was so close. She may have passed this building on the way to the ship."

He picked her up and swung her around, then set her down quickly, splaying his hand across her stomach. "I should be more careful."

She placed her hand on top of his, and they exchanged a glance so full of love it warmed her bones.

Worried, she chewed on her bottom lip. "Our Laurel will be aboard a ship. Do you think she'll fare well? I cannot bear to think of her being sick."

"She's her mother's daughter. And you're the strongest woman I know." He tucked her into the crook of his arm.

"I feel many things right now. But strong isn't one of them."

She nestled his shoulder. "What's our plan?"

"I've booked passage on a schooner leaving Sunday. Laurel is aboard a cargo ship with two scheduled stops, so it's very likely we'll catch up with them before they reach Baltimore."

They sat with Mildred and Robbie, who beamed with anticipation.

"You're going on a sea voyage, sir?" Robbie asked with the eagerness of a puppy.

"Yes."

"Would it … could I go with you?"

He considered his request. "I'm not sure, lad. What would your father say?"

"I suspect he would agree," Robbie responded quickly but then frowned. "I'm not as sure about my ma."

Lilyan couldn't resist responding to the obvious plea for support in Robbie's eyes. "It seems that Robbie's been smitten."

Nicholas looked puzzled, and Robbie's face flushed.

"He's discovered the ocean," she explained.

"I see," Nicholas said with a glint of understanding in his eyes.

"And." She reassured young Robbie with a smile. "I think Mr. Forbes would honor whatever decision you make in his stead. After all, dear, you trusted me to his care, and he got me home safely."

"True. And so I am in his debt." Nicholas rubbed his thumb across the corner of his lip. "I'll consider it and let you know my decision soon. Does that suit?"

"Aye. It does, sir."

Nicholas began to fill in Mildred and Robbie on the plan to find Laurel, but Lilyan's thoughts stole away from their conversation. It was Thursday, and the grand jury was to hear her case on Saturday. Nicholas would leave Sunday. Could she be cleared in time to join him? If the hearing didn't go smoothly, it would take a miracle.

Lord, dare I ask for such a miracle?

Later that evening, without her husband's steadying presence, Lilyan's emotional compass went awry. Like a ship sailing in a tailwind, her heart sped with hope. *I might hold my child once again.* And then doubt battered her high-flying optimism. *But I face a hangman's noose. Surely they wouldn't execute a pregnant woman. Of course, they'd wait for me to have my baby. Wouldn't they?* But Nicholas had promised he would save her from such a fate. *What if someone got hurt … killed … in such an attempt?* Anxious about the jury's verdict, afraid for her life, she clung to the edge of a vortex that threatened to suck her down into a pit of despair.

Because neither she nor Mildred could sleep, she voiced her fears to her friend. "If they find me guilty and sentence me to death …" She swallowed. "They would not harm my child, would they?"

"Law says they can't," said one of the female prisoners sitting nearby.

Lilyan watched the woman push herself up from one of the bales of hay and walk toward them, her lumbering gate a sure sign of her condition. She stopped so close Lilyan could see that the buttons of her tattered woolen coat stretched taut across her stomach seemed ready to pop loose at any moment.

"My name's Fianna, and I couldn't help overhearin'."

Lilyan found Fianna's strong Irish brogue pleasing, as well as the combination of her bright red hair, green eyes, and the freckles splashed across her nose. Her hands itched for her brushes to paint the vibrant-looking young woman. "I'm Lilyan, and this is Mildred. Please, won't you sit down?"

Fianna rubbed the small of her back and then dropped with a heavy groan onto the bale beside Lilyan. "'Bout all I'm good for now. Sittin' that is."

On closer inspection, Lilyan realized that the woman must be in her late twenties—much younger than she had first thought. "You were saying something about the law?"

"Aye. Law says you can't hang a woman who's in the family way." She folded her arms and rested them on her stomach. "You're to plead your belly."

Lilyan pressed her hand to her barely swollen stomach. "Plead my belly?"

"Aye. Plenty of women have done it. Jenny Diver, the woman who taught many a street criminal how to filch a man's wallet." She grinned. "She's long gone, now, but she passed her skills on down to the likes of me."

She started counting off on her fingers. "Then there's Anne Bonney and Mary Read."

Unfamiliar with the names, Lilyan cocked her eyebrow.

Fianna gawked. "Don't tell me you ain't never heard of the fiercest women pirates that ever lived. And Anne Bonney from right here in Charlestown."

Mildred snorted. "I don't think Lilyan would have been around the kind of company to hear of such things."

"Oh, right, love." Fianna winked. "Anyways. Just tell the judge you want to plead your belly. He'll know your meaning. That's what's put off my hanging."

Lilyan gasped. "You are to hang?"

"Aye. My fault. All of it. Couldn't keep me fingers out of other people's pockets. Got caught in London and sent to Newgate. It being my first offense, they shipped me off to the colonies." She crossed her swollen ankles. "Thought me and my gang—other pickpockets like me—were coming to the same place, but my man was sent on to Georgia. Surprise that was. Anyways, water under the bridge, as they say."

Fianna stopped talking for a moment to watch her stomach pitch and roll. "Won't be long now, though. This one's wanting to make its presence known. Sad, don't you think, that I won't get to know the babe who gave me a few months' reprieve?"

Her sparkling emerald eyes held a strange combination of knowing and innocence.

Lilyan suddenly felt very sad. "I'm so sorry. I wish I could help you."

Fianna fidgeted with one of her coat buttons. "There's something I want to ask."

"Yes."

"You're a Christian, right?

"I am."

"I've seen you reading your Bible. But more than that I've watched how you treat other people. You're a true gentle woman." She cocked her head. "I can't help but wonder. If I'd met someone like you, when I was young. You know, before I took a wrong turn. Would things have been different?"

A feeling of expectancy tingled through Lilyan's body. Something profound was about to happen. Fianna was reaching out, searching for answers. *God, how do I help guide this person to you?*

"Fianna, have you heard the gospel? That Christ came to us in the form of man to lift the burdens of our sins from us? He sacrificed His life for us, and if we accept His gift, our debts are paid. And when we pass, we will go to be with our Father in heaven."

"I've heard the words, but I didn't pay them mind. Besides, only times I was ever in church was to look for marks sitting on the pew with me. Many a person left services lighter in their pocket because of me. I've done some awful things. I bet you never done anything bad in your life."

Lilyan locked eyes with Fianna. "I killed someone."

"Yes. I heard you talking. A British officer. But you did it to save your friend."

"Nonetheless, I took his life. Something I begged God's forgiveness for."

"And you believe that He forgave you?"

"With all my heart."

Fianna shrugged and held out her hands palms up. "Do you think God could ever forgive me?"

A big breath left Lilyan's body, and she shared a smile with Mildred, whose eyes swam with tears.

Lilyan clasped Fianna's hands. "I think God forgave you the moment you said those words."

"You hens going to keep up your cackling all night?" a man yelled from across the room. "Blast. You'd think I was in a church, not a prison."

Lilyan was stunned by the man's crassness.

Fianna slid to the edge of the bale. "Can't blame him for wanting to sleep. I used to feel the same. But somehow, sleep just ain't that important to me anymore." She stared deeply into Lilyan's eyes and must have seen some of the sadness there, for she patted Lilyan's shoulder. "Don't worry. I'm sure everything will turn out well for you."

Lilyan gulped. "Good night, Fianna. We'll talk more tomorrow."

Lilyan curled up under her blanket but sleep eluded her, so she and Mildred continued their whispered conversation throughout most of the night until the same man yelled at them to stop their gabbing. That request was followed by scuffling and muted groans. She couldn't see anything and wondered at the noises. Her curiosity was satisfied in the morning when, while waiting for breakfast, she spotted Mr. Gilbert glaring at a man at the back of the line who sported a newly acquired black eye.

The day dragged on until, finally, Mr. Martin arrived and announced it was time for Mildred to go.

Mildred stood at Lilyan's elbow as he approached them. "Everything'll be fine, I'm sure. Like it was for Constance and Sally."

They had received news that morning that both their friends had been given benefit of clergy and they were free. Sally had recited Psalm 51 perfectly.

Lilyan fluffed her friend's cap and tucked in a stray tendril of her hair. "Remember, you are to go with Robbie to my house and are welcome to stay for as long as you like."

Mildred hugged her. "I don't know how I'll ever repay you."

She held out her hands for Mr. Martin to secure the cuffs. At the bottom of the steps, she turned. Her lips trembled, and her eyes focused on something behind Lilyan. "I'm glad your guardian angels are with you."

Lilyan looked over her shoulder to find that Gilbert and his compatriots had closed ranks behind her. She held out her hands, palms upward. "Mr. Martin, would you be kind enough to let me know the verdict for Mrs. Lewis?"

"I will, ma'am. Soon as I'm able." He turned away, pressed his hand into the middle of Mildred's back, and escorted her up the stairs.

Lord, be with my friend. She is one of Yours. Give her courage, please. No matter the outcome.

Lilyan was exhausted and kept to herself, passing the afternoon by taking sporadic naps. She wondered why Nicholas had not come to see her.

Mr. Martin delivered the good news at suppertime. Mildred had been granted benefit of clergy. Mr. McCord had stood for her and had not charged a fee, and she was safely ensconced with the Camerons. Lilyan felt as if a boulder had been lifted from her chest.

Finally, after supper, Nicholas came to see her, bearing an armful of packages. But after only a few minutes' conversation, he took Gilbert, Thompson, and Bell aside. They huddled together, Gilbert casting furtive glances at the other prisoners.

She couldn't hear what they were saying, but she had a good view of her husband's face, illumined by a nearby torch. His eyes almost seemed feral, his countenance grim. She had seen that look many times during the war as he headed out with Marion to do battle.

Irritated with being excluded from plans she knew regarded her, she confronted them. "What's happening? I insist you tell me."

He took her by the elbow and walked with her to a bench, but she refused to sit, so he turned her back to the wall and shielded her body from the others.

"You've heard about the unrest? The accusations people are making about you?"

Anxiety gripped Lilyan's stomach muscles. "I've heard."

"Tomorrow morning, you'll be riding in an open wagon with three other prisoners. I've been enlisting help from friends, former militia, the people who worked with us against the British during the occupation. Anyone I can trust. We're going to line the three blocks to the courthouse. That's where you'll be the most vulnerable."

His words hurt. "They hate me that much?" She rested her hands on his chest.

He curled his hands around hers. "It's mob thinking. Like an epidemic, eating its way through the city. Patriots routing out loyalists. People who lost everything in the war hating those who profited from it. Elites looking down their noses at working people. Charlestown is a tinderbox."

She chewed on her lip and pressed down the corner of his shirt collar. She stared at him as fear and panic took turns bludgeoning her.

"Don't look at me like that, Lilyanista." He slid his arms around her. "I promise, I won't allow any harm to come to you. To our child."

"I know. I worry too much. But …" She clutched his forearm. "I know you think I'm brave, but right now, it's so much easier to keep hope when you're near."

"I put a plan in place should the hearing not end as we hope. Callum, Andrew, and Robbie will see it through, get you to safety."

He stared at the ceiling and then held his arms stiffly at his sides. "I'm torn, my love. I want to stay with you. But I must follow after our daughter. Have I made the right choice?"

She struggled for words that would let him know he had made the right decision. "As much as I want you by my side, you've got to find our precious daughter and restore her to us."

"Captain," Mr. Gilbert said from behind them, "they'll make you leave soon. We have to talk more about tomorrow."

Nicholas turned to go, but Lilyan put her hands on his shoulders. "There's one thing I would ask."

"You have only to say it."

"When this is all over. When—Lord willing—our family's back together again, safe in our home, promise me we'll find things to laugh about, and we'll live each day as God intended, with joy and gladness." She ran her fingers across his lips. "It's been ages since you laughed. It's such a wonderful sound. I want to hear it often."

He responded with a soft smile. "That's a promise I'll be most happy to keep."

When Nicholas left, Lilyan sat on her makeshift bed and opened the packages he had brought. One held a pristine white shift tucked inside a sapphire-blue bodice and skirt. A second package contained stockings and a pair of blue shoes. In the last, she found a starched white linen mobcap with a blue band and bow. Inside the cap was a piece of paper that had been folded into a small packet. She opened it and discovered two silver combs embellished with chamomiles. She followed the words on the paper with her fingertips.

Beloved Wife,
Remember the rebel flower? The more it's trod upon, the stronger it comes back.
Wear them in your hair for me tomorrow.
Your Most Adoring and Obedient Husband.

Lilyan held one of the combs in the palm of her hand, tracing her fingers across the finely wrought petals. *Thank you, dearest husband, for this symbol of courage. I'll need all I can muster tomorrow.*

CHAPTER 17

Let the sighing of the prisoner come before thee; according to the greatness of thy power preserve thou those that are appointed to die.
Psalm 79:11 KJV

Flanked by Mr. McCord and the sheriff, Lilyan crossed the threshold of the dungeon and into the street. The sun immediately blinded her, and she blinked, her eyes watering.

"There she is," a man yelled. "The Tory woman."

People gathered at the building entrance started grumbling, the sound like the low-pitched growl of a stalking predator. Their animosity slid down her spine like liquid tar.

"Steady," Mr. McCord murmured, taking her by the elbow.

Lilyan ducked her head as her eyes slowly adjusted to the sunlight. A wagon, drawn by two horses, stood nearby and held the three prisoners who had preceded her. Someone had placed a crate on the ground as a stepping stool. Prodded by the sheriff, she took a few steps toward it and spotted Nicholas standing at the back corner of the wagon. He looked splendid dressed in shiny black boots, buff-colored breeches, a cravat, and a cream waistcoat underneath a fawn-brown doublet. His curly, recently washed hair was raked into a queue tied with a brown ribbon. The look he gave her, the wonderful smile that was hers alone, bolstered her, and she straightened her spine.

She was about to put her foot up on the crate when a man broke free from the crowd. Nicholas reached for the pistol stuffed underneath his coat, and when the sheriff and Mr. McCord closed in, Lilyan's muscles tensed from head to toe. But then her husband's posture relaxed, and his smile encouraged her.

The short, swarthy man bowed, offering her his hand. "May I have the honor, Mrs. Xanthakos?"

Startled at first, she quickly recognized the man and realized that Nicholas, Mr. McCord, and the sheriff knew him as well.

"You're too kind, General."

He took her by the elbow and helped her into the wagon. He glared at the prisoners with a silent, unnerving warning that made them duck their heads and then looked back at Lilyan with a reassuring smile. "You will be safe. You have my promise."

"Thank you." She found it startling that his promise of safety seemed to make it so.

He stood back and tapped his brow in a salute. "Your servant, Madam."

"It's Marion!" someone shouted.

"What's he doin' here?" someone else asked.

"Marion's her friend?" another inquired, incredulous.

Lilyan could hear the news being passed along from one person to the next down the thoroughfare, news that seemed to restrain the crowd for a moment. When she was seated, the sheriff threw the crate in beside her, shut the wagon gate, and fastened it with a rope. She returned the general's nod and watched him turn to Mr. McCord.

"Sir." General Marion reached into his waistcoat and withdrew an envelope with a red wax seal. "I believe this is what you require."

"Thank you, Senator. You're most gracious."

Mr. McCord slipped the note into his coat, exposing the pistol hidden inside. Surprised, Lilyan stared at it and then shared a glance with him. His only response was a slight lift of the corner of his mouth.

Marion stepped away and motioned for Nicholas to join him. "Captain, I have something for you as well."

The difference in their heights obliged Nicholas to lean down to catch what the general was saying. Her husband's face, his movements, his demeanor—all reflected his deep respect for his former commander. Among his acquaintances, she had never met another he revered more. After a few moments of conversation, the general passed him an envelope and stepped back into the crowd.

The driver snapped the reins, lurching the wagon so hard Lilyan held onto the back gate to keep from falling. Nicholas strode forward and slid his hand underneath hers. Her shackles clanking, she clasped the seat underneath her knees with her other hand and studied her fellow prisoners. All were filthy with long, shaggy hair, scraggly beards, and ragged, dirt-encrusted fingernails. One wore the blousy pants and Monmouth cap of a sailor. The others were dressed in the coarse linen jackets of laborers. They had brought the prison stench with them and sat hunched over with their eyes downcast. She guessed the sailor's age to be late twenties, but his brown eyes ringed with dark circles seemed ancient. He gave her a fleeting look, drawing one side of his mouth up in a smirk full of irony. Just then, someone yelled something she couldn't make out. She saw rakes lifted high, and her mouth went dry.

"Shut your yap or I'll comb your ears from your head," came a familiar voice.

Lilyan leaned out to find Sally brandishing a rake toward a man a few feet away. Beside her stood Constance and Mildred, who smiled broadly at her and tipped their rakes when she passed by. As the wagon slowly progressed down the straight shot to the courthouse, she scanned the swarms of people, astonished to see men she recognized—her "guardian angels" who had been in prison with her and Nicholas's fellow militiamen. Here and there she heard people start to yell only to be cut off, followed by the sounds of fisticuffs. She observed one man being knocked to the ground and hurriedly dragged from the street.

Turning to Nicholas, who kept vigil, his eyes darting from one side of the road to the other, she caught his attention. There were so many things she wanted to say. How safe he made her feel, despite her dire circumstances. How proud she was to have a husband so well thought of that his friends would come to his aid. How very much she loved him.

But she only managed to murmur, "Thank you."

They finally came to a halt below a balcony on the Meeting Street side of the courthouse. The thought flitted across her mind that it was here, seven years ago, that the Declaration of Independence had been read aloud to the people of Charlestown. She had been fifteen. How much had happened to her since that time. And now, here she was in the same place again for another momentous occasion, on trial for her life.

The people nearby seemed subdued. She realized why when she spotted Samuel, standing straight with his arms crossed over his chest, his glower as formidable as any she had ever seen. Intimidated, the crowd gave him a wide berth.

When Nicholas helped her from the wagon, she heard someone whisper, "That's Marion's niece."

So, she realized, word had spread through the throngs of people, passed from one to the other, changed and embellished until, instead of Marion's friend, she had become a cherished relative. That thought pleased her so much, she wished it were so.

She surveyed the crowd once more. "Nikki, I didn't see Callum or Andrew?"

Before he could answer, Mr. McCord approached them. "Trust me, Nicholas," he said, reaching for Lilyan's arm.

Lilyan found herself being relinquished from her husband's care as he patted her hand and stepped beside Samuel. With Mr. McCord at her side, the sheriff escorted them into the courthouse.

Pausing in the doorway, she looked over her shoulder at Nicholas, who mouthed the word *courage*. She pressed her fingertips against one of the chamomile combs underneath her mobcap and struggled to tamp down her fears.

Mr. McCord, who had followed her gaze, said, "He cannot come with us. None can enter the courtroom but witnesses."

They passed through a spacious entryway and into an anteroom at the back of the building, where maroon velvet curtains hung from paned windows and draped onto loblolly floors polished to a high sheen. The strong scent of beeswax permeated the air.

"I have to leave you now,' said Mr. McCord. "The grand jury will be hearing four cases today, and I must find out where we are on the docket."

The panic that ricocheted through her insides must have shown in her eyes for he squeezed her fingers and added, "You'll be fine."

As he and the sheriff left through the prisoner's entrance into the courtroom, Mr. Martin hurried into the room, seated the others on a long mahogany bench, and then unlocked Lilyan's handcuffs.

"No need for these. Don't care what the sheriff says." He hooked the chains onto a ring hanging from his belt and then stationed himself at the side door of the building.

One of the prisoners held his arms toward the deputy. "And us?" he asked with a sneer.

Mr. Martin scowled. "Quiet, you beetle-browed, bracket-faced oaf. Or I'll chain up your feet as well."

Relieved to be rid of the heavy shackles, Lilyan perched on the edge of a nearby chair. Soon she would know her fate—a fate that rested in the hands of a jury comprising, according to her attorney, the elite of South Carolina. Would they be sympathetic? Would Mr. McCord plead her case, make them believe that, even though she had taken a life, she did it to save her friend from harm and for self-defense? Would her name be cleared? If found guilty, she could hang or be sent to a penal colony. With that, her hands began to tremble, and she balled them into fists, pressing them into the arms of her chair.

The whirring and clicking of a grandfather clock, followed by deep *bongs*, signaled nine o'clock. The sheriff threw open a door, and Lilyan jerked her head at the sound. Massaging her taut neck muscles, she watched him stride across the room, his boots clacking loudly on the wooden floors, punctuating the pounding in her heart.

He stopped before the sailor.

"Come on, lad," the sheriff said gruffly as he pulled the young man to his feet. Grasping the irons, he dragged him into the courtroom and shut the door behind them.

The other prisoners started mumbling. She couldn't hear what they were saying, but she could tell by the lines furrowing one's brow and the frown dragging down the other's face that they suffered from nerves as much as she.

"No chattering," Mr. Martin snapped, putting an end to their conversation.

It seemed only a few minutes passed when the door to the courtroom swung open once more. The sheriff shoved the sailor onto the seat.

"That was quick," said the prisoner charged with burglary and arson.

"Quicker than a bosun can swill a mug o' ale," said the sailor. "None o' them would look at me, neither. Not one question among 'em. Seemed in a hurry to get it over with."

"What's going on?" one of the prisoners asked in a loud voice that crackled from tension.

"Keep it down, Carleton," said Mr. Martin, who leaned against the wall, one ankle propped atop the other.

"The jury's votin'. Everyone but them got cleared out," the sailor responded.

Not ten minutes later, the sheriff came and hauled the sailor back into the courtroom. Upon their return, the look on the young man's face was pitiful when he slumped down onto the bench.

"So?" asked Carleton.

"Indicted me for murder," the sailor mumbled, moving his head back and forth in a daze. "My trial's Monday."

Carleton blew out a breath. "Things're moving mighty fast."

"Yep. They keep it up and …" The sailor dropped his face into his hands. "This time next week, I'll be already hung and shoved into my grave."

Lilyan could feel the blood draining from her face, and her heart pounded so loud in her ears that she couldn't hear the rest of what was said.

"Quiet," Mr. Martin warned.

The sheriff signaled to Carleton, who stood and, without looking back, preceded him from the room. Carleton's case took longer, and with each quarter-hour chime of the clock, Lilyan's throat became more parched until it hurt to swallow. At the mark of the hour, she pressed her hands to her chest, crushing against her skin the picture of Laurel she had tucked inside her chemise. A vision of her daughter came to her in vivid details—perched on her father's shoulders, her legs dangling down either side of his neck as she scooped his thick hair into spikes and laughed out loud while he mimicked a woodpecker. Fighting the tide of melancholy that swelled up inside of her, she pictured Nicholas and herself standing on the deck of a schooner, his hair tossed by the wind, a smile on his face as they sped nearer and nearer to Laurel.

Finally, the sheriff escorted Carleton back into the room to await the jury's vote. It didn't take them long to present a true bill indicting him for burglary and arson, also a hanging offense. He and the sailor sat stoop-shouldered and grim-faced. All semblance of swagger or bravado had vanished, their lives spent.

Red-faced and irritated, the sheriff sidled up to her, and her heart leapt. "You got a visitor," he ground out the words. "No one's supposed to be back here, but seein' as who it is, the judge allowed it. It ain't the custom, but …"

Thinking it might be Nicholas, Lilyan swiveled on the chair to find an elderly woman striding through the doorway, her back straight despite her age, her carriage stately as if she ruled all in her path. Maybe an inch taller than the sheriff, she wore a sky-blue satin dress with a mantua skirt draped open and attached with silver satin ribbons to reveal an underskirt of pale-blue silk embroidered with silver daisies. Her hair was tucked up under a frilly, white, lawn mobcap topped by a cocked hat the color of lapis lazuli. Her features, Lilyan thought, if studied individually, were not attractive. But viewed together, they became one of those faces her hands itched to paint. Lilyan slid off the chair and stood.

With eyes the same hue as her hat, the woman scanned Lilyan from her head to her toes. "Mrs. Xanthakos, I presume?"

Lilyan curtsied. "Yes."

The woman returned her curtsy, bobbing silver-streaked, light-brown ringlets on either side of her face. "Jimmy was right. 'Diamond of the first water,' he called you. You are quite lovely."

"Thank you," Lilyan answered, wondering who Jimmy was.

"You don't have a notion who I am, do you?"

"I'm sorry—"

"I'm James McCord's grandmother, Agnes McCord. Thought I'd keep you company for a bit." Motioning to a nearby window seat, she smiled, and deep laughter lines radiated in small parentheses from her eyes. "Come, let's sit together awhile."

Lilyan detected a hint of gardenias as they sat, knee to knee, in the small alcove. She glanced over her shoulder at the crowd that still milled about outside and bit her lip.

Following her glance, Mrs. McCord patted Lilyan's hand. "Never you mind them. They'll change their tune soon enough." She studied Lilyan's face. "Jimmy says you're an artist."

"Yes. Murals. Portraits. Lately, I've worked pottery."

"And how did you come about this skill?"

"When I was thirteen, my dah noticed some of my drawings and liked them so much, he hired a teacher—an artist from England. I studied with him for three years and then with an Italian teacher until I was eighteen. The pottery, I recently learned from my sister-in-law, who is Cherokee."

Mrs. McCord turned over Lilyan's hands and stroked her fingertips across her palms. "You have strong fingers. Very capable hands, I should say. A time ago, mine were like that." She glanced at her own manicured nails and laughed. "You wouldn't think it now, but once, I could hoe a field, milk a cow, and wield an axe as good as—no, better than—my husband. Speaking of which, I met your Nicholas outside. Fine-looking man you have there. Made my heart skip, even at my age."

Lilyan met the woman's twinkling eyes. "He's a very fine man."

"And the Indian with him? So stern looking. Gave me gooseflesh."

"That's Samuel, my husband's best friend."

"From what I hear, you and your husband are suffering through quite an ordeal. Especially with your daughter. Laurel, is it?"

"Yes." Ordeal seemed such a tepid word. Torment, anguish, and nightmare described it better. A powerful undertow of frustration threatened to snatch her feet out from under her.

"I can see that just hearing her name causes you pain." She crossed one foot over the other, exposing the toes of her sapphire-blue satin slippers. "We have much in common, you and I. I lost my first child when I was seventeen, not much younger than you."

Lilyan flinched. "How awful—"

"Not to worry, my dear." Mrs. McCord lifted her hand. "I married my first husband when we were both sixteen. The courtship and wedding were hurried-up affairs, as my husband was eager to set out to make our home in the backwoods. I thought I loved him, but looking back, I see that I was drawn to the adventure. I had no notion whatsoever of what true love really is. A year later, I found myself hoeing cornfields out in the middle of the wilderness with a two-month-old strapped to my back." She knitted her brow. "And then, one night they came. Indians. Killed my husband. Struck me down and left me for dead. Set our cabin ablaze and ran off with my little boy, Henry. I never saw him again."

The words, spoken so bluntly and without embellishment, stirred up the terror that resided in Lilyan's chest, but she managed to stammer, "I'm so sorry."

"Eventually my heart and my mind mended. In my thirties, I met my second husband, James, the love of my life, who gave me eight beautiful children." She slid her locket back and forth across its chain. "That is not to say the eight took the place of the one. For years, I envisioned little scenes where I would run into my Henry: walking into a trading post, fishing by a stream, docking a boatload of deerskins here in Charlestown."

Lilyan was amazed by how the woman's thoughts mirrored her own.

"To this day, I wonder if my son lived to be a man, to have a family of his own. I tell you this so you will know, should you—God forbid—not find your Laurel, one *can* survive the terrible, unspeakable pain of losing one's child. It took me a while, but I came to know that God will sustain us if we let Him."

Mrs. McCord was the second person in a week to talk to her about losing a child. Lilyan believed that God often brought messengers into his children's lives to warn them, protect them. Was He trying to tell her something?

What had Mrs. McCord just said? *With God's help, one can survive the terrible, unspeakable pain of losing one's child.* Lilyan believed it. Mrs. McCord and Mildred were both living proof. But she also knew if she survived never seeing Laurel again, it wouldn't be as the same person. A growing dread curled in her stomach. She was so deep in thought she jumped when Mrs. McCord spoke.

"Jimmy tells me you met your husband when you were both working for the patriots. When you rescued your brother from a prison ship."

"That's true."

"You lived as a camp follower with partisans after killing the fiendish British officer who attacked your friend?"

"I did." Lilyan wondered how Mr. McCord was able to share

with his grandmother so many details about her life, when she herself had not talked with him about it.

"So, you are courageous and determined, as well as pretty."

Lilyan looked down as Mrs. McCord curled her fingers around her hand.

"How I wish my Jimmy could find someone like you. You and your husband are the kind of people this country will need if we're going to make something of ourselves. God-fearing. Strong. Hardworking. Brave."

"I don't feel brave." Lilyan looked into the woman's eyes that were so like her grandson's. "I'm afraid, Mrs. McCord."

"Please, call me Agnes. And there's no need for fear. You'll be free soon. My Jimmy will see to that. After all this is done, you'll find that little one of yours. And," she winked, "if my eyes serve me well, you'll have more."

Lilyan pressed her hand against her stomach and wondered when this new one would make its presence known. No movement. Yet. But it was still early.

Not so for Fianna.

A vision of the young woman's candid green eyes came to mind, and Lilyan was overwhelmed by the urge to help her. "Agnes, we have only been acquainted these few minutes. But in that time I think I have come to know that you are a warm, generous woman. I would hate to presume, but I have a request of you."

Captivated, Agnes slipped forward to the edge of her chair. "What may I do for you, child?"

"It isn't for me. But for someone I met while in prison. A young woman. Her name is Fianna. A spirited, courageous woman who, I am sure, fell victim to adverse circumstances. She made some very bad choices."

"I should hate for someone to make an accounting of the unfortunate choices I have made in my life. How did this young person come to be in prison?"

"She was a pickpocket. A member of a gang of street criminals in London. Imprisoned in Newgate and sent here to the colonies."

Agnes raised an eyebrow.

"Despite all of that, I found her charming. Honest. I liked her. In other circumstances, I think we could have been friends."

"Quite a compliment for her. I must say. Your friendship would make for quite a prize, I'm thinking."

"I don't know about that."

"Simply speaking the truth." Agnes laced her fingers together in her lap. "Your request regards this person, Fianna?"

"Yes. She has been sentenced to hang."

"What a tragedy."

"It is. A terrible tragedy. And what is worse, she is with child. Due any time now. And as soon as it is born, the sentence will be carried out. I don't know what will happen to the babe." Near tears, Lilyan pressed her hands to her heart. "I … is there a way? Would you?" She gulped and dropped her hands to her lap. "I apologize. It makes me so sad I can barely manage to speak."

Agnes cleared her throat. "Not to worry, my dear. I will look into this matter. I promise. I will see that the child is cared for. You honor me. After all, God has instructed us to care for the orphans. Has He not?"

Just then, the door to the courtroom opened and the sheriff approached Lilyan. "You're next, Mrs. Xanthakos."

She stood and hugged Mrs. McCord, taking comfort from the strength that emanated from her sturdy, solid frame.

Mrs. McCord caressed Lilyan's cheek. "I wish I could go with you. But know this. I will be praying for you. And dear, my Jimmy is a fine attorney, and he has pledged by his honor to set you free. All will be well. I just know it."

"Thank you, Agnes." Lilyan reluctantly turned to the sheriff, who swept his arm toward the door.

With legs so wobbly she wondered if they could support her, she followed his lead.

Into the lion's den.

CHAPTER 18

I consider trial by jury as the only anchor yet imagined by man by which a government can be held to the principles of its Constitution.
Thomas Jefferson

Inside the courtroom, the sheriff motioned for Lilyan to stand behind a table. She hadn't been there long when she felt someone at her side and looked up to find Mr. McCord, his face unreadable, as usual.

The two attorneys for the state, one of whom was Daniel Chambers, took their places at the table beside them. Chambers's colleague, a gaunt middle-aged man, stared at Lilyan with intense brown-green eyes like an eagle eyeing a field mouse, patiently waiting for its dinner.

A hundred thoughts roiled in her mind, like kernels of oats whirling and tumbling, rising and falling, caught up in water on the brink of boiling. She scanned the room and noted the bench where the attorney general, who served as presiding officer and judge, chatted with the clerk as if unaware, or uncaring, that her life hung in the balance. The jurors—three rows of them—sat with legs crossed, lounging back in their chairs. Some seemed bored while others casually examined their fingernails or tucked kerchiefs into their coat cuffs.

How can they be so detached? Dear God, don't they realize how important this is? Sit up. Pay attention.

Mr. McCord had provided her with only a few details concerning what was about to transpire. He had explained that because the war had only recently ended, the judicial system was in turmoil. Though procedures were in place, they weren't always followed. It was up to individual judges to determine what went on in their courtrooms. That knowledge doubled Lilyan's uncertainty. Her hands trembled so hard, she clasped them together in front of her, closed her eyes, and lifted up a prayer for strength. She didn't realize how far her thoughts had drifted until Mr. McCord cleared his throat.

The clerk stood and addressed the court. "Hear ye, hear ye. A quorum of twenty-three members of the grand jury having been summoned, swearing an oath binding them to inquire diligently and objectively into all evidence without malice, fear, hatred, or other emotion, this day the sixteenth of June, in the year of our Lord 1783, to investigate charges against one Lilyan Allison Grace Cameron Xanthakos, that she, not having fear of God before her eyes and being moved and seduced by the instigation of the devil, did willfully, wickedly, and maliciously, on the twentieth of February in the year of our Lord 1781, destroy the life of one Captain Remington Bradenton, second son of the Earl of Bradenton of Great Britain, an officer in the recently vanquished forces of King George III, causing him to perish. A heinous and high-handed offense and infamous crime contrary to the peace of the laws of the state of South Carolina."

Lilyan cringed at the formal, direct language that punctuated the dreadfulness of her crime. *I killed someone.* That realization took form once again like a piece of driftwood spewed up on the shore, bloated out of shape by barnacles and pockmarked with worm holes.

If Mr. McCord had not tugged on her elbow and instructed her to sit, she may have pitched forward.

The judge pushed his round spectacles up on his nose and sat up straight, adjusting his white wig that draped down his red robe like spaniel hound ears. "Are the representatives for the state prepared?"

"We are," responded the attorney, who remained standing as Mr. Chambers scraped back a chair and sat.

"Is the representative for the accused prepared?" The judge's formidable voice rang in Lilyan's ears.

Mr. McCord bowed. "I am."

The judge gave Lilyan a cursory glance, but she claimed his attention for a moment longer by staring back. *He has kind eyes.* His face relaxed for an instant before his countenance grew solemn once again and he pronounced, "Mr. Gregg."

"If it pleases the court," Mr. Gregg began, "I should like to call our first witness, Mrs. Abigail Steadman."

Lilyan recognized the name of the neighbor who lived directly across the street from her house. A door at the back of the room opened, but she didn't turn around. Instead, she waited as Mrs. Steadman, guided by the sheriff, sat in a wooden spindle-backed chair between the bench and the jury.

The judge pointed his gavel toward the witness. "You have been duly sworn by the jury foreman, madam?"

"I have, sir." Mrs. Steadman, a rail-thin, elderly woman, fidgeted with a fold in her skirt and then grasped the tabs of the kerchief draped around her shoulders.

The judge swung his hound-dog eyes toward the foreman, who nodded. "Proceed, Mr. Gregg."

Mr. Gregg cleared his throat. "If you would, please, Mrs. Steadman, inform the jury of your relationship to the accused."

"She and her family—the Camerons, that is—has been my neighbors since my husband and me moved to Charlestown nigh on to ten years ago."

Although Lilyan now stared directly at her, the woman still had not looked her way.

"And how would you describe the Camerons?"

"Nice, but sometimes a bit snooty for my taste."

"Snooty?"

"You know, thinkin' 'cause they have money, they's better than everyone else. Lookin' down their noses at us cause we have slaves. Course, that didn't stop them from bringing that Cherokee gal into the house."

"Cherokee gal?" Mr. Gregg asked.

"Miss Elizabeth, they called her. Brought to tend to the children after their ma died."

The mention of her friend tugged at Lilyan's heart. It had been almost three years, but the loss still hurt.

"Miss Elizabeth and Mrs. Xanthakos. Did they get along?"

"I suspect so."

"Yes or no, Mrs. Steadman."

"Yes. Yes. They got along as far as I could tell. Though, sometimes they had words about how to handle Andrew."

Where is this leading? Why is he asking about Elizabeth?

"Who is Andrew?"

"Mrs. Xanthakos's brother. The one what ran off to fight for us at Camden and wound up on one of them ungodly British prison ships."

"So, Mrs. Xanthakos's sympathies lay with the patriots?"

"You would think so, with her brother and all ..." The woman flicked a glance at Lilyan for the first time.

Animosity had turned the woman's eyes into dark orbs. *She hates me. But I hardly know her.*

The attorney momentarily looked at Lilyan before focusing on the witness. "Yes?"

"She was much too friendly with the officer that was billeted in her house. Walking on the streets, in public, with him. Smiling. Laughing. It was a shame."

One of the jurors seated in the second row raised his hand. "I would request some clarification. Is now the proper time?"

"You may direct your question through the foreman, or pose it yourself," the judge spoke sharply, as if irritated by the interruption.

The juror, a youngish gentleman dressed in the latest fashion, leaned forward in his chair. "Mrs. Steadman, did Mrs. Xanthakos ever speak to you directly about this officer?"

"She did. Once."

"And what did she say?"

"Said she was ever so grateful because he was helping her brother recover from his wounds."

The man sat back, folded his arms across his chest, and tapped his fingertips together. "So could not her cordial attitude toward this man who was our enemy—as he was—have had its origins in gratitude?"

The woman snorted. "Not likely, I say. 'Cause treatin' him special wasn't even the half of it."

Mr. Gregg swept his arm toward the jury. "Please, enlighten us, Mrs. Steadman."

"When the Brits hightailed it out of our city, they took everything they could that wasn't nailed down, including our bells at St. Michael's." She sighed. "Stole all my family's valuables. Silver. My precious departed mother's jewelry. They even ransacked everyone's kitchens. Ceptin' *hers*." She jabbed her bony, arthritic-knobbed finger toward Lilyan. "Some British soldiers boarded up her house and nailed up a special order of protection so's no one would plunder *her* belongings."

The note on my door! Though Lilyan appreciated the kindness behind the gesture, she regretted the coals of resentment and hatred heaped upon her family as a result.

"What reason would they have for that?" asked Mr. Gregg.

Mrs. Steadman sneered. "She had a reputation, you see. Saved that same officer from getting killed when some patriots rescued our boys from a prison ship. Took a knife wound in his stead, she did. Brits even called her the *Heroine of Charlestown*. Huh!"

The elderly man sitting next to the young juror asking questions leaned forward. "Am I to understand that Mrs. Xanthakos saved the life of a British officer?"

"You understand rightly." The woman grinned so wide she exposed her gums. Her eyes were alight with triumph.

The elderly juror turned to the younger one. "Saved his life aboard a prison ship. Why would a lady of character have been in that situation in the first place?"

"Confusing to me," said another juror. "Saving one enemy officer. Killing another?"

Mr. McCord uncurled his tall frame and stood. "May I ask my learned colleague what this questioning has to do with the charges at hand?"

The jurors started mumbling among themselves, shaking their heads and pointing fingers at Lilyan.

They're turning against me. Panic sprang from her stomach and pushed bile into the back of her throat, making her cough.

The judge rapped his gavel against the desk. "I'll have order, gentlemen. And straightaway." He wobbled the gavel back and forth before pointing it at the attorney. "Mr. Gregg, I'm inclined to agree. What does all this have to do with our matter at hand?"

Mr. Gregg bowed. "I beg indulgence. I'm trying to establish the impulsive nature of the accused. Someone who allows passion to override reason."

That's not me. She stiffened her back and glared at Mr. Gregg, resenting his implications and hating the inability to respond. Why wasn't Mr. McCord saying more?

The judge put down his gavel. "Well, get on with it."

The young juror raised his hand again, and the judge sighed. "Yes?"

"I do apologize for being obtuse, but I have heard quite enough about the lady's character and about which side she favored. I don't think there's a person in this room who does not have a family member or acquaintance who chose to side with the Tories. It was, after all, a civil war. Brother against brother. Neighbor against neighbor. One need only look at Kings Mountain. There were only a handful of British present. The combatants were mostly colonials."

Some of the jurors glared at him, and others stared at him as if he had grown sea oats out of his ears.

"I think," he continued, "that I would very much like for us to get on with finding out exactly how the crime was committed. Did you witness it, Mrs. Steadman?"

She grimaced. "No."

The young man dusted a nonexistent piece of lint from his breeches leg. "Then I should prefer if we hear from someone who did."

Several of the jurors muttered in agreement.

"In that case," said Mr. Gregg, "I would like to call our next witness. Unless my colleague has questions of Mrs. Steadman."

Mr. McCord shook his head. "I do not."

"Very well, then," said the judge, nodding to Mrs. Steadman, "you are dismissed."

The woman jumped up and scurried past the table where Lilyan sat, turning her face to avoid eye contact.

"Call your next witness, Mr. Gregg," the judge ordered as he irritably rearranged his wig, which had become lopsided.

"We call Mrs. Oliver M. Laurens on behalf of Poseidon Laurens."

Lilyan's back went rigid. She spun around to watch a tall, elderly man lumber into the room, not looking to either side, but straight ahead, the tip of his cane tapping on the wooden floor. Leaning on his arm was a petite white-haired lady whose head barely reached his chest.

It had been over two years, but she remembered every detail of the last time she had seen Poseidon. After the horrible night of Captain Bradenton's death, Lilyan, Elizabeth, Callum, and her young assistant, Gerald, had huddled together in a cave the original plantation owner had used as a hideaway from Indian attacks. The cave was connected to the main house through a secret passageway Lilyan had discovered when she was preparing the dining room wall for a mural. The little band of refugees spent over a week in the cave, waiting for a chance to get away and avoid the British soldiers combing the area.

Lilyan spent those nightmarish days trying to come to terms with the death she had caused and praying for forgiveness. Guilt kept her in a constant state of tension. Her spirits remained as gloomy as the craggy gray walls of their chamber, as if a giant veil had been lowered in front of her, separating her from the others. She yearned for Nicholas—a yearning that induced a soul-deep loneliness that frightened her so much she would sit on the top step leading to the outside, seeking warmth from the sunshine that barely filtered through the thick hammock of trees hiding the entrance.

Poseidon had saved them. He snuck them their belongings, food, and water. Most importantly, he brought them news of the outside world and made contact with a nearby dairy farmer, a patriot sympathizer, who eventually secreted them in his root cellar.

The evening of their escape, Poseidon had led Lilyan and the others out of the cave and through a forest. Gooseflesh ran up her arms as she recalled the yellow glow of a full moon filtering through the dense pines overhead, the wind that fluttered the branches like quivering fans, and the snap of twigs that sent prongs of fear shooting up her spine. She had said good-bye to Poseidon on a secluded country road. But, before she climbed into the back of a wagon to hide under a pile of hay, she had turned to catch him standing with a tin lantern placed on the road between his feet.

His countenance was the same then as now, dignified and courageous. As he walked by, he stopped and gave her a reassuring smile, and Lilyan was shocked to see how much he had aged. He escorted Mrs. Laurens to the witness chair and walked to the back of the courtroom, where he sat on a lone chair that had been shoved against the wall.

The judge leaned forward as Mrs. Laurens settled in the chair. "You have been sworn in?" he asked.

She turned to him. "I have."

The judge looked again at the foreman for confirmation and said, "We will proceed."

"Mrs. Laurens, will you identify yourself to the jury?" said Mr. Gregg.

"I am Mrs. Olivia Laurens, mistress of Violet Plantation."

"Near Haddrell Point?" asked Mr. Gregg.

"Yes."

"You are here today in what capacity?"

"Since my houseman, Poseidon, as a Negro is prohibited from testifying, it is my duty to relay to the court the things he has said to me relative to this investigation." She paused and leaned toward the bench. "I was told I could do that—speak on Poseidon's behalf, that is."

"You are correct," said the judge. "We are more lenient about hearsay in the grand jury than in other courts."

Mrs. Laurens smiled at him and nodded, then turned a leery eye toward Mr. Gregg.

Mr. Gregg cleared his throat. "We appreciate your assistance, madam. And how long has Poseidon served you?"

"Since he was a boy."

"Is Poseidon a free man?"

"Going on ten years now."

"So, Poseidon was present on the night in question, the night that Captain Bradenton was murdered?"

"'Twas no murder, sir."

Mr. Gregg frowned. "Answer yes or no, please."

"Yes. He was there."

"And why was Mrs. Xanthakos at Violet Plantation that evening?"

"Mizz Melborne, the British woman who took over my plantation like it was her own and shoved me out without a 'by your leave,' hired Mrs. Xanthakos—she was Mistress Cameron to Poseidon at the time—to paint a mural."

"Why was Captain Bradenton at the plantation?"

"He and two others had come to dinner that evening."

"And what was the accused's relationship with Captain Bradenton?"

Mrs. Laurens puffed up. "I'm not exactly sure what you're insinuating."

"Were they cordial? Friendly?"

She sniffed. "As Poseidon tells it, the captain wasn't the kind for being friendly. Mean spirited. That's how Miss Elizabeth described him."

Mr. Gregg stepped closer to the bench. "Miss Elizabeth?"

"Mrs. Xanthakos's companion. Her friend."

"What was Miss Elizabeth's relationship with Captain Bradenton?"

Mrs. Laurens looked toward Poseidon, who shifted his weight and stretched out one leg.

"From what I understand, the captain was attracted to Miss Elizabeth. Worried her to death with it."

Lilyan remembered with revulsion how the man had taken every opportunity to touch Elizabeth, leaning close to her at the dinner table, relentlessly turning their conversations toward her, making inappropriate remarks about her being his "little Indian princess."

"Ah-ha!" exclaimed Mr. Gregg smugly. "So, he was not attracted to Mrs. Xanthakos, but to her friend. Did Mrs. Xanthakos mind?"

"Mind?"

"Was she jealous?"

Jealous! What rubbish. Lilyan pressed her hands against her hot cheeks.

Mrs. Laurens snorted. "Truth be told, Poseidon was of the opinion that she wished him to perdition."

Mr. Gregg turned pointedly to the jury. "She wished him to

perdition."

Couldn't Poseidon have kept that one opinion to himself? She studied the jury's reaction. Several had swiveled in their chairs, and others seemed more intent. Mr. McCord searched through his notes.

Mr. Gregg faced Mrs. Laurens again. "Please, if you would, describe for the jury what Poseidon saw the evening of Captain Bradenton's death."

"He had been down at the chicken house, making sure everything was all right and that the Brits hadn't taken off with anything." She grinned. "They were quite proficient at that, you know."

Several jurymen guffawed.

"As Poseidon conveyed to me, he heard a scream and went running. He saw a light coming from the gazebo and headed over. That's when he saw Mistress Cameron—Mrs. Xanthakos—and Miss Elizabeth. Miss Elizabeth was crying and was barely able to stand up without Mrs. Xanthakos's help."

She harrumphed. "Come to find out later on that the captain had hurt Miss Elizabeth terribly." She took a handkerchief from her purse and fluttered it in front of her face. "He was so violent, he'd pulled her shoulder from its socket."

Mr. Gregg cleared his throat. "What else did Poseidon see?"

"According to him, it started raining. He saw blood on Mrs. Xanthakos's arms. He looked around behind her and saw the captain, lying on his back, blood pouring out of his head."

The young juror who had been asking questions earlier raised his hand, and the judge, scowling again, spun his hand, spurring him along.

"Poseidon did not personally see the act?" the young man asked, his brow wrinkled with a frown as he looked from Mrs. Laurens to Poseidon and back.

Poseidon shook his head.

"He did not," Mrs. Laurens responded.

"Huh!" The juror took a handkerchief from his sleeve and

pressed it to his nose. "Are we *ever* to hear from someone who *actually* witnessed the crime?"

"B-but," Mr. Gregg stuttered.

Mr. McCord took that moment to uncurl his tall frame from his chair. "The court has waited patiently as my client's honor and character have been impugned, her motives brought into question. And I am inclined to agree with the learned juror. Are there any witnesses who can testify to what truly happened that night? Of the three people who could shed light on this for us, Mrs. Xanthakos is the only one living. Do you expect her to testify against herself?"

At that moment, Daniel Chambers jumped up from his chair and smiled. *No*, Lilyan thought, *he smirked*. He pulled a piece of paper from his pocket, waved it at the jury, and hunched his shoulders like a cat arching to pounce on its prey. "She already has."

CHAPTER 19

Reputation is what men and women think of us;
character is what God and angels know of us.
Thomas Paine

Mr. Chambers waggled the paper toward Lilyan. "I have in my possession a letter written to me from the accused in which she confesses to murdering Captain Bradenton."

Mr. McCord turned to Lilyan. *Why did you not warn me?* She read the message clearly in his dark eyes now rife with accusation. His stare intensified, pinning her like a bug specimen on a slab of wax.

"I protest," Mr. McCord said, raising his voice over the din of the chattering jurors. "I must be allowed to see this document."

"I will see it, too," the judge said and then rapped his gavel. "Order. I will have order."

The jurors hushed as Mr. Chambers walked to the bench, followed closely by Mr. McCord and Mr. Gregg. He gave the document to the judge, who dipped his head down and studied it over the top of his glasses. When he finished, he passed it to Mr. McCord.

The room was so quiet Lilyan could hear only the rattling of the paper as he pulled back the folds of the letter and began to read.

She thought back to the day she had written the letter. Chased by bounty hunters, she, Andrew, and Callum had fled the coast of South Carolina and into the backwoods. She and her brother were alone in an abandoned cabin in the middle of the wilderness somewhere between Camden, South Carolina and the North Carolina mountains. Andrew was desperately ill, having recently recovered from a bout of influenza that nearly killed him. He could barely walk, and riding through the treacherous mountain trails in his condition sapped what little strength he had. Callum had left them to seek out anyone willing to carry Andrew on a stretcher—something her brother had sorely hated agreeing to.

Lilyan remembered how her thoughts seemed to tumble one over the other. Andrew had almost died, and she still ached from the death of her dearest friend. Racked with guilt, she wondered how Captain Bradenton's family would receive the news about him. Something inside her had yearned for their forgiveness, especially from his mother. After much soul searching, she decided to write the Bradentons through Mr. Chambers.

Andrew had advised her to let things be. She recalled every word of his sincere entreaty when he reminded her of David's trials in the Bible and how, even though he was being hounded by King Saul's men, hiding in caves as they themselves had been, David still called God his hiding place. His protector. He reminded her that God had rewarded David's faith by giving him inner peace and a sense of well-being. Her wise-beyond-his-years brother reminded her that God was not only her source of strength, but also the source of her joy. And that she must explore and feel that joy and quit taking on the responsibilities of everyone around her. Notwithstanding all of Andrew's good advice, for peace of mind she needed to write the letter and had gotten Callum to enlist someone at the nearest trading post to carry it to Charlestown.

Praying that Mr. McCord was not too angry with her, she watched as he finished reading and clasped the missive in his hand. "I would request that this be read aloud to the jury."

Mr. Gregg sputtered. "There is no need to read past the first paragraph."

Mr. McCord looked pointedly at Lilyan. "And I would request permission of the court for my client to read it aloud. In its entirety."

The judge took a moment before answering. "We see no problem with your request." He then directed Mrs. Laurens to step down.

Poseidon helped his mistress from the chair, and as they exited, he passed by Lilyan as Mr. McCord accompanied her to the witness chair. "Sorry 'bout all this, ma'am. I'll be prayin' for ya."

Too nervous to respond, she gave him a tremulous smile.

Once she was seated, Mr. McCord handed her the letter. "If you would be so kind."

Lilyan's hand shook as she took it from him. She cleared her throat and began.

Dear Mr. Chambers,

As I pen this letter, I am filled with such profound regret. I find it difficult to express myself regarding Captain Remington Bradenton and the ending of his life by my hand. I shudder with remorse at those terrible words.

I do not know how the circumstances of his death were portrayed to you, but I feel compelled to give you the true and factual account as I know it.

Captain Bradenton, my friend Elizabeth, and I became acquainted at the home of Mrs. Melborne. It was there that the captain began to display an ungentlemanly and, I assure you, unwanted attention to Elizabeth.

On that dreadful evening, while searching the grounds for Elizabeth, who had sought escape from the captain's advances, I came upon the captain as he had begun a most savage attack upon her. I say savage because, in attempting to subdue her, he had pulled her arm from its socket. In desperation and to prevent the captain from accomplishing his purpose—

Tears pooled in her eyes, blurring her vision.

I picked up a statuette and struck him. It is a memory that has burned itself indelibly into my mind.

Elizabeth and I fled the nightmarish scene, thus beginning a series of desperate events, ending most recently in her death. My most beloved, most precious friend was killed by the very bounty hunters who carried your missive at the behest of the captain's family.

I have laid this terrible sin before my Maker and have received some solace in the blessed assurance that I am ...

She took in a deep breath.

... forgiven. Notwithstanding, my deed lays heavy on my mind and heart. So much so that I implore you, sir, in the name of Christian benevolence...

Tears began to roll down her cheeks.

... please convey to the captain's parents my deep and abiding sorrow for having taken the life of their son. Tell them that I beg their forgiveness with all my heart.

I will leave it to you to determine how much of the details you wish to disclose to them, as I know it would be painful indeed to hear such a despicable report about one's beloved son.

I remain, your most abject and sincere servant,
Lilyan Cameron.

She dropped her hands into her lap, tightly clutching the letter. Terrified to face the jury, she kept her head down. Mr. McCord took the letter from her, handed it to the judge, and then escorted her back to the table.

He bent low, and pressing a handkerchief into her clammy palm, he whispered in her ear, "Well done, Lilyan."

Thank heavens, he isn't angry with me after all.

"And now," he reached inside his tunic, "I have a letter of my own I would share, if it pleases the court."

"Come forward," said the judge.

Lilyan's emotions had been pent up for so long, her chest nearly burst open as Mr. Chambers and Mr. Gregg once again moved to the bench. Mr. McCord handed a letter to the judge, who seemed to consider each word, adjusting his spectacles several times.

"Gentlemen, if you would return to your stations." He removed his eyeglasses and sat up straight. "Mrs. Xanthakos, please rise."

Lilyan, her heart racing, stood beside Mr. McCord. *What's happening? Lord, whatever it is, please, give me strength.*

The judge addressed the jurors. "Gentlemen, we have here a statement from one of our most revered and honored citizens, Brigadier General, now Senator, Francis Marion. A man of sterling credentials, held in the highest esteem by this court, who, in the most ardent terms available at his command, vouches for the character of the accused. With the highest of praise he commends her and advises us that, while at the Violet Plantation, she served under his command to gather information for the patriot cause. It is his belief that Mrs. Xanthakos displayed an act of heroism by defending her friend and herself from harm, and he most fervently requests that we drop the charge levied against her."

Lilyan looked up at Mr. McCord, who smiled and winked at her. *He winked!* For the first time that day, she allowed herself a glimmer of hope.

"Mrs. Xanthakos." The judge reached for his gavel. "We are inclined to agree. And, so, with the power vested in me by the state of South Carolina, I hereby dismiss the charge of murder placed against you."

Joy, pure and sweet, flooded through her veins in such a rush, she clasped Mr. McCord's arm.

The judge turned to address the jury. "Gentlemen, we have one additional case to hear this afternoon. I am ordering a recess. We will reconvene in an hour."

He rapped the gavel on the desk so hard, Lilyan jumped. *Is it really over?*

Rising from his chair, the judge bowed to Lilyan, and, looking into her eyes with the kindness she had spied earlier, he said, "You are free to go, madam. And may I add, we express our gratitude for your service to this country and wish you Godspeed."

Just then, the door to the anteroom flew open and Nicholas strode into the room. He sped toward her, threw his arms open, and she stepped into his embrace.

Home again.

"My love. My love," he murmured over and over as he stroked her hair and her back as she pressed her face against his chest. He tucked her into the crook of his arm and held out his hand to Mr. McCord. "Thank you. I don't have the words. I can never repay you."

Mr. McCord smiled broadly. "It was my honor."

"I do have one question." Nicholas clasped Lilyan even tighter. "Mr. Martin was kind enough to allow me to listen from the anteroom so that I heard most everything. If General Marion's letter was so powerful as to sway the judge to dismiss the charges, why did you not produce the letter at the beginning?"

Gathering his papers, Mr. McCord explained, "I was given to understand by your wife, sir, that she desired a full airing of all the accusations against her name. By waiting, we were able to bring those to light and repute them."

"I understand." Nicholas shook his hand again. "If I can ever be of assistance, you have only to ask."

"Jimmy," Agnes McCord called out as she hurried toward them, followed by Mrs. Laurens walking slower and leaning on Poseidon's arm.

"So proud of you, dear boy." Agnes kissed her grandson on his cheek and then cupped Lilyan's chin in her hand. "I told you all would be well."

Agnes motioned to the other woman. "I would like to introduce you to my dear friend, Candice Laurens. Candice, meet Lilyan and Nicholas Xanthakos."

Lilyan and Nicholas bowed to the woman, who smiled at them with lovely gray eyes and said, "When Poseidon was identified as a witness, I feared for him, but I knew we must come and help in whatever way we could."

Lilyan took her hand. "Thank you, Mrs. Laurens," she said and then met the old man's eyes. "What a shock, Poseidon, when I heard your name called."

Mrs. Laurens clutched Poseidon's arm. "It has been quite a shock to all of us."

Lilyan motioned to Nicholas. "Poseidon, this is my husband, Nicholas."

Poseidon started to bow, but Nicholas released Lilyan to take hold of the man's hand with both of his. "I'm forever in your debt."

"Not at all, sir."

"I do confess," said Mrs. Laurens, "I was very curious about you, Lilyan. When you were at my home, Poseidon kept me apprised of everything. He—and Agnes—speak so highly of you. It's nice to finally meet you."

"The pleasure is mine." Lilyan surveyed the room. "Though maybe not so pleasant for you in these circumstances."

Mrs. Lauren's eyes twinkled. "We haven't been part of such excitement since the British threw Cousin Henry into the Tower of London for trying to enlist the Dutch into the American cause."

"What a time that was," Agnes exclaimed. "Finally got him out of there, though." She curled her fingers around Mr. McCord's arm. "Jimmy helped with the negotiations to exchange Henry for one of our prisoners—Lord Cornwallis. I'd say we got the better part of that bargain."

Exhaustion washed over Lilyan, sapping her strength, and she dropped her head onto Nicholas's shoulder. These were such dear people who had come to support her, and she loved being with them, but she had to get away.

Nicholas clasped his arm around her waist. "I must get my wife home."

Mrs. Laurens moved aside with the others. "Of course, dear man. What an ordeal this has been. Thank God for such a heartening outcome."

"Where are Andrew, Golden Fawn, and Callum?" Lilyan asked as Nicholas guided her through the front doorway of the building.

"At home," he responded, concentrating on the crowd dispersing in the streets.

She stopped on the top step of the stairway. "I would have thought they would be here. Is there something wrong?"

"Callum wasn't feeling well."

Panic stirred her stomach.

"Don't worry, my love. He was tired is all."

Before Lilyan could respond, Agnes hurried toward them. "Just one more moment," she began, breathless from her sprint. "I was speaking to Candice about your daughter."

Lilyan dug her fingers into Nicholas's arm.

"Bramble—that is the name of the people who have Laurel. Is it not?"

"Yes."

"Candice says there's a family that lives not too far from her that has relations named Bramble."

Nicholas tightened his hold on Lilyan's waist. "We have information they are sailing with Laurel to Baltimore."

"Wonderful that you have news of her!" Agnes clapped her hands. "Well, Candice wanted you to know that they are a fine family. And, if they are the same people, your baby is in loving hands."

Lilyan shared a glance with Nicholas, knowing that if they didn't leave quickly, she would start crying.

"Thank you, Mrs. McCord," said Nicholas. "I leave tomorrow on a ship bound for Baltimore, and your words will be of comfort on my journey," he said, watching Lilyan closely as he emphasized *my* journey.

She flashed him a rebellious look. *On our journey, you mean.*

CHAPTER 20

Wives, submit yourselves unto your own husbands, as unto the Lord.
Ephesians 5:22 KJV

Lilyan was never happier than when she crossed the threshold of her house and into the loving arms of her family and friends. Hugs and kisses abounded. They all gathered in the parlor, where even Callum, who sat in a chair looking pale and exhausted, managed a loud cheer.

She and Nicholas slumped down on the settee, where he curved his arm around her and gathered her close. With her head drooped against her husband's chest, she listened while he patiently dealt with the questions that peppered him.

Finally, when everyone grew quiet, Lilyan leaned forward. "I want to thank each of you for being there for me. For caring for me and praying for me. And you, my dearest." She paused to look up at Nicholas and lace her fingers through his. "You are my rock."

He drew her hand to his lips and kissed it.

She scanned the faces of the people she loved most in the world. "While we're gathered, I'd like to tell you about something Nicholas, Andrew, and I have talked about. Once we find our

Laurel," her heart skipped with hope as she said those words, "we plan to return to North Carolina straightaway. We don't want to give up our house here, though, as we'd like to return from time to time. If you choose to—Mildred, Constance, and Sally—we'd like for you to live here, as our housekeepers."

"Oh my!" Sally squealed, clasping her hands to her heart. "I do. I do want to."

Constance, her eyes alight with joy, echoed Sally.

But Mildred, who stood beside the settee, shook her head. "If you wouldn't mind, Lilyan, Mr. Xanthakos, I'd just as soon come with you. I don't have no ties here, and I sure would like to start my life over in a new place. Isn't there something I could do in North Carolina? Work your vineyard? Keep house? Tend your children?"

Lilyan was humbled by the affection she read in her friend's eyes. "I'd love that. Nikki?"

Nicholas smiled. "I'd like that too."

Lilyan's heart swelled at the happiness on Mildred's face, but she realized she had put her husband in a spot. Had he already considered that such an idea would necessitate building another cabin?

Poor darling, his family keeps growing by leaps and bounds.

Out of the corner of her eye, she spotted Samuel and Robbie passing the doorway and heading upstairs. They had slipped out earlier, and she wondered what they were doing. "We've also decided we'll get word to Gerald that we'd like to give him half ownership in my shop. He's been so faithful to keep it going." She glanced at Nicholas. "It would make a grand wedding present for him and his bride, don't you think?"

He squeezed her hand.

Lilyan had just slumped back into the curve of Nicholas's arm when Samuel and Robbie came in and whispered to Golden Fawn.

Her sister-in-law grinned. "We have a surprise. We've filled a tub with hot water. And, there are fresh linens on the bed, all ready for you to take a nap."

Nicholas rose and held out his hands to pull her up. "Come, my sweet."

"Thank you." Lilyan managed to squeak the words through her constricted throat as she and Nicholas departed. "Thank you all so much."

Weary to her bones, she almost collapsed at the bottom of the stairs. Nicholas swept her into his arms and carried her to the bedroom, where he gently set her on the bed, removed her shoes and stockings, and helped her to stand. Her body drooping like a rag doll, she struggled to keep her eyelids open while he undressed her and helped her step into the tub.

The warm water enveloped her like mulled cider. She wriggled her toes as Nicholas washed and rinsed her hair twice and scrubbed her body with a sea sponge until her skin tingled, finally free from the terrible smell of the dungeon. He draped her hair over the rim of the tub, rubbed it with a cloth, and brushed it until it was only slightly damp.

"Please, tell me you found no nits," she said with a shudder.

"No. Not to worry." He started massaging her scalp.

"Hmm," she murmured. She reached for his hand and kissed his palm. "The entire time in the dungeon, I couldn't free myself from the fear that bugs were crawling all over me."

"Let's not talk of that terrible place ever again." He stood and held open a towel for her to step into. "There's a tray by the fireplace with cheese and bread. Are you hungry? Or would you rather nap?" he asked, patting her body with the towel.

"I think I'll sleep a bit." She reached for the chemise that lay across the end of the bed.

He took it from her, and when she lifted her arms, he paused a moment, taking her in from head to toe. He caressed her stomach. "All is well?"

She smiled. "We're fine."

He leaned down and kissed her slightly swelling belly.

"I am beyond happy that you're home, my Lilyanista," he said as he slipped the chemise over her head.

"Home. What a beautiful word." She leaned back against him, loving the feel of his arms as they enveloped her.

"Let's get you into bed."

He held open the covers for her, and she slipped into the bed and stretched her languorous body.

Her eyelids drooped as sleep permeated her muscles. "Stay with me?"

"Most assuredly." He climbed on top of the covers and curled around her.

"I'm free. I'm home. And soon I'll hold our little girl once again." She sighed, arranging her long tresses across her shoulder. "And what about you, my love?"

"What about me?" He draped his arm across her and slipped his hand underneath her stomach.

"You've suffered too." She pulled her arm from under the covers and draped it across his. "You've struggled to be strong for me. I want you to know I'm aware of that and appreciate it with all my heart."

He kissed the back of her neck. "Get some rest. It's already late afternoon, and I must leave in a while. There are things that must be done before I sail."

Before he *sails. He's said that twice. But* I *am going too.* Those were the last thoughts her exhausted brain managed to string together before she fell into the beckoning arms of slumber.

* * *

She awoke to the sounds of a carriage passing by and breathed in the salty, loamy breeze wafting through the curtains. Nicholas must have opened the window to provide relief from the sweltering, humid, July air. Sitting on the side of the bed, she watched as the brilliant sunset bathed the room in a rosy glow. She stood and, stretching her aching muscles, spotted the luggage that had been stashed beside her dressing table.

Looking at the trunk, she recalled that her father had given it to her long ago during their travels together. He had purchased it because the sealskin casing would keep the contents dry and secure through river crossings and stormy weather.

She shoved it and the portmanteau into the center of the room and sorted through them, pulling the clothes she wouldn't need from the trunk and rearranging Nicholas's clothes in the portmanteau. Although the bodices of all her dresses were adjustable, she selected two she knew would be more comfortable for her expanding waist and sore breasts. Just as she finished tucking Laurel's doll and the white blanket Miriam Greene had given her into the trunk, the bedroom door opened slowly.

Nicholas crept into the room, obviously expecting to find her still asleep. "What are you doing?"

She swiveled around on her knees. "Packing."

"But you aren't going anywhere."

She jumped up, causing her head to swim. Steadying herself against the foot of the bed with one hand, she pressed the other onto her hip. "Why would you say that?"

"Look at you. You can barely stand."

"I stood up too fast, is all." She let go of the bed to prove her point but quickly grasped it again. "I'm perfectly fine."

His arms fell rigid at his sides. "Fine enough to withstand life aboard a ship? To endure—well, God knows what—in Baltimore? Arduous walks? Bone-cracking carriage rides?"

Lilyan's irritation rose in direct parallel to the volume of his voice. "I don't think any of that compares with what I've endured already."

"You just made my point for me. Look at what you've been through already."

"And I'm still standing," she countered, though her limbs grew weaker by the minute.

He snorted. "Just barely."

She set her chin. "I'm going with you to find our baby."

She moved to the side of the bed. He approached her and took her face in his hands, searching her eyes with his own. "Please. Listen to reason. It would be so much better if you stayed here. Safe."

She almost fell prey to his eyes, so dark with entreaty. Almost. "I'll be safe with you. And besides, can you not see how horrible it would be for me here? Not knowing what was happening to you? To Laurel?" She pressed her palms against his chest. "You know me well enough to realize that I'd worry myself sick."

He jerked away and paced, arms folded in front of him as he mumbled Greek words she probably didn't want to understand. Finally, he stopped again, directly in front of her. "I am the head of this household, and it's your duty to obey me."

Anger like a raging predator surged through her with such intensity that she balled her hands into fists. "You would use that argument against me?"

He threw back his head and stared up at the ceiling. "It seems the only argument I have left, Mrs. Xanthakos."

"Well, it won't work. I'm going with you tomorrow, *Mr. Xanthakos*."

He blew out a breath, spun around, and, shouting in Greek, stomped from the room, slamming the door behind him.

Frustrated, she flopped down on the bed and wrapped her arms around her stomach. "What a stubborn father you have."

In all honesty, she knew she was acting as stubborn. What would she do if he unequivocally demanded she stay home? As her husband, he had every right to lock her in her room. Would he do that to her? *Surely not.* But then, did she really know him that well? After all, they had been separated more than they had been together. They had met only a month or two before they married.

The first two months of their time together as husband and wife, he was a partisan with General Marion. He would leave her for days at a time and return exhausted. Their evenings were spent with her tending his wounds, mending his clothes, and making sure he had enough to eat. Unwilling to talk about the war, he had shared his hopes for their future with her. She recalled some of those conversations that took place huddled together in front of a campfire or snuggled in each other's arms in their tent. The memory of the light in her husband's face when he talked about his plans for a vineyard kept her warm on many lonely nights.

And then came the time she was forced to leave him to avoid capture by bounty hunters—the most horrible months of her life. But he found her, as he had promised. He had stayed with her only long enough to build their cabin and make sure she was safe and settled before he left again to finish out the war.

Then came the glorious day when she stood on the cabin porch and spotted him walking on the valley road. He had been home only six short months when Laurel was taken from them. That thought sent a chill through her, stirring up the sadness that permeated her bones like a cancer.

But to answer her own question, yes, she knew him that well. Knowledge, not due to the amount of time they had been together, but from his sterling character that shone from his heart, his courage, his actions. Her husband was a fine and decent man.

And what about her duty to subject herself to his will if he demanded she stay home? She owed him so much, this man that God had brought into her life to be her constant help, her earthly shelter from life's storms. The one who had not only gained her everlasting love, but who had earned her respect.

Her mind wrestled with those tumultuous thoughts until finally, mentally exhausted, she came to a decision. If her husband said the words, "You may not go," she would do his bidding with as much grace as she could muster. He deserved that much from her.

I do like my way, though, Lord. Forgive me.

She'd been sitting awhile when she noticed the door being opened slowly. She hoped to see her husband, but it was Golden Fawn who peeked inside, her face a portrait of worry.

"May I come in?"

"Please."

Golden Fawn crossed the room and sat beside her. "We heard the shouting. But I couldn't understand what Nicholas was yelling about when he left."

Lilyan's shoulders drooped. "Dear sister, I do so love my husband, but he can be a trial sometimes."

"Do you want to share with me?"

"Of course. He doesn't want me to go on the ship with him to find Laurel. He wants me to stay home."

"I see no harm in you going."

Lilyan squeezed Golden Fawn's fingers. "I knew you'd understand."

There was a tap on the door, and Mildred and Constance came in followed by Sally, who carried a tray loaded with a teapot, cups, and scones.

"Thought you could use some cheering up," Sally said, setting the tray on the bed steps.

Piling up the pillows and tucking them behind Lilyan, Mildred bade her to scoot back under the covers. She spooned sugar into a cup, stirred it, and held it out.

Lilyan cradled the cup in her hands, inhaled the steam rising above the rim, and took a sip. "Mmm. Tea."

After Mildred poured for the others, she sat on the side of the bed.

Lilyan popped a piece of scone into her mouth and downed it with a swallow of tea. "Heaven."

Constance and Sally sat on the other side of the bed, and soon they were all engaged in conversations about anything and everything. Lilyan glanced out the window and noticed that the sun had set. The moon was partially veiled by a somber, overcast sky—in contrast with the happy group of women gathered around her. The room grew dim, but no one moved to light a candle.

As they chatted, she studied them, her interest captured as the evening light softened the angular features of some and added mystery and character to the others.

I love them. How tender and engaging they were, these dear, dear friends who had circled around her, taking on the yoke of her wounded spirit. Theirs was a special relationship—born of shared suffering, proffering nothing but kindness and support. *This must be how Naomi and Ruth felt about each other.* Of course, she loved her husband, but his was a different kind of love. She and Nicholas were a part of each other—but these women *were* her. They had a depth of understanding for one another that no male could ever know. Soon their sweet, soft voices and gentle laughter drifted around her and seemed to lift her up and cradle her, rocking her to and fro until her eyelids drooped and her head dropped back onto the pillow.

It must have been hours later when she awoke and heard the door latch. Through partially closed eyes, she watched Nicholas slip inside and blow out a candle, wafting the scent of bayberries that tickled her nose. Lying on her side with her knees very nearly hanging over the edge of the bed, she feigned sleep and listened as he removed his clothes and slid under the covers. First he lay on his back, then turned away from her on his side. He switched sides again, flopping his arms. A few minutes later, he whirled one way and then the other. Finally, with a groan, he wrapped his arms around her waist and pulled her to his side of the bed, tucking her into the curve of his body.

"You came back," she murmured.

"Go back to sleep," he whispered in a voice not nearly as stern as before.

What would the morning bring?

CHAPTER 21

*Red sky at night,
sailor's delight;
red sky at morning,
sailor, take warning.*

To Lilyan's relief, when they awoke, Nicholas never spoke the
words she dreaded to hear. Instead, in a sulky mood, he agreed
that she could accompany him. Against his better judgment, of
course.

To catch the tide, they left home moments before daybreak,
accompanied by Golden Fawn, Andrew, Robbie, and Samuel.
Robbie, who was to sail with them, whistled a merry tune while
he fairly skipped alongside with Lilyan's trunk balanced on one
shoulder and his canvas bag slung across the other.

Callum, still feeling poorly, had decided to remain at home,
but Lilyan was at peace knowing that her friends cared for him.
Despite his protests to the contrary, she knew he reveled in having
three women at his beck and call.

Most of the inhabitants of the city still slumbered as the little
party trod the cobblestone streets tinted pink from the bright red

colors of dawn. Several times, she caught Nicholas glancing at the sky with a frown. Though the brilliant colors were pleasant to look at, they did not bode well for the weather.

When they reached the wharf and the schooner, *Muirgheal*, Robbie quickly said his farewells and bounded up the gangplank. He was so excited, Lilyan couldn't help but smile at their young friend.

Nicholas dropped his portmanteau on the ground and clasped Samuel's forearm. "You'll watch over everyone?"

"You have my pledge. Good luck, my friend."

Samuel stepped close to Lilyan. "Pleasant journey," he said with a wink, his only acknowledgement of Nicholas's sour humor.

Nicholas waited for her to hug Andrew one last time before escorting her up the gangway. She hoped he would come out of his mood soon, as the close quarters aboard the schooner were not suited to bad attitudes. She wanted to pinch him. Didn't he realize how near they were to getting their Laurel back? *This should be a happy time, not one clouded with hurt feelings and stiff necks.*

As her feet touched the deck, a gust of wind shot across the bow, rippled across her skirts, and whipped strands of hair across her face. The familiar aromas of salt, fish, wet hemp, and tar teased her nose. Pelicans pushed against the air currents, poised as if suspended above the tightly furled sails of the two masts that loomed overhead. Seagulls dove for scraps the cook was dumping overboard, their cries barely audible over the creaking of the rigging. It was a tidy ship—scrubbed deck planks, tightly coiled ropes, a highly polished brass signal bell—which spoke well of its master.

She filled her lungs with the warm morning air, welcoming the sense of well-being that washed over her. Her attention was drawn back to the cook, now seated atop a barrel and gazing at other vessels already setting sail. Curious, she studied his striped balloon canvas pants, vest, and slope-shouldered shirt and realized there was something oddly familiar about him. The moment she spotted the frizzy, bright-orange curls haphazardly stuffed under a cap, she knew.

"Evelyn?" she called out.

"As I live and breathe!" the woman shouted, jumping from the barrel.

She ran headlong toward Lilyan, arms open wide. They hugged and kissed each other on the cheek and stood back, then, giggling, they hugged again.

Lilyan looked into the lively blue eyes she remembered so well. "It's wonderful to see you."

Lilyan turned to Nicholas, who had been watching with his arms folded across his chest. "It's Evelyn Stewart. Do you remember? From Marion's camp?"

He bowed. "I do remember. It's good to see you again."

Evelyn did her interpretation of a curtsy and grinned. "Handsome as ever, I see. Lilyan, you broke many a woman's heart when you married him, you know. Fortune smiled on you when you caught this one."

Eying the scowl on her husband's face, Lilyan raised an eyebrow. *Right now I'd like to throw him back.*

As if he knew what she was thinking, he pursed his lips.

Evelyn's knowing look indicated she had missed nothing. "Surely you aren't the people my husband's taking to Baltimore? Please, tell me you aren't the ones … the ones whose child was taken."

Lilyan took a hesitant step toward Nicholas.

"My dears. It fair took my breath away when my Walter shared your story with me. But, he never once mentioned your name. 'Twas sad before, but even sadder now that I know it's your child.

"But it's a happy thing that it'll be me and my husband who'll be taking you to rescue her." She clapped her hands like a child.

Evelyn's good humor was contagious, and Lilyan chuckled. "You're married to the captain of this ship?"

Evelyn's vibrant eyes sparkled. "Over a year now." She spotted something behind them, and, if possible, her face lit even brighter.

"Here he comes."

The man walking toward them, though he carried himself with confidence, was not an imposing figure. He was short by most standards, not more than an inch taller than his wife. His features came together in an ordinary way. But his eyes captivated Lilyan's attention. Hazel, more green than brown, they were bright with intelligence and an appealing openness. He gazed at Evelyn with such affection that Lilyan knew right away why her friend loved him.

"Captain Sinclair," said Nicholas, "permit me to introduce my wife."

"A pleasure, Mrs. Xanthakos," the captain said with a bow. "I see you already know my wife."

Lilyan curtsied. "Indeed, we're the best of friends."

"You didn't mention the surname of our passengers, sir, when you told me about their plight." Evelyn slipped her arm around Lilyan. "I came aboard to offer what sympathies I could, and what a nice surprise to see my friends again. Now, I'm doubly glad I insisted on sailing with you."

"And I, dear lady, am always glad of your company," said the captain.

Catching the adoring look that passed between them, Lilyan glanced at Nicholas, but he seemed to be studying the sails.

"Come," said Evelyn. "Let's get you settled in."

Lilyan followed her friend down ladder stairs into the ship's hold, through a cramped corridor, and into a cabin that could be spanned three strides one way and by four the other. A narrow berth had been built into an alcove, and a bench ran along a side wall. Two large hooks hung from the ceiling for netting to hold their luggage or to string a hammock for a third occupant.

Evelyn sat on the bed and patted the mattress. "Tell me about your little one."

Lilyan sat beside her. "It's been forty-six days—long and terrible and awful days—since Laurel was taken from us. It was the day before her first birthday. She was visiting with my sister-in-law—Andrew married a Cherokee woman—"

"Andrew. Married? I'll be … but go on."

"They were at Golden Fawn's village when slavers attacked and kidnapped most of the women and children." She fingered the folds in her skirt. "When I heard our Laurel was among them, I nearly lost my mind. If it hadn't been for Nicholas, I may have. There's not a day that goes by that I don't cry. I try not to let him see, though, because his heart is broken as well. And he feels responsible, as if he didn't do his duty … taking care of his family."

"My dear friend, my heart hurts for you both."

"Anyway, Nicholas and I, along with Samuel and a group of volunteers, followed their trail, but they kept splitting up. Finally, we found out that Laurel had been given to a family that was leaving the backcountry. They're headed for Baltimore. Apparently, their ship, *Resolution*, left two days ago."

"I know it. A big, lumbering cargo ship."

"Yes. It's making two stops before Baltimore, so we should catch up with it." Her heart leapt with anticipation.

Evelyn grinned. "Knowing my Walter, that'll be faster than you think."

The captain shouted orders to cast off the lines, and the ship began to sway.

Evelyn sighed. "It'll be good to be out to sea again."

"One step closer to Laurel."

"Won't be long now." Evelyn squeezed Lilyan's hand. "You can rely on Walter."

"It's good to see you so content. Tell me about him."

"Well, when we were with Marion—you recollect my son, Devin?"

"I do." Lilyan envisioned the tall, lanky young man with the same brilliant orange hair as his mother.

"He was wounded—shot in the leg—not too long after you left us. So, I brought him back home to Mount Pleasant. The doctor had to take his leg off at the knee."

"I'm so sorry."

"Don't worry yourself. It took a while, but he's fine now. We met Walter at the home of an acquaintance, and he took to Devin right away. Had a ship builder friend make him a peg leg, taught him how to sail, and now he's a first mate on one of Walter's ships." Evelyn giggled. "Course Walter took to me right away, too. Fairly swept me off my feet. We got married two weeks after we met. And, in the bargain, I exchanged one good Scot's name for another." Her eyes grew luminous. "He's a grand man, my Walter."

"I thought so the moment I met him."

"I'm glad to hear it. And he loves me. Lets me wear this getup whenever I want. It's so freeing for me—though he does ask that I present myself properly attired at meals. Lets me have my way most of the time on shore, but makes sure I know he's the boss when we're at sea."

She pressed her fists onto her hips. "You know, I've never felt this way about anyone, even my first husband. Don't mistake me. I loved Devin's father and mourned deeply when he passed. But this is different. Walter and I are … we have … I'm not sure how to say it. We have a deep connection. We're the best of friends. We finish each other's sentences. He taught me how to play cribbage, and I taught him how to knit socks. Sometimes we sit together for hours, never feeling the need to say a word." She blushed. "I'm going on, aren't I?"

Lilyan tapped her friend's chin. "I know exactly what you mean, and I couldn't be happier for you."

"Tell me if it's none of my business, but Nicholas seems to be … well … bearish." Evelyn punched the lumpy mattress. "And if you're having problems, you might want to sort them out before tonight, because this bed's so narrow you couldn't slip a piece of parchment between you. Might make for an uncomfortable night."

Lilyan sighed. "I guess you couldn't help but notice. He didn't want me to come on this trip. Wanted me to stay home where I'd be safe."

Evelyn cocked her head. "And why is that?"

"I'm in the family way."

"How wonderful!" Evelyn hugged her. "I'm so happy for you. How far along are you?"

A vision of a waterfall and thousands of fireflies came to Lilyan's mind. "Close to six weeks, I think."

Evelyn looked dreamy eyed. "I'd like to have a child with Walter, but alas, it's not to be. I'm far too old."

"Such nonsense."

"Maybe so." Evelyn stood and walked to the door. "I'd best be going. Walter likes me to stand beside him till we can't see land anymore."

The ship pitched slightly, and they braced themselves. Lilyan's stomach rolled too, and she crossed her arms over her waist.

"You going to be all right?" Evelyn said with a frown.

"I think so. Normally, I'm a good sailor. I hope the pregnancy won't change that."

"Do you want to come topside?"

"Let me get settled. I'll join you later."

"Good. Walter may even let you take the wheel."

They heard a clattering noise and spotted Robbie juggling cases at the doorway.

"Do you think he'd …? The captain, that is. Let me take the wheel?"

Evelyn laughed heartily. "You finish your work, and he just might." She winked at Lilyan. "Why don't you pull your shoes off and rest awhile? If you're not topside by luncheon, I'll send someone to fetch you. I'll change from this." She indicated her clothing. "But what you have on is fine."

"Where do you want the baggage, Mrs. Xanthakos?" Robbie asked, hauling it through the doorway.

"Leave it right here, please, so I can get to it."

While Robbie arranged the luggage in front of the bed, Evelyn lit the teapot lamp suspended from the ceiling, and then they left, closing the door behind them. Lilyan sorted through Nicholas's portmanteau, pulled out a clean shirt and breeches for him, and hung them on wall pegs. The ship lunged forward, and she held onto the pegs. Suddenly aware of the tremendous mass of the sea around her and feeling as if the walls were closing in, she donned her straw hat, tied the ribbons underneath her chin, and stumbled up to the deck to find the mainsails blowing full, pushing the vessel through the water as if flying.

Her heart fluttered when she spotted Nicholas talking to Evelyn, Robbie, and Captain Sinclair at the helm. Her husband was so handsome, braced against the wind, the collar of his shirt lifted up against his neck, his eyes alight, exhilarated. She hadn't seen him this content in a long while and spent a few moments watching him until Evelyn saw her and waved. When she joined them, Nicholas rested his arm across her back, using his weight to balance her. They made a happy party, chatting amiably, the jovial captain entertaining them with stories of his adventures at sea. They broke away long enough to go below to the captain's quarters to eat luncheon, a feast of she-crab soup flavored with sherry and just the right amount of pimenton picante to give it a bite, followed by lightly fried dolphin steaks and dark, crusty bread, cheese, and pears. After more pleasant conversation, they returned on deck to find that the overcast day was turning gloomier by the moment.

Lilyan lumbered to the starboard side of the ship, chuckling at the sensation of one leg being shorter than the other. She rested her arm against the rail, fascinated by a heavy black cloud in the distance, pouring rain down on the ocean in a dark shaft. Pulling off her hat, she reveled in the blustery wind as it lifted her hair off her shoulders.

Nicholas stood beside her and braced his hands on the rail on either side of her. "Wind's picking up."

She turned to find him studying her eyes and her mouth.

"Lilyan—"

"Nikki—"

They spoke at the same time.

She smiled. "Go ahead."

"I've been watching you, the wind flirting with your hair. Looking lovelier, more beautiful than I've ever seen you. It made me want to tell you that, despite everything, I'm happy you're here with me."

She leaned her forehead into his chest. "I'm sorry I was so … so …"

"Difficult?" he said with a laugh.

She toyed with his collar, her eyes roaming up his chin, past his smiling lips, and on to his eyes. "I want you to know, had you ordered me to stay home, I would have. I was prepared to honor the vow I made to obey you. Not from a sense of obligation, but because, dearest, you deserve my respect. Can you forgive me for the way I acted?"

He leaned down as if to kiss her but stopped and glanced around, realizing that some of the crew gathered around the scuttle cask were watching.

"Later?" he asked, his voice full of promise.

She nodded, then faced the bow again and leaned back against him. "Do you remember our first argument?"

"I do. You were getting ready to leave me to get away from the bounty hunters. You were trying—not with much success, I might say—to disguise yourself as a man. And you insisted that you cut your hair. I couldn't believe you would even consider such a thing. But I won that argument, as I recall."

"You did. And it was because of Evelyn. Remember? She solved our dilemma by finding a skullcap and man's wig for me to wear." She turned around to face him. "I said something very silly at the time."

"You did?"

"That arguing was great fun when one could make up the"

way we did afterward. But, dear one, arguing isn't fun. It hurts. Anything that makes me feel the slightest bit of distance between us is unbearable. Please, let's not do that again."

He chuckled. "I'll do my best, my love."

A tendril of her hair, as if it had a life of its own, floated on air and wrapped itself around her neck. Nicholas caught it in his fingers and pushed it back over her shoulder. "Do you think we've missed anything special?"

Knowing exactly what he was referring to, she answered, "She may have cut one or two more teeth."

"I'll never forget when she sat up by herself that first time," he said, a faraway look in his eyes.

Nicholas had been home only a month from the war when, one morning, Lilyan awoke to the sensation that someone was staring at them. And someone was. Their seven-month-old daughter was sitting up, her two bright-green orbs full of mischief, peering at them over the edge of the cradle next to the bed. Nicholas veered up and glanced at Lilyan, who feigned sleep, waiting to see what he would do. Pulling off the covers, he told Laurel in the tenderest of whispers to be very quiet so as not to wake her ma. To Lilyan's astonishment, he changed his daughter's wet napkin and gown, wrapped her in a blanket, and carried her into the front room of their cabin, gently closing the door behind him.

Curious, she had sprung from the bed and pressed her ear against the door. When she couldn't make out what he was saying, she cracked open the door and watched him poke the fire in the fireplace back to life and then settle himself on the rug with Laurel lying in front of him. Leaning forward, he kissed her tiny, rosebud mouth. "You're going to be a beautiful woman, just like your ma," he said and then chuckled as Laurel wove her fingers into strands of hair that hung down the sides of his face. He tried to sit up, but she wouldn't let go.

"You've captured me, little one," he said, freeing his hair.

And then, in what seemed an instant, Laurel rolled onto her

side and pushed herself into a sitting position. When he clapped his hands and told her how proud he was of her, she grinned, wrinkling her nose like a bunny and exposing her newly-cut teeth.

"What a charmer you are!" he exclaimed. "And so smart."

He pulled their baby onto his lap, leaned her against his chest, and they both seemed captivated by the flames. Rubbing his fingers across her dainty ones, he apologized to her for not being there when she was born and for missing the first six months of her life. He assured her it was his plan, God willing, never to leave home again and to be there whenever she and her ma needed him. "Manari mou," he whispered and bent to kiss Laurel's tiny earlobe.

My little lamb. Lilyan sighed deeply and scanned the undulating ocean. *Lovely memory.*

She had sorely missed her husband when he was away fighting. Once he was home, he told her often how sorry he was he hadn't been with her for their daughter's birth. He had planned to be home in time, but a gunshot wound in his shoulder had curtailed his homecoming. Thank heavens, Samuel had been there to follow through on Marion's surgeon's orders to dress the wound each day. Nicholas recovered, not like many others whose wounds became septic. It was shameful that men like him and Samuel, who had fought years for their country's independence, had returned home wounded, with only their rifles and the clothes on their backs. But then, she and her husband were the fortunate ones. They had their house and their vineyard. Some leaders, like Marion, had lost everything—their fortunes had vanished, their homes had been ransacked, and their property and fields had been burned.

Thinking of Marion jogged Lilyan's memory. "What was in the letter General Marion handed you before the trial?"

Nicholas grinned. "You remember how I told you, no matter the verdict, you were going to be free—one way or the other?"

She nodded.

"Had things not gone in our favor, I determined you wouldn't spend one more day in jail. Marion sensed that. In his letter, he told me of several houses near Beaufort that have secret rooms built in them—rooms where friends had hidden him after he broke his ankle, just before the British took Charlestown. Inside the envelope were letters of introduction to those friends, who, according to Marion, would have helped us."

Lilyan shivered at the thought of being a fugitive again. *Thank You, God, for the outcome we had.*

Suddenly, she spotted something in the distance. "Look!" she pointed behind him.

"Spout!" one of the crewmen called out from the rigging.

Crewman gathered around them, and they all stood in awe as, several miles away, a giant black cloud rolled and dipped down until the end of it narrowed into a misshapen funnel. Moving lower and lower, the writhing twister agitated the sea beneath. The ocean rose, becoming a mound that continued upward until it met the end of the funnel, and together they became a spiraling tube. The cloud grew blacker, and as quickly as it had formed, the waterspout thinned into a thread until, in a thundering roar, the connection was broken. The tail ascended once more into the sky, and the bulging sea fell back down like a soiled scrap of cloth, freeing Lilyan to expel the breath she had been holding in.

Nicholas scanned the horizon. "Seems like there are black skies and storms all around us. Let's talk to the captain."

When they joined the captain, he turned over the helm to the first mate and walked with them to the bow.

In response to Nicholas's concerns, Captain Sinclair nodded. "Don't like the look of things much either. But the skies are clearer to the north. We're making good headway, and I'm hoping the storms will blow themselves out before they reach us. Thunderstorms come up quick and play out fast most of the time."

"And if they don't?" asked Nicholas.

"Ye never can tell what you're in for until it hits you. But," he said, looking directly at Lilyan, "the *Muirgheal's* a sturdy ship, and we've come through many a storm together."

"What about staying close to shore? In case we have to take refuge?" Lilyan asked.

The captain shook his head. "Not a good strategy once we near North Carolina. There are shoals with sandbars that are here one day and gone the next. And then there are the shipwrecks—of which there are a plenty around Hatteras." He smiled. "Anyway, don't you worry, Mrs. Xanthakos. You leave that to me. Now, let me get back, and we'll talk more at dinner."

But that evening, the subject of the storms was never broached. Lilyan thought the fish muddle with shrimp, scallops, and monkfish was so perfectly prepared, she asked the cook for his recipe. The man beamed as he shared his secret ingredient—saffron.

When they had finished their meal, Captain Sinclair stood and raised his wine glass. "A toast to the ladies. Two of the finest, most excellent women I know."

Nicholas and Robbie raised their glasses. "To the ladies," they said together.

"And now," said the captain, retrieving a violin from the corner of the cabin, "'tis a bonnie night for music. Don't you agree, my dear bride?"

Chuckling, Evelyn took her husband's elbow and led the party topside.

As soon as Lilyan stepped on deck, she heard an unusual sound, clear and lilting, something between a violin and mandolin. Searching for the origin of the music, she spotted one of the crewmen playing an instrument she had never seen. Oval in shape, with two small, semi-circular sound holes, it had three strings stretched across its long neck. The man struck the strings with a bow from which dangled several round bells that kept time with the melody.

Heading toward the man, she and Nicholas passed groups of sailors who were smoking, playing cribbage, or simply enjoying the balmy, moonlit night. Several of them jumped up, but the captain signaled them to relax. When she and Nicholas reached the musician, he stood and greeted them in Greek. Nicholas responded, and a big smile lit his face. Though she knew a few Greek phrases, she could not begin to understand what they were saying. At the look of delight on her husband's face as he conversed in his native tongue, she made a mental note to learn even more and to teach their Laurel.

Nicholas motioned toward the man. "Lilyan, this is Thanassis. He is from Crete. Thanassis, this is my wife."

The man stood and bowed. "Honor-red, Kyreea."

Lilyan curtsied. "What is the instrument you're playing?"

The man looked to Nicholas, who translated her question and his answer.

"Thanassis offers his apologies for not speaking English. He is learning, he says. But this is a lyra."

"Please," Lilyan said, "continue. It's delightful."

Some of the crewmen rolled kegs into a circle for seating. Lilyan and Evelyn sat, but Nicholas stood behind her, resting his hands on her shoulders. When Thanassis began playing, the captain joined in with his violin, while one sailor kept time pounding a tin pan with wooden spoons. It was a lively tune that had Lilyan tapping her toe. Suddenly, one of the crewmen jumped up and started to dance, arms in the air, waving a kerchief, tapping his heels and toes on the deck.

To her amazement, Nicholas ran around her to join him but turned back to her.

"May I?" he asked. He took the wrap she held in her lap and tied it into a sash around his waist.

Standing side by side, he and the other man entwined their arms, and, resting their hands on each other's shoulders, they began a series of intricate steps, swaying left to right, and then bending at the knee and kicking their feet. As the tempo increased, they separated. Facing each other, they continued the lively movements, several times locking their feet together and whirling in a circle to Thanassis's enthusiastic shouts of *Opa!*

Lilyan clapped her hands and watched, fascinated by this newly discovered side of her husband. He was happier than she had ever seen him. His joy was contagious, and she joined in with the others, laughing and shouting, "*Opa! Opa!*"

And then, too soon, it was over. Nicholas shook hands with the other dancer and with Thanassis. He untied the sash and, breathing heavily, he draped it around Lilyan's neck. Notwithstanding the crowd, she jumped up, threw her arms around his neck, and kissed him, all to the rousing shouts of *Opa!*

The captain and Thanassis played several songs that were more familiar, with Lilyan, Evelyn, Robbie, and some of the crew singing along.

Lilyan gazed at the sails billowing in the soft breeze, the reflection of the half-moon dancing across the gentle ocean swells, and the lamplight illuminating the faces of those gathered around, some singing, some smiling, and some with faraway looks. All seemed caught up in this special evening, one she knew would become a treasured memory that would stay with her a lifetime. No one seemed to want the night to end, but, finally, the captain reluctantly gave the order for lights out.

Later, in their cabin, lying in her husband's arms, she envisioned him smiling and the two of them dancing to the music of his homeland.

She drifted off to sleep only to be jarred awake, wondering why she hadn't pictured Laurel with them.

CHAPTER 22

Diamond Shoals, the graveyard of the Atlantic ...

After breakfast the next morning, Lilyan climbed the stairs to discover layers of ominous, dark clouds shifting overhead, almost completely blocking out the sun. The balmy, genial air of the previous night had turned raw. The sea was becoming choppy as little wave tops broke off and blew backward.

The ship rolled in the increasingly turbulent water, and Lilyan staggered across the deck toward Nicholas. When she reached him, she nestled into the crook of his arm. They had been staring out to sea a while when she spotted a long, slow swell of water coming their way.

"Mr. and Mrs. Xanthakos," Robbie shouted as he ran toward them, holding onto Evelyn's elbow. "Captain says we're to go below. Batten everything down and hold on. A bad storm's on the way. He'll try to outrun it. But just in case—"

Nicholas didn't wait to hear more but took hold of Lilyan's hand and raced with her down the stairs and into their cabin. Inside, he pushed the mattress and pillows up against the wall. While Robbie threw everything he could into the netting that hung overhead, Nicholas bundled Lilyan and Evelyn into the bed. He instructed Robbie to sit beside him on the edge of the bed, and they both braced their arms against the walls.

Her heart pounding in her ears, Lilyan held Evelyn's arm with one hand and gripped the waist of Nicholas's breeches with the other.

Twice, large swells lifted the ship straight up and hurled it back down. The lamp overhead swung back and forth. The ship yawed in a zigzag until the lantern swung crazily in circles, just like the contents of Lilyan's stomach.

"The lamp, Robbie!" Nicholas yelled.

Robbie jumped up and doused the flame, throwing them into darkness. Though the blackness was frightening, Lilyan understood it was necessary—fires, not storms, were the worst enemies at sea. Robbie returned to the bed and, for what seemed like hours, they huddled together, trying to buffer each other from bumping against the cabin walls as the ship rolled, pitched, and yawed. Then suddenly, something crashed against the hull, bringing the ship to a standstill and throwing them all forward, tossing them about like rag dolls.

The ship's violent shudder loosened Nicholas's vice-like grip on Lilyan's arm, and she toppled over the edge of the bed. But before she could hit the floor, Nicholas threw his arms around her and shoved himself underneath her, taking the brunt of her fall. They heard a loud groaning, then a tremendous snapping sound, followed by a crashing thud that sent tremors throughout the hull.

The cabin door was wrenched open, and one of the crew stuck his head inside. His lantern cast macabre shadows across his face, lighting the channels of rain pouring down his head and onto his shoulders. Lightning flashed in the hallway, followed by a deafening clap of thunder. Frightened, Lilyan clasped her hands to her ears.

The crewman hunched his body against the onslaught and spun away. "We've hit another ship! Wedged against a sandbar! Lost the mainmast and the foremast. Captain says abandon ship!" he yelled over his shoulder as he headed toward the stairs.

Nicholas pulled Lilyan to her feet and yelled, "Come. Robbie, see to Evelyn."

They clambered up the stairs where the heavens dumped rain on them like a high-mountain waterfall. Lilyan's eyelids almost closed with the force of the cold liquid. Bolts of lightning illuminated a scene she could never have conjured up in her wildest nightmare. The foremast lay across the deck in a tangle of wood splinters, tattered sails, and ropes and tackle whipping in the relentless wind, which was so strong it sucked the air from her lungs. With Nicholas leading the way, they scrambled toward the lifeboats, weaving under and over the debris. Her clothes stuck to her like a second skin, and she stumbled. Several times, Nicholas had to let go her hand to jump over rigging and then reach across, pick her up, and drag her over.

"Where's Walter?" Evelyn shouted.

Lilyan glanced back, and for the first time noticed blood dripping down her friend's face.

"Nikki! Evelyn's hurt," she yelled, but the wind ripped the words out of her mouth.

She tried to slow down, but Nicholas, in a relentless rush toward the lifeboat, pulled her by her arm.

When they reached the bow, she realized that the ship had broached, turning edge to the wind, and huge waves now slammed against the hull and thundered over onto the deck.

Several of the crew had managed to rig up a pulley and struggled mightily to crank the boat over the side. When it was low enough, Nicholas leapt in and held his arms open for Lilyan to jump. She leaned forward but stopped, fearful of the churning, writhing water below.

"Now, Lilyan," he shouted.

Her eyes riveted on her husband's face, she leapt overboard and landed in his waiting arms. After he pushed her onto a seat, she cupped her hands over her brow, shielding her eyes from the rain, and spied Evelyn faltering at the edge of the ship. One of the crew swept her up in his arms like a babe and tossed her overboard. She landed in a heap beside Lilyan, who tried with every ounce of strength she had to pull her to a sitting position. A few moments later, Robbie and three of the crew jumped aboard and started lowering the boat. The pulley slipped, and then became taut, jerking them about. Just as Nicholas reached for the pulley, a giant wave washed over them, ripping loose the rope attached to the bow, and they found themselves hanging perpendicular to the sea. In the blinding rain, groaning and gasping bodies tumbled past Lilyan, clutching at her skirts and bumping against her leg entangled in a rope that ripped and burned her skin. She heard Nicholas scream her name, and to her horror, she saw him grasping the oar hinges, struggling to reach her. Another wave crashed against them, and in an instant, Nicholas was gone.

Dangling by her ankle, blood rushing to her head, Lilyan fought against the blackness that threatened to overcome her.

God. Have mercy.

The lifeboat rammed against the hull once again, freeing her leg, and she found herself flying through the air, tossed into the raging waves and a terrible abyss that opened its mouth and swallowed her.

CHAPTER 23

Hear my cry, O God; listen to my prayer. From the ends of the earth I call to you, I call as my heart grows faint ...
Psalm 61:1-2

Lilyan's first conscious thought was of being lifted up and settled back down. Something scraped the side of her face, and she breathed in wet sand and coughed, searing her lungs as if someone had stuck a hot poker into her ribcage. Then came the horrible somersault in her stomach that emptied itself through her mouth and nose, tasting of hot pickle brine. She rolled onto her side and retched until there was nothing left. When it was over, she drew her knees toward her chin.

Forcing her crusty eyelids open, she found she was lying on a beach, tossed up on shore like flotsam. Her hair, like slick ropes of kelp, clung to her face and shoulders and coiled around her torso.

With rubbery arms, she pushed herself into a sitting position and used the hem of her dress to wipe the sand from her eyes. Even that took too much effort, and she flopped back down on the sand with a groan. Growing more and more conscious of her body, the throbbing in her ankle, the ache in her shoulders and neck, the sting of open cuts and scratches, she slid one hand up across her stomach.

My babe?

Trying not to panic, she lay perfectly still and breathed in and out deliberately, slowly taking inventory of her muscles. No pains or cramps in her stomach or back. Good signs.

Nikki?

She clamped her eyes shut against her last memory of him clinging to the boat, his fingers clawing at the rope that ensnared her. Moaning, she sat up again and peered down the shore to her right, her left, and over her shoulder, spying not one other soul. Crawling like a child, she dragged herself out of the ebbing tide until, too exhausted to move, she stared up at the afternoon sky that held no trace of the storm. She closed her eyes, listened to the unnatural, slow beat of her heart, and waited for the words that whirled in her mind to slow enough for her to string together a coherent thought.

"Lord," she pleaded as she rose onto her knees. Cupping her hand over her brow, she searched the ocean again. She spied the shattered remains of the ship in the distance, and her heart tripped. As she watched the tattered sails flapping in the wind, something in the water near the shore caught her eye.

With legs like sacks of flour, she stood and realized that she wore only one shoe. She groaned and pulled it off, wobbling in her stocking feet. Gasping from the pain that shot through her leg, she dropped to the ground and gingerly ran her fingers across her ankle beneath the shredded remnants of her stocking. It wasn't broken or sprained, but the lacerated skin was raw and bloody. Relieved, she focused once again on the object deposited onto the beach. A body.

Her ankle throbbing, she sloshed through shallow wavelets only to discover two more bodies cradled in the gentle surf. They were crewmen, all dead. She wanted to drag them from the water, but she found it difficult to breathe, as if someone had laid an anchor on her chest. Fleeing from the carnage, she staggered down the shore, heading southward, though she knew not why. She stumbled several times, and each time it was harder to get back up.

And then a thought came that struck her down. *Is Nikki dead?* Completely spent, she fell prostrate onto a thick layer of shell shards that scraped her hands and arms.

Dear God ... I'm frightened ... So alone.

Hot, salty tears slid down the sides of her face, searing the open wounds on her cheeks.

If my Nikki is with you ... if I lie very still, very quiet ... would you ... please ... come and take me too?

She waited, resolved, her breathing labored, listening to her heartbeat grow faint. She wasn't sure how long she lay there before a thought crashed into her consciousness—her babe nestled in her womb. With that remembrance, hope—fragile at first, like the delicate petals of a bramble rose slowly unfurling—curled around the roots of her despair.

"I'll not give up, little one," she whispered.

I cannot.

Using her last remnant of strength, she lifted her head and willed herself up onto her elbow, astonished to feel two arms, warm and strong, slide around her shoulders.

"Dear lady," came a strange male voice. "Have courage. You are not alone. Permit me to help."

The man sprawled on the sand, propped her against his chest and held a canteen to her lips. "Take a swig of this water and slosh it around in your mouth and then spit it out."

She followed his instructions, coughing as the cool, fresh water hit the back of her throat.

"Now, take a drink."

She took a big swallow. It tasted wonderful, so she clasped the canteen and drank her fill, taking big gulps that almost choked her.

"Enough?" he asked when she finally let go.

She nodded and glanced up at him for the first time. He was an elderly man, his sun-bronzed face crisscrossed with wrinkles and his hair as white and feathery as an egret's wing.

"If I may," he said, studying her with clear aquamarine eyes, "let me cleanse your face."

She lay still while he poured water on her eyelids, gently removing the grainy, itchy particles with his thumb and rinsed shell fragments from her cheeks and neck.

"More?" He held the canteen to her lips again.

This time she sipped the water.

"Your people are coming now," he said, cradling her shoulders until she settled back down.

He let go of her and stood, and her heart hammered against her ribcage as she rolled onto her side and spotted a group of people making their way toward her.

"I'll be going, but I'll leave this with you." He corked the canteen and leaned it against her.

"But ... I ... your name," Lilyan sputtered, watching him walk away.

"No need," he called over his shoulder and disappeared behind a dune covered in sea oats.

"Lilyan!" a very familiar, very dear voice cried out.

"Nikki!" she screamed, bursting with joy at the sound of her husband's voice.

He swept her onto his lap, and she rejoiced at the way he rained kisses all over her face. Running his fingers from one end of her body to the other, he murmured over and over, "Are you hurt, dearest? Are you hurt?"

She wanted to laugh, to reassure him, but she didn't have the energy to do that.

He took her face in his hands and studied her eyes. "Our baby?" he whispered.

Her eyes misted, and she managed a smile. She tried to wrap her arms around him, but they wouldn't cooperate, dangling by her sides like limp rags. Secure in his arms, she gazed up at him and found herself drowning once again, only this time in a pair of vibrant, adoring eyes. And then the world went black.

CHAPTER 24

*"The grapevines on the coast covered every shrub and climbed
the tops of high cedars. In all the world, a similar abundance
was not to be found."*
Sir Walter Raleigh's explorers, 1580s

Lilyan woke on a down-filled mattress in one of the most elegant rooms she had ever slept in. She lay in a huge, mahogany bed with ornately spindled posts that almost touched the ceiling. Sunlight filtered through lace curtains billowing from a gentle breeze. A bowl of sunflowers graced a round table next to the window. The yellow petals were mirrored in cheerful paintings hung across from the bed. She turned her head and breathed in the smell of lavender on her pillow.

Nicholas, still asleep beside her, had thrown an arm and a leg across her, as if afraid she would get away from him again. But that simply was not going to happen. If she spent the rest of her life attached to his hip, she would be content, but she dispensed with that happy notion the moment she realized she needed to use the necessary.

Inch by inch she untangled herself from Nicholas and slid from the bed. Favoring her sore ankle, she slipped behind a Chinese print screen to discover a chamber pot that was so ornately decorated she hesitated to make use of it. Minutes later, she stood before a mahogany marble-topped washstand and poured water from a pitcher into a washbowl, moistened a towel, and patted her face, avoiding the scrapes and bruises. The gauze secured around both hands made bathing such an ordeal, she unwrapped the bandages. When the soap touched the open cuts, the stinging was so severe she bit her lip to keep from screeching. She studied the lacerations on her hands, thankful that the ointment had kept the wounds from festering. She found a brush and comb in the washstand drawer, and, lightheaded, she crept past the bed and eased down onto a ladder-back chair.

The prospect from the window was so splendid, she missed her paints and canvas. The two-story house hugged the edge of a round bay circled by a chain of twenty or more cottages and houses in various shapes and sizes. At the narrow mouth of the inlet, two schooners were anchored among smaller sailing vessels and fishing boats in the aqua water that flowed into the sound on the west side of the island. Leaning her arm on the sill, she wondered what sights her little girl had awakened to.

Until today, she had comforted herself by picturing Laurel in familiar surroundings—the rolling hills of the Piedmont, the lush green backcountry crisscrossed by dancing rivers, the crowded streets of Charlestown. But she had never been to Baltimore. It was unsettling not to be able to envision Laurel and what she might be doing, so she closed her eyes and pictured her daughter's impish smile that crinkled her nose and lit her eyes.

Sighing, she began to undo her braid, still damp from washing it the night before. She didn't remember much after finally coming to, riding in the back of one of the wagons that the Ocracoke Islanders used to transport Nicholas and her to the village. One thing she did recall was the soothing tone of Mrs. Hortensia Garrish, who walked beside the stretcher while men carried Lilyan up the stairs. She lay motionless like a helpless child as the tall, gaunt woman bathed her, washed her hair, spread ointment on her cuts, and bandaged her hands and ankle. The chemise Mrs. Garrish dressed her in was fashioned of the finest white lawn and lace.

The brush caught in a tangle of hair, slid from her hand, and clattered to the floor. Nicholas sat up, poised to spring out of the bed until he spied her.

"Come," he said, holding open his arms.

Careful of her ankle, she hopped onto the mattress and into his arms. His day-old beard scratched where he rubbed his chin across her forehead. She threw her arms around his waist, digging her fingers into his nightshirt.

"Woman," he said with a chuckle, "you're squeezing the life out of me."

"I'm sorry, dear sir, but you're going to have to suffer for a while."

He chuckled. "That I should suffer this for the rest of my days."

Lilyan released her hold and rolled onto her back. Though dreading the answer, she had to ask the question that plagued her since waking. "What news of the others?"

He tucked his arm closer around her. "Evelyn and Robbie survived, though she suffered a cut to her forehead. Robbie has some minor bruises. Only five of the twenty crew made it."

"Only five of twenty?" She rose up on her elbow. "And the captain?"

He gazed into her eyes, his face somber. "No. Not the captain. His body washed ashore near where the rest of us gathered."

Lilyan remembered the last time she saw the captain. He stood braced against the wind, gripping the helm, guarding Evelyn with his eyes as she followed his orders to seek safety below decks. "Such sad news. He was a splendid man."

They lay quietly for a few moments.

"Poor Evelyn. She loved him so. I should go to her." She started to rise, but he clamped his arm tighter.

"No. You stay here. Your body has taken a beating, and you have to rest. Besides, she's probably sleeping. She was up most of the night. Robbie and I tried to console her, but we could not."

Lilyan realized it could just as easily have been her mourning the loss of her husband. The thought was sobering, and she snuggled closer to him. "What do we do now? How do we get to Baltimore? How much longer until we can leave?"

"I'll ask Mrs. Garrish. I'm sure she can tell us the fastest way to find passage to Baltimore."

"I'm so anxious. It seems that our journey has been blocked at every turn. As if for every one step we've taken forward, we've taken two steps back."

He kissed the top of her head. "We'll find our Laurel. And soon."

Turning on his side and pulling her back up against his chest, he tucked his knees under hers. "Go back to sleep."

With that, she gave herself over to sleep, awakening several hours later to a grinding noise in her stomach.

Nicholas chortled. "Thought there might be a lumberyard nearby."

They were still chuckling when someone tapped on the door.

"Yes?" he called out.

The door opened just a crack, and a young woman peeked into the room.

"Good day," she greeted with a bright smile. "I'm Sarah, the housemaid. With my mistress's apologies for interrupting, would you care to come downstairs and partake of some oyster stew?"

"Tell Mrs. Garrish we'll be down straightaway." Nicholas sat up on the side of the bed.

"But," said Lilyan, "we don't have clothes."

Grinning, the maid stepped into the room and bowed. "I've brought some things. What with all the shipwrecks that happen 'round here, there's always plenty to go around. The missus picked out some right fine things for you."

She draped the clothes over the end of the bed and placed some shoes at the footboard. "I'll see you downstairs," she said, closing the door behind her.

Lilyan left the bed to admire the pale yellow chemise and matching skirt, which she held against her. "I must say, I wish she hadn't told us where these clothes came from. It's ghoulish, don't you think?"

Nicholas joined her and picked up a pair of breeches. "Not really. Many people who live in areas like this make their money salvaging. It's a normal part of living for them."

"I imagine so."

She sat back down on the edge of the bed, prepared to enjoy watching him shave as he stood in front of the washstand, but when he pulled his arms from the nightshirt and the garment dropped to his waist, he exposed purple and blue splotches spattered across his shoulders and arms.

"You're bruised." She slid off the bed and stood beside him. "Are you in pain?"

He turned around and chucked her chin with his knuckle. "I'm fine."

She ran her fingertips across his torso. "There's a particularly distressing one, almost the size of my hand, here at your waist."

He curled his hands around hers and brought them to his lips. "We're here, aga'pi mou. We survived to find our little girl. Let's dwell on that. Hmm?"

"You're right."

Her stomach chose that moment to growl so loudly, she giggled.

He grinned down at her. "Let's get you downstairs, woman. You and the little one need some food."

They dressed quickly, he tightening the strings at the back of her dress, and she tying his cravat.

She retrieved a pair of yellow slippers and sat in the chair by the window, but before she could put them on, he bent on one knee in front of her.

"The swelling's almost gone," he said, running his fingertips over her foot and anklebone. He slid the shoe onto her foot. "Any pain?"

"It's a bit sore."

She studied him as he touched the bandage beneath her stocking. If only she had her paints. One swooping motion of her brush could portray the angle of his neck, the line of his shoulders and muscular forearms, so familiar and so dear. For a moment, she wondered why she had never done his portrait.

She reached down and combed her fingers through his hair. "Husband?"

"Yes," he answered, slipping her other foot into a shoe.

"I don't think I've told you today how very much I love you."

He glanced up then, giving her one of his most charming smiles. "No, you haven't. But then, if you never spoke the words again, I would know it anyway."

He rose and helped her to her feet, then followed her to the washstand. He stood behind her as she used the mirror to adjust her mobcap and drape tendrils of hair on either side of her face. She gingerly touched the scratches on her cheeks and forehead and frowned at the scrapes on her hands, hoping they weren't too unsightly.

Nicholas caught her worried look in the mirror. "Lovely," he said and then kissed the palms of her hands.

She took his elbow and they headed out the door. Downstairs, Sarah escorted them into a dining room decorated with the same splendor as their bedroom. Sixteen mahogany chairs with fine needlepoint cushions circled a dining table covered in an ecru lace cloth. The bobbing bright heads of beeswax candles reflected in the pewter plates and mugs lined on shelves that stretched across one wall.

"So happy to see you up and about," Mrs. Garrish greeted from the doorway. "And a mighty handsome couple as I've ever seen."

Lilyan curtsied and Nicholas bowed.

"It's very kind of you to take us in, Mrs. Garrish," said Nicholas. "I apologize for the lateness of the hour."

"Nonsense," said Mrs. Garrish, a cloud of lilac perfume wafting about her as she entered the room. "You sit to my right, Mr. Xanthakos. And you to my left, dear."

"Will Evelyn be joining us?" Lilyan asked, waiting at her designated place.

"I'm afraid not. She asked that we send for a clergyman. She's with him now. Bless her."

Nicholas pulled out a chair at the head of the table and waited for Mrs. Garrish to take a seat before seating Lilyan and then himself.

"Your ankle? It pains you?" asked Mrs. Garrish.

"Just a bit. Most of the swelling's gone. Though the rope burn will take a while to heal, I'm afraid."

Sarah came forward with a sapphire-blue tureen and set it on the table. When she lifted the heavy lid, the aroma that drifted across the table tantalized Lilyan's nose and teased her tongue. Nicholas returned her wide-eyed stare, and she wondered if they would be able to keep themselves from drooling.

Lilyan could barely take her eyes from the creamy liquid in her bowl. "It smells heavenly."

"Mr. Xanthakos, would you do us the honor of blessing our meal?" Mrs. Garrish reached for their hands and curled her cool, slender fingers around theirs.

Lilyan bowed her head while Nicholas said grace, adding her own unspoken prayer for her family and friends.

As the first taste of stew slid over Lilyan's tongue, she closed her eyes. "It tastes even better than it smells. If that's possible."

Mrs. Garrish's smile lit her pansy-brown eyes. "'Tis an old family recipe. Oysters, potatoes, mushrooms, milk, and just a hint of tarragon leaves."

During the course of conversation, their hostess discovered, to her great delight, that she and Nicholas shared a passion for wine, especially muscadine wine. They were soon immersed in an animated conversation that allowed Lilyan not only to enjoy her stew, but also to study the unusual, more-than-likely rare objects decorating the room. In one corner stood a three-foot-tall Chinese vase. Beside that was a trestle table, which displayed a collection of jade statuettes. Sitting in the center of the lime-green and aqua pieces was a beautifully crafted rose that seemed out of place, since it had been carved out of wood.

"What say you, Lilyan?" asked Nicholas, drawing her back into the conversation.

"I'm sorry, dear?"

"Mrs. Garrish says that while we're waiting for passage, she has a man who will sail us to Roanoke Island to get root cuttings from a vine that grows golden muscadines—only they call them scuppernongs. Golden, not purple. Can you believe it?"

Lilyan shook her head but was captivated more by her husband than the thought of getting back on a boat again.

"So, we'll go?" he asked.

Lilyan smiled. "Of course."

"Very good then," said Mrs. Garrish. "I'll make the arrangements."

"Mrs. Garrish, I couldn't help but notice the unusual carving there on the trestle," Lilyan said, pointing to the flower.

"The rose? That was carved by a local man. Jason."

"It's beautiful. Does he have others like it?"

Mrs. Garrish placed her napkin on the table and slid from her chair. "If we are finished, let's retire to the sitting room where we can converse more comfortably. Shall we?"

Nicholas offered his arm to Mrs. Garrish, who waved him away and told him to care for his wife. Lilyan took his arm as they followed her into a cozy room with a lovely prospect of the bay. While Nicholas and she sat together on a settee covered in an Oriental pattern of blue willows, their hostess seated herself in a sky-blue velveteen high-backed chair and rested her feet on a matching footstool. Lilyan tried to drape one ankle over the other, but her skin was so ravaged she grimaced and quickly placed both feet flat on the floor.

"We were speaking of Jason," said Mrs. Garrish, taking a carved ivory fan from the table next to her and fanning herself. "Yes, he has many other carvings. All made from wood taken from shipwrecks."

Lilyan clamped her eyes shut and struggled against the disturbing memories of the shipwreck.

"Jason—that's what everyone calls him. No last name. Owns most of the property on the southern tip of the island. That's where a great deal of the wreckage comes ashore."

"Why no last name?" Nicholas asked.

"It's a thorny history, but I'll try my best to explain." She closed the fan and rested it in her lap. "You see, most everyone on this island makes money from salvaging. From the ships that crash into the sandbars or get caught in the gales that plague this area. It's a reputable practice, but Jason's family were tricksters. What some called 'pirates without ships.' They would tie a lantern around the neck of a lame horse and let it wander up and down the shore at night. Ships spying the lantern bobbing up and down believed it was another ship, making them also believe that they were farther away from shore than they really were."

"You mean they deliberately lured ships into the sandbars?" asked Nicholas.

"I'm afraid so." She gently fluttered her fan back and forth, lifting the tendrils of her hair around her face. "Jason grew up deeply ashamed of his family and their deliberate ensnaring of poor innocents into their traps. When he inherited the property, he renounced his family name and began to insist that the islanders address him only by his given name. Now, when there's a bad storm, he walks up and down the beach, seeking survivors."

Lilyan gasped. "Nikki, there was a man … man who gave me water just before you found me." She stared at Mrs. Garrish. "An older man? Tan, leathery skin? White hair?"

Mrs. Garrish nodded. "Sounds like our Jason."

Lilyan shook her head. "I wondered for a while if I had imagined him. I even thought him an angel."

"I guess you could call him a guardian angel of sorts. He

keeps everything he finds in a huge warehouse on his property. Catalogues it, seeks out ships' manifests to find the names of the passengers, and tries to return as much of the salvage that he can to the survivors or to the families of those lost."

"It's possible he has some of our belongings, then?" Nicholas asked. "I had some papers. My debt books. Some money."

"So, should we go visit Jason? See if he has some of our things?" Lilyan asked.

Mrs. Garrish shook her head. "One doesn't visit Jason. He's as elusive as a ghost. You'll have to wait for him to come see you."

Nicholas pressed his fists into his thighs. "I hope it's not a long wait. We'll need money to travel on to Baltimore."

"That was your destination?" asked Mrs. Garrish. "You have business there?"

Nicholas nodded. "The business—if you can call it that—of getting our child back."

"I'm all astonishment." Mrs. Garrish stopped moving her fan. "You must explain."

Nicholas spent the next few minutes recounting Laurel's kidnapping and their efforts to find her. Sarah, who had entered the room carrying a tea tray, stopped to listen.

"That is why we sailed out of Charlestown. In pursuit of the *Resolution*, the ship our daughter is on," said Nicholas, finishing his story.

Lilyan heard Sarah's gasp and caught her sharing a panicked look with her mistress.

Something's wrong, thought Lilyan, rubbing the back of her neck where the skin prickled.

"The *Resolution*? Are you sure?" Mrs. Garrish did not take her eyes off Sarah.

"I am." Nicholas clasped Lilyan's fingers tighter as if he, too, sensed something amiss.

Mrs. Garrish snapped her fan shut. "Sarah, if you would, please, fetch Reverend Whitehouse."

CHAPTER 25

A time to weep ...
Ecclesiastes 3:4

The *Resolution* had sunk during a storm two days prior. All souls aboard lost.

Lilyan demanded the pale, spindly, young reverend repeat himself over and over, until, finally, his words crashed through her, wreaking havoc like a hurricane, leaving behind a swath of devastation. Even so, she could not, would not, completely believe what she was hearing. Something inside her refused to connect the horrible news with the proper feelings she should be experiencing. As the others slipped from the room, she crept onto Nicholas's lap and wrapped her arms about his shoulders. She had gone cold. Bone cold. As if someone had plunged her into a frozen mountain lake. Beyond crying. She held on to Nicholas, who dropped his face into the crook of her neck and cried for both of them. When his shoulders stopped shaking, she rubbed his back and dried his face with the hem of her dress.

His eyes, full of anguish, swam with tears. "She's gone."

Lilyan gulped, her throat constricted.

"Our sweet baby girl." He covered his face with both hands. "How can this be? What did I do to displease God so much that He would punish me in such a way?"

Lilyan cupped his face with her hands. "Dearest, don't take blame where none is warranted. 'Twas no fault of yours."

"You don't blame me? For not finding her before … before …?" He stopped, tears running down his cheeks.

She wiped away his tears with her thumbs. "Do you blame me for letting her go with Golden Fawn?"

Because I do.

He blinked, stunned. "Of course not."

"And I don't blame you. You did everything you could."

"Then why? Why did God let this happen?" He dug his fingers into her shoulders. "Make me understand. I need to understand why."

His questions haunted her. Night and day they plagued her. They niggled at her soul days later as she stood on board a schooner to witness Captain Sinclair's body committed to the deep. She found them in Evelyn's eyes as her grieving friend leaned on Robbie's arm.

A week slipped by, then two. They waited not only for a ship to arrive to take them back to Charlestown, but mostly because they couldn't bear to leave for home without their daughter. Days were bearable only because she and Nicholas would steal away to the beach, where they stood arm in arm, braced against the winds. She found it comforting near the ocean with its familiars and constants. Life continued, despite her tragedy. Seagulls splashed down into the swells only to rise again with fish caught in their shiny beaks. Waves ebbed and flowed as they had done since their creation, and the sun rose new every morning. She forced herself to remember that the God of the beginning and the end would see them through their suffering and bring healing.

In contrast, the nights brought with them tortured doubts and confusion. Her inability to completely absorb her daughter's death and her husband's need to share his grief became a mental tug-of-war. What was wrong with her? Why couldn't she concede to the facts her husband had accepted? Had something severed between her heart and her mind? When emotions overwhelmed her, she would fall on her knees and pray for relief. Yearning for answers, she combed the Bible. She knew that God would not have taken the life of their precious child to punish or to prove some point. The God she worshiped wasn't like that. She came to the conclusion that they might never comprehend why He allowed it to happen … if it had happened.

If it had happened? How could she think such a thing? The doubt was making her ill.

One morning, she found herself saying that very thing when she and Evelyn sat in Mrs. Garrish's garden. The change in her friend was startling, for she wore her sorrow like a heavy mantle. Her responses, like a dirge, came slow and measured.

Evelyn wilted onto the willow branch settee where they both sat looking at the bay. "I don't think I'll ever be the same. Were Walter and I too happy? Was God jealous?" she asked, twisting a handkerchief in her fingers.

"Oh, no. I cannot think that. We're His children, and He wants only good for us."

"That only makes it more difficult for me to understand why this all came about. My Walter? Your Laurel? Why? What earthly good can come of it?"

"My dear friend," said Lilyan, "I'm afraid I have many more questions than I have answers. But the one thing I cling to is the knowledge that, no matter what happens, God will be there with us. He'll never forsake us."

Evelyn's usually sparkling eyes clouded with sadness. "Would that I had your faith."

They sat in silence until Nicholas entered the garden.

He stood before them and bowed to Evelyn. "Good morning.

I hope you fare well."

Lilyan's heart lurched at her husband's somber appearance and the wounded look in his eyes.

"As well as could be expected," Evelyn responded, her gloomy countenance belying her words.

"I'm on the way to the village to make arrangements for passage back to Charlestown and thought you ladies would like to accompany me."

Evelyn shook her head. "If you'd be so kind, would you arrange for me, Robbie, and the crew as well? I'll provide my note, if necessary, until we reach Charlestown."

"I'd be honored." He held Lilyan's hand as she rose from the bench.

"We'll talk again." Lilyan slipped her arm through Nicholas's.

As they departed, Evelyn paid them no heed, her attention drawn to a patch of sunflowers beside the bench.

On the way to the harbor, they were greeted by villagers who doffed their hats, stood quietly to the side, or offered condolences. Lilyan clung to her husband's arm and worried how they were going to break the news to their family, especially Callum and Golden Fawn.

At the docks, having found a captain who agreed to take his promissory note, Nicholas signed for their group to board a ship that would leave for Charlestown in a week's time. On the return walk, he broached the subject she dreaded.

"Lilyanista, I should like very much to hold a memorial service."

When she didn't answer, he guided her off the road and onto a trail through the dunes. They continued in silence until they stepped onto the beach.

"Since this is where she lies," he swept his hand to encompass the ocean, "this is where the service should be." He removed his hat and tucked it under his arm. "I spoke to Thanassis. He said he'd be honored to assist."

The young sailor had visited Nicholas many times since the

news about Laurel. He and Nicholas spent hours conversing in Greek, something she knew gave her husband comfort.

They reached the water's edge and stood a few minutes watching a lone fisherman casting a net, his small boat bobbing in the gentle swells.

She sucked in a deep breath. "I don't think I'm ready—"

"What?" He bent his head toward her.

She curled her hands around his shoulders. "I have a feeling. Or maybe it's a feeling I *don't* have." She faltered. "Oh! I can't find the right words."

Sharing his anguish, she dug deep down inside for a way to express her uncertainty. "When a mother loses a child, there should be ... a sense that part of her is no longer there. A knowing."

He continued to stare at her, puzzled.

She grasped the sleeves of his waistcoat. "I find it impossible to let go of her."

"But you mourn?"

"I have grieved the *idea* of her death."

He looked incredulous. "You don't believe she's dead?"

"I can't accept it."

"But to think this ... to harbor such ..." He shook his head. "It will be like an open wound. Festering. That's never allowed to heal."

He scrubbed his hand through his hair then splayed his fingers toward her. "Why would you torture yourself ... us ... so?" He balled his hand into a fist. "I cannot believe this!"

His accusation stung and, at once, all her heartache and confusion formed into a lump in her chest that threatened her breathing. "And I cannot believe how readily you accept it," she shouted, putting into words a sentiment she had been unaware of until that moment. Her heart ached at what she must say. "We've not seen her ... her body. How can you be so sure?"

"You dare say such a thing to me?" He leaned over to stand nose to nose with her, clenching his hat in both hands.

Lilyan blanched as his body shook with fury.

He stepped back. "Would the fact that I spent five years of my life fighting a war have something to do with it?" His voice was taut, his temper barely held in check. "I cannot count the mornings I sat around a campfire with my men, only to be told that evening that they had been killed in battle and I would never see them again. The first year, I wrestled with hope. Thinking maybe, just maybe, a friend would have survived and would walk into camp any moment. Do you have any notion how difficult that was? How I became resolved—no, conditioned—to death, without proof, without a body? Do you even know how many friends I lost … how I finally learned to hold myself apart when new men came under my command?" He stepped back, holding his arms stiff at his sides. "It was my love for you and Laurel that finally brought me out of that pit of hell. And now, for you to accuse me … to say I find it easy to accept my precious child's death …" He choked on the words, but he straightened his spine. "'Tis a cruelty I would not have expected of you."

Never once in their marriage had they confronted each other in such a manner, and it terrified Lilyan. Their turmoil ran deep like a river threatening to branch in two as it strikes against an insurmountable boulder. With tears burning the backs of her eyes, she looked up at him. "I'm simply asking for a little time …" She stopped, watching his expression change as he focused on something behind her.

She turned around to find Jason heading toward them, his gait steady and purposeful.

"I hope I'm not intruding," he said, standing beside them.

Nicholas looked out to sea.

Lilyan dried the corners of her eyes with her knuckle and curtsied. Struggling to sound composed, she said, "I'm grateful for the opportunity to thank you for helping me."

He bowed. "It was the least I could do."

"Nicholas, this is Jason, the man who found me on the beach

and gave me water. Jason, this is my husband, Nicholas Xanthakos."

The two men bowed.

"I'm in your debt," said Nicholas.

"Not at all." Jason reached into his pocket. "Mrs. Xanthakos, your daughter's name was Laurel, was it not?"

Lilyan nodded.

"I have something for you."

Proof? She braced her arm muscles, preparing for a blow.

"Here." He handed her a palm-sized wood carving. "It's something I do."

She studied the small sculpture, captivated by its intricate pattern and the delicately shaped petals of a mountain laurel. "It's exquisite."

Jason looked at the carving. "The wood came from the *Resolution*."

She held it out to Nicholas. "Isn't it lovely?"

Taking it from her, he avoided eye contact. "Beautiful. It's a fine gift, sir."

"Keep it for us, please," she said to Nicholas, who tucked it inside his waistcoat.

"Jason," said Lilyan, hesitantly. "Mrs. Garrish says you store the salvage from shipwrecks. Is it nearby?"

The man pointed southward. "About a quarter mile."

"Things from the *Resolution*?" Nicholas asked.

"A great deal. It was a four-master."

"Could we see it?" Nicholas still avoided eye contact with Lilyan.

Jason stood to the side and motioned for them to accompany him. No one spoke as they walked along the shore. Lilyan remained quiet because she knew Nicholas was absorbing what she had been so inept at expressing. She gathered that Jason didn't talk because that was his way.

They continued on until Jason motioned for them to follow him through a patch of dunes and along a path that took them through a marshy, flat area and then on to a group of rustic buildings surrounded by marsh grass swishing in the afternoon breezes. Lining the pathway, clumps of pussy willows drooped their heads in a gloomy greeting.

Jason motioned toward the nearest structure. "This holds salvage from the *Resolution* and from your ship, *Muirgheal*." He pushed on the wide wooden doors that opened with a creaking, tortured sound. "Course, stuff is still coming in."

He led them to the side of the building, where row upon row of barrels and crates were lined up next to piles of lumber, neatly stacked according to size. Lilyan couldn't believe the amount of materials. How could all of that have survived and not one person? With gooseflesh moving across her arms, she couldn't shake the feeling that she was standing before an open coffin, except the deceased was a skeleton.

She and Nicholas wandered along the rows of salvage until they came upon an area where baggage was stored.

She spotted two small trunks and pointed to them, her fingers shaking. "Could we open these?"

Jason nodded.

The outside of one trunk was covered in a thick casing of ocean salt and sand. The lock was already beginning to corrode. Nicholas reached down and shoved open the lid, revealing a stack of clothing. While she searched one of the trunks for something—anything— that would help her face the unthinkable, Nicholas searched the other, looking, she knew, for something—anything—that would put him in touch once again with his little girl. Neither found what they sought.

"Over here's the salvage from the *Muirgheal*." Jason swept his arm toward another, smaller stack of debris.

Something caught her eye and she hurried toward it. "My sealskin trunk!"

Nicholas got there first and pried open the latch and flung open the top.

Lilyan dropped to her knees and seized the white lamb's wool coverlet and Laurel's rag doll and snuggled them against her face. She remembered the joy when packing them, the promise that both objects held.

Nicholas reached over and touched the cover. "It's dry. Completely dry. No damage at all."

Unlike our hearts.

Scooping the doll and cover under her arm, she searched further and found Nicholas's money pouch and bank papers.

Grimacing, Nicholas perused the wreckage. "At least we won't have to worry about funds."

He slipped the pouch inside his waistcoat, returned the cover and doll to the trunk, and shut the lid. "May we take this, Jason?"

"Of course, it belongs to you."

They stayed until the reminders of such terrible loss became too sad to bear.

Nicholas tossed the trunk onto his shoulder and offered her his arm. "We'll go now."

Outside, Jason closed the doors and led them back through the marsh and out onto the beach. They hadn't gone far when she heard a sound like thunder, at once familiar and peculiar.

"Look!" said Nicholas, pointing down the beach.

She turned to see a band of about a dozen horses racing toward them, their manes flying straight behind them as they plunged knee-deep through the shallows, splashing beads of water around them like sparkling diamonds. Her heart pounding as loudly as the horses' hooves, she watched them slow down and then halt a few yards away. Smallish, standing only thirteen hands at the withers, they had chestnut coats, except for a stallion that had dun coloring. Their foreheads were broad and their chests were deep and narrow.

"Where did they come from?" she asked.

"They're wild. They roam up and down the islands when the tide is low, often swimming from one to the next when the tide is high," said Jason. "That one there ..." He pointed to a chestnut mare. "She's the dominant one, the leader."

"Do they belong to anyone?" she asked.

"No one. The story is that they descend from horses that were on board one of Hernando DeSoto's ships that ran aground during one of his expeditions."

Nicholas stepped closer to Lilyan. "Are they dangerous?"

"No. They're quite friendly. The only threat they pose is when they dig shoulder-deep holes in the ground when they're searching for fresh water."

Nicholas put down the trunk and observed one of the mares snatch a frond of sea oats in her teeth. She pawed the ground with her hoof and tossed the stem back into the water.

Nicholas leaned down and whispered, "Would that our Laurel could have seen this."

Lilyan lamented the profound regret in his voice. "Yes."

Lord, please, do not let regret overtake our lives.

* * *

Later that evening, seated once again with Evelyn in the garden, Lilyan recounted the argument she'd had with Nicholas. She watched a variety of emotions play out on her friend's face as she contemplated a response.

After a time, with a frown wrinkling her forehead, Evelyn looked her in the eye. "I sympathize with you. I do. But I beg you to consider in your heart of hearts the need your husband has for this service."

Lilyan's body drooped.

"Could you not put aside your own feelings to grant him this comfort? After all, he gave in to you when you insisted on joining him on the voyage from Charlestown."

Recalling Nicholas's face as he accused her of cruelty, Lilyan grimaced. "You think I'm being unkind, as well?"

"Not in the least. But I am saying there's a time to give and to receive. And this is a time I think you must give." Evelyn sighed, folding her hands in her lap.

"But attending such a service would be a form of acceptance." Lilyan trembled at the thought.

"But it's a way to stand by your husband. To console him."

"To put his needs before my own? That's what it comes down to, does it not?"

Evelyn sank back against the seat. "Yes, my dear friend, I believe it does. Would that I had my dear Walter here once more. I'd take back every harsh word I ever spoke to him. We had such a brief time together, I regret every moment of discord I may have brought about between us."

It took only a moment for her friend's advice to soften Lilyan's heart. Her thoughts turned back to the confrontation with Nicholas, and she ached, remembering the pain she had inflicted on her beloved. She had known all along what she should do, but it had taken Evelyn's confirmation to remind her that above all things in this world, she longed for her husband to be content.

Spurred by a thought, Lilyan leapt from the bench. "I need to find Thanassis. He can tell me what I must do. Will you come with me?"

"That I will." Evelyn stood, and for the first time in weeks, she smiled.

They found Thanassis in a tavern near the docks. Astounded and humbled by their visit, he stammered his introductions to his two companions, Paul and Presis, who looked like their friend with the same swarthy skin and dark hair and eyes. They all stood before her and Evelyn, heads downcast. Lilyan invited them to be seated again and tried her best to put them at ease. With Paul's help interpreting, she was able to explain to Thanassis about her husband's desire for a service. Once he understood, Thanassis propped his chin on his hand and sat quietly, giving her request deep concentration.

"The captain wants. But you do not?" Thanassis asked in broken English.

"It doesn't matter what I want. This is important to my husband."

Thanassis turned to Paul and began a rapid conversation with him.

Lilyan leaned forward. "What is it? What's he saying?"

"Dear lady," Paul began. "Thanassis has struck upon a solution that will surely comfort your husband and calm your heart as well."

Evelyn met Lilyan's glance. "Tell us, young man. Straightaway, please."

"There is a service done in our church called the Trisagion." He grimaced. "'Tis not easy to explain. It is not a funeral service, but one performed before the funeral. A kind of remembrance."

Thanassis nodded. "That is so. A remembrance."

"Family and friends greet each other with the words *memory eternal*. There are special songs sung and words spoken."

"Could you? Would you help us with those?" asked Lilyan.

Paul bowed. "It would be our honor."

They spent another hour making plans to hold the service at dawn. As she bade them good-bye, Lilyan breathed easier, as if someone was gently removing the brick wall of grief that surrounded her heart.

When Lilyan returned to Mrs. Garrish's home, she looked for Nicholas everywhere only to discover that he had left an hour earlier, headed for the beach. On feet that could barely move fast enough, she took the familiar trail, stopping at the dunes to search the shore. Her heart tripped in her chest when she spotted him in the distance plodding along the beach, his hands jammed into his pockets, the sleeves of his shirt billowing in the wind.

He looks so forlorn.

She waved her arms over her head and then cupped her hands around her mouth. "Nikki!" she called, but he didn't respond.

She took off running, only to stop a few yards shy of him. He looked up then and stared at her, holding back and guarded.

Chancing his rebuff, she opened her arms to him. "Forgive me?"

He quickly closed the distance between them and stepped into her embrace.

***

The next morning, standing beside her husband and clasping his forearm, Lilyan, blinking back her tears, stared at the horizon as the sun seemed to ease up out of the water. Horizontal lines waved across the fiery ball, promising clear blue skies.

No red skies. No threat of storms this day.

They were a large party. She and Nicholas, Evelyn and Robbie, Mrs. Garrish and her maid, Sarah, the five crewmen from the *Murgheal*, a handful of sailors she didn't recognize, and the islanders who had taken part in her rescue. As if in a dream, she heard Nicholas respond to the Greek sailors who repeated the somber greeting, "Memory eternal." Thannasis began to sing, his voice a pure and clear baritone. She couldn't understand the words, but the sentiments behind the notes massaged her heart and spread like a balm across its ragged edges. She looked up and was startled to find tears running down the faces of several of the sailors.

Are they sad for my Laurel? Though they didn't know her?

A thought struck her. This was perhaps the only opportunity the sailors had to mourn the loss of their shipmates lost at sea.

The service has brought comfort. Not only to my beloved, but to others. What a blessing.

CHAPTER 26

For ye have need of patience, that, after ye have done the will of God,
ye might receive the promise.
Hebrews 10:36 KJV

Two weeks later, sitting in the parlor of her Charlestown home, Lilyan held Callum's hand, rubbing her fingers across his calloused ones. Her old friend had taken the news very hard. She had never in her life seen him cry, and it was distressing. Golden Fawn had taken to her room for days, but Andrew was finally able to coax her out.

It was Lilyan's hope that everyone would fare better once the family returned to the vineyard. It would take them about twelve days' travel, and by the time they arrived, the muscadines would be ready for harvesting. Maintaining the house and the lands was backbreaking work compared to their sedentary lifestyle in Charlestown, which gave one too much time to dwell on painful thoughts.

Nicholas avoided the subject of a formal memorial service, and once, when Andrew brought up the question in front of the others, he shared an understanding glance with Lilyan before telling his brother-in-law that they weren't ready. Maybe when they returned to the vineyard, he offered.

Mildred, Constance, and Sally bedded down in the attic and spent their time preparing meals, cleaning the house, and taking turns consoling each family member. Evelyn and Robbie, who had moved into Evelyn's home, visited often. They had become a cloistered group, not venturing out even for Sunday services, except for Nicholas, who was making arrangements—buying wagons, horses, and supplies—for them to leave for home as soon as possible. One of the wagons would carry the dozen or so scuppernong root cuttings Mrs. Garrish had arranged for them to take. She had met them at the ship as they were leaving Ocracoke. Nicholas was moved by the gift and made her a promise to write and let her know how the vines fared. The promise of new beginnings seemed to lift—at least for a short time—some of the pall surrounding them.

Their household felt even more somber compared to the festive mood taking over the city, which was in the midst of incorporating and changing its name from Charlestown to Charleston. Though Lilyan couldn't begrudge the people their joy, the changes to her birthplace were unsettling. She longed even more for the tranquility of her mountain cabin.

The day before they were set to leave, they had a visit from Agnes McCord and Candice Laurens, escorted by James McCord, who had come to share condolences.

Agnes had barely stepped over the threshold when she pulled Lilyan aside to inform her that she had already begun making inquiries about Fianna. Delighted and relieved, Lilyan embraced her so tightly that Agnes complained her bones might break.

Nicholas warmly greeted James and took him outside in the backyard of the house, where they talked while Nicholas supervised the loading of the wagons.

Agnes seated herself beside Callum, and they soon enjoyed a lively conversation. Since the rest of the household was engaged in packing, Lilyan was left to entertain Mrs. Laurens.

"I cannot tell you the effect the news about your child had on us, my dear," said Mrs. Laurens. "Agnes and I have become very fond of you, and your loss is ours."

"That's very kind." Lilyan appreciated the woman's genuine concern but wished she wasn't having this conversation.

"At the courthouse, before you left, I told you that the Brambles are neighbors of ours."

"Yes, I recall."

"Well, I'm leaving Charlestown in a week or two to return to my home at Mount Pleasant. I thought I'd pay a visit to the Brambles and offer my condolences for the loss of their relatives." She leaned forward. "If I may have your permission, I'd like to tell them about you and your family."

Lilyan nodded. "Offer them my condolences as well, if you would. And please let them know how much I appreciate the care … any kindnesses the Brambles showed my daughter."

"Certainly."

Agnes scooted forward on the settee. "Lilyan, Jimmy and I have brought you a gift."

When Agnes started to rise, Callum stood and gave her his hand. "It was really Jimmy's idea." She motioned toward a package leaning against the wall. "But I'd like some credit too."

Lilyan retrieved the bulky package and sat down to untie the twine and unwrap the burlap cloth. To her delight, she discovered a set of paintbrushes, a box containing small crocks of paint, and a sheaf of rolled-up canvases. The canvases were impressed with the name *Lefranc & Bourgeois,* a company in France from which she had ordered art supplies in the past.

"It's a fine gift, Agnes. Thank you very much." She rose and gave the woman a kiss on both cheeks.

Agnes tilted Lilyan's chin with her fingers. "I thought they would help occupy your time. But Jimmy, he said he'd love a portrait of me. I told him I wasn't sure we could arrange that, us being so far apart once you leave Charlestown."

"I have your comely face committed to memory, my sweet friend. I think I can manage a portrait once I get back home." She reveled in Agnes's delight. "And you could come visit, could you not?"

"Jimmy might be against my making such a long journey." Agnes looked around as if plotting a conspiracy. "But I often have a way of convincing him to my side of things."

I can believe that.

"And what is it that you would be convincing me about, Grandmother?" asked James as he and Nicholas joined them.

"Oh, nothing, dear boy, just women's talk."

"Nikki," said Lilyan, "come and see the gift that James and Agnes gave me."

Nicholas stood beside her as she showed him the art supplies. "You couldn't have given my wife anything that would please her more. Thank you."

He turned to James, who was helping his grandmother prepare to leave. "We have something else to thank James for. He has agreed to be our representative here in Charlestown. He'll see to our accounts, counsel Gerald about the wallpaper business, and make sure Constance and Sally have the funds they need to keep the house going."

Lilyan held James's hand in both of hers. "Our affairs couldn't be in more capable hands."

"Capable enough to coordinate the trip my grandmother is already planning?" he asked with a wink.

Agnes laughed. "You heard me after all. Though I would love to see the vineyard, it likely won't be for some time."

But Agnes's visit would happen sooner than any of them expected.

CHAPTER 27

Love beareth all things, believeth all things,
hopeth all things, endureth all things.
1 Corinthians 13:7 KJV

At the edge of the forest near their cabin, Lilyan finished tearing vermillion flower petals into tiny pieces and sprinkled them across the freshly-cut tree stump Callum had selected.

"Now." Callum waved his hand toward the stump. "Spread the honey all across the top, and then we'll go behind the trees. If we stay real still, the bees will come."

She did as he asked and walked with him behind the trunk of a large oak. Helping Callum with his beekeeping was only one of the myriad chores he had coaxed her into since they had arrived at the vineyard four days ago. She knew what he was attempting to do, and she loved him even more for it.

As a young girl, she had learned from Callum how to lure bees with honey, then observe as they left, taking note on a compass the direction in which they flew. Since bees always flew in a straight line back to their hives, they were easy to follow. Once he located a hive, he would cut down the branch in which it had been built and transport it to his hiving area. There he would suspend it from a pole at the same distance from the ground it had been originally. Because of his failing eyesight, he had come up with an ingenious idea of putting flower petals on the stump along with the honey, so that when the bees landed the vermillion pieces would stick to their legs.

They didn't have long to wait for the bees to arrive, and, watching them fly off with tiny red specks attached to their legs, she recalled Laurel's fascination with birds and butterflies. *How she would giggle at these comical-looking insects.*

She shied away from that thought and concentrated on Callum as he noted the beeline. Afterward, they walked arm in arm back to the front porch of the cabin. He eased down into a rocker, and she sat on the top step.

Spotting something on the valley road, she cupped her hand over her brow to shade her eyes against the afternoon sun. "Wagons are coming."

"Who is it?"

"I can't imagine."

She reached behind her and picked up the telescope from the worktable, slid the lens open with a *click*, and trained it on the road. "My goodness. It's James McCord, riding a horse. He's escorting a wagon with ... I can't believe it. It's Agnes and Candice."

She jumped up and dropped the spyglass onto the table. "I know Agnes said she wanted to visit, but you would expect her to write ahead of time."

"Must be something awful important, lass, to bring them here like this," he said.

Puzzled, she pulled off her apron, flung it over the back of a rocking chair, and gave a furtive glance at the edge of the woods where Nicholas and several of the vineyard workers were clearing land for another cabin. She ran her hand over her mobcap and down the braid draped over her shoulder. "Oh, dear, I'm not prepared for guests."

She ran to the bedroom, pulled one of Nicholas's shirts from a wall peg, and threw it over her shoulder. In the kitchen, she gathered a cloth and a pan of water and headed out the door. Hurrying across the yard, she glanced often at the unexpected company slowly drawing nearer.

"Nikki!" she called out. "People are coming."

He jerked around, buried his axe into a log, and ran toward her.

"What people?" He took her by the forearms, sweat running down his neck and onto the taut muscles of his bare chest.

"The McCords."

"The McCords! Here? Now?"

"Yes. Hurry." She doused the cloth into the water and scrubbed at the grime and sweat on his shoulders.

He plunged his hands into the water and splashed it on his face and down his chest. He leaned over and let her toss the rest of the water across his back. After sponging him dry, she helped him slip the clean shirt over his head. On the way to the cabin, he tucked in his shirttail and retied his queue with a piece of rawhide. Inside the cabin, they raced around straightening up, shoving things they weren't sure what to do with into a trunk next to the fireplace. Breathless, they ran back outside and joined Callum at the bottom of the steps to greet the unexpected visitors.

"We'll need more fish and a couple more squirrels," she said, waving back to James as he topped the hill. "And where are we going to put all these people?"

"The fish and the squirrels I can manage. The accommodations I'm not so sure about," Nicholas said, waving his arm in greeting.

Callum harrumphed. "Watch out, lad, or she'll have you building a cabin for guests. One more cabin around here and it'll be like living on Meeting Street."

She and Nicholas shared a glance. They were still smiling when James rode up, dismounted, and greeted them with a bear hug and a huge smile, so unlike his usual reserved manner.

" James." Nicholas slapped him on the back. "What a surprise."

"It's nothing compared to the surprise we have for you," James said with a grin.

"You promised you'd let me tell them," Agnes called out as the wagon neared.

"Tell us what?" Lilyan asked as James helped his grandmother and Candice down from the wagon.

Agnes, hunched over, her muscles obviously cramping after her long trek, took a few hesitant steps. Lilyan and Nicholas hurried to her side, and she gave Lilyan a kiss on both cheeks, her eyes bright and eager. "There's something in the back of the wagon you both have to see. Show them, James."

Holding Nicholas's hand, Lilyan followed James and waited for him to unlatch the backboard and lay it flat. Inside, a woman Lilyan had never seen before reached down into a wooden box and picked up a bundle wrapped in a quilt.

"Lilyan. Nicholas." Agnes stood beside them, her eyes dancing. "This is Mrs. Rubie Bramble. And this, my dears," she said, taking the bundle in her arms and extending it to them, "is your Laurel."

Lilyan found herself looking down at the face of her daughter, who was sound asleep.

Yes, the same beautiful face. The coils of red hair. The sweet, sweet smell.

"Dear God in heaven. My Laurel. My darling baby girl," she shrieked, startling Laurel awake.

She and Nicholas cried and laughed at the same time. They unwrapped the coverlet and clutched their startled child against them, kissing her hands, her face, her arms, her neck.

Laurel's face puckered, and she began to squall at being so rudely awakened. Lilyan thought it the most wonderful sound she had ever heard. Then, as if she sensed she was home, Laurel quit crying. Her eyes swimming with tears, she looked calmly from one parent to the other, reached out her fingers, and pulled on her mother's bottom lip.

"Can it be?" asked Nicholas, tears streaming down his face. "Is this a dream or some kind of miracle?"

Andrew, Golden Fawn, Mildred, and some of the vineyard workers joined them, and they all began to laugh and talk at the same time.

Callum lumbered around the wagon, stopped short, and stared at them. "What's going on here?"

When he spotted Laurel in her parent's arms, he clutched the side of the wagon. "Glory be!" he shouted and threw his arms around the three of them.

With Laurel clasped to her breast, Lilyan and Nicholas hurried inside the cabin, where she slumped into a rocking chair and he knelt beside them. Again, their daughter waited patiently as they checked her from head to toe, not finding the first bruise or sign of the ordeal they had lived through the past months. When they were done, she gave them one of her grins that crinkled her nose.

"She remembers us," said Lilyan, her heart filled to bursting with joy. She slid off the rocker, and they sat together on the rug in front of the fireplace. "Nikki, get her dolly."

He jumped up, went to their bedroom, and came running back with the doll, which Laurel took from his hand. Grinning, she stuffed it under her arm, more interested in wrapping her fingers around Lilyan's braid.

Their family and friends gave them about a half hour before they slipped in through the door and gathered around them.

Nicholas tried to speak but could only cough. He tried several more times before he could get the words out. "How did she survive the shipwreck?"

As the others found a place to sit, Agnes came forward and sat in the rocker beside them.

"She was never on the ship," Agnes said triumphantly. "Rubie, you tell them."

The middle-aged woman, short and plump with hazel eyes magnified by her round spectacles, knelt on the floor.

"First off, I hope you know that we'd never have taken your

daughter had we any notion you were still alive. We were told you'd been killed by Indians and that she was an orphan."

Nicholas caressed his daughter's head. "We know."

"We treated Abigail—that's what we called her—as our own," she said, speaking directly to Lilyan. "Loved her as if she was our own."

"She was happy?" Lilyan's vision suddenly blurred with tears.

"I think so. She ate and slept well. She acted content. Always greeted me with a smile, though sometimes she would look past my shoulder as if expecting someone else."

"She didn't suffer?" asked Nicholas warily.

"No." Rubie shook her head. "The only thing that worried me was that she never would talk. Hard as we tried, we couldn't get her to say anything."

"Why weren't you on board the ship?" Lilyan asked.

"The morning we were to leave for Baltimore, when we crossed over on the ferry, we ran into a patch of mosquitoes. Must have been hundreds of them, and they all seemed to be drawn to Laurel. Anyway, by the time we reached the ship, she was squalling, miserable, and hot. And covered with red bumps. Some she had scratched until they bled. The ship's purser took one look at her and thought it was measles and told us we couldn't board. We told the silly man what had happened, but he wouldn't believe us. Said he couldn't take any chances."

Lilyan kissed the top of Laurel's head, imagining what it must have been like for her.

"It was then that my husband made a … terrible … decision." Rubie sighed. "He said he'd continue on to Baltimore and find us a home. Told me to take the child back to his brother's house at Mount Pleasant and wait for a letter from him telling us all was ready."

Andrew stepped forward. "You have our family's sincere condolences upon your loss, Mrs. Bramble."

Golden Fawn clasped her husband's arm. "And our undying

gratitude for taking care of Laurel. For bringing her back to us."

Lilyan noted that her sister-in-law looked happier and more relaxed than she had in some time. Offering Laurel up to her, she asked, "Would you like to hold her?"

Golden Fawn rushed forward and took Laurel into her arms, cuddling her and kissing her.

Mr. McCord took that moment to leave his grandmother's side and approach Lilyan. "You are happy, Lilyan?"

"Ecstatic." She smiled up at him. "Nicholas and I have much to thank you and your family for."

He waved his hand as if to make nothing of it. "I have other news that Grandmother insists I relay. It's about your friend, Fianna."

"Good news, I pray."

His dark blue eyes grew darker. "Not good for Fianna, I'm sad to say. Her sentence was carried out."

"Oh!"

"But we were able to find a home for her daughter. She's now the only child of my grandmother's seamstress and her husband." He winked. "I'm told they treat her like a princess."

"Was Fianna told before …?"

"We were able to tell her. And there's something else. She left strict orders that her child was to be named Lilyan."

"Oh, dear." Lilyan's eyes welled with tears. "Thank you, James. I've thought about Fianna often. Now I can be at peace about it."

The rest of the evening, Laurel, who was passed from one person to the other, seemed to thrive on the outpouring of love, thoroughly enjoying being the center of attention. While the others ate dinner, Lilyan's and Nicholas's eyes never left their daughter, except for the times they would gaze at each other with such joy and love that the corner of Lilyan's apron grew wet with her tears.

When Callum finally pressed her little girl's drooping body into her arms, Lilyan looked up to discover Rubie stealing out the door, quietly pulling it closed behind her. Nicholas, who had noticed the woman's departure too, nodded his head toward the door and held his arms open for his daughter.

Lilyan stood, straightening the wrinkles from her skirt. "I think I'll get some air."

She picked up a lantern from the trench table and slipped out the door. Outside on the porch, she found Rubie sitting in a rocking chair. She set the lantern on the top step, pulled her workbench close, and sat down.

"Rubie, I know I've said this many times," she began, "but if I said it a thousand times, it would not be enough. I can't begin to thank you for what you've done. That you became a mother to my child will be a forever bond between us."

Rubie's smile was captured in the glow of the lantern. "I like that thought, Lilyan. It makes me happy to see that Laurel has such dear parents and a large and loving family."

"And what of you? Is there family for you somewhere?"

Rubie shook her head. "Not really. My parents passed quite a while back. We were only returning to Baltimore because Jonathan's first business was there, and I was feeling so very lonely in the backcountry. Of course, there's Jonathan's brother and his family in Mount Pleasant." She looked up at the night sky. "They're kind enough, but I often feel like an interloper among them."

"Would you like to stay here? With us? Become a part of our family?"

Rubie remained silent, fingering a ruffle in her skirt.

"That way, you could be close to Laurel, be a kind of aunt." Lilyan winked. "Lord knows, she needs another doting person around."

"I wouldn't accept charity," Rubie said, her chin set. "I'd have to make my own way."

"Of course. You wouldn't believe what all has to be done around here. Another set of hands would be appreciated."

Rubie's eyes lit up. "But do you have room for me?"

"If you'd be so inclined, I could ask Mildred if the two of you could share her cabin." Lilyan stood and pulled Rubie from the chair. "You'll give it some thought?"

"Don't have to think anymore. I'd love to stay. There is one thing …" Rubie wrapped her arms around her waist. "There'll be two more mouths to feed instead of one."

Confused, Lilyan stood silent for a moment, until realization dawned. "You're in the family way?"

"Yes. My husband and I … we prayed for such a long time. We thought it would never happen." She put her hand on her stomach. "Will this change anything?"

"Oh, my dear friend. My heart aches that your husband isn't here to share this with you. But between my relatives and all the vineyard workers, we make for a huge family. One that the both of you will fit right into." Lilyan cocked her head. "I'm delighted!" She rested her hands on her own stomach. "'Twill be another bond between us."

Laughing, they returned to the cabin to share the good news with all gathered inside.

* * *

Much later in the evening, Lilyan and Nicholas lay on their bed, curled toward each other with Laurel between them lying on the lamb's wool cover Miriam Greene had given them. They took turns cooing over their child, often picking up her dainty fingers and kissing them one by one.

Noting Laurel's drooping eyelids, he whispered, "Should I put her in the crib?"

Laurel's eyes popped back open, and she clasped her parents' hair in each hand. "No! Mine!" she said, clearly and loudly.

"Well." He chuckled. "Our daughter is home and has made her wishes known."

At that moment, Lilyan clasped her hand to her stomach.

Nicholas froze. "What? What's wrong?"

The quickening had startled her at first, but surprise soon turned to joy that permeated her body. "It's our other child making its presence known."

He grinned. "I'm so happy. With everything that has happened, I was worried …"

"Our son is fine."

"Our son?"

"Just a feeling."

"If I've learned one thing from all this, it's never to doubt your feelings."

They both looked down at Laurel, who had finally given in to sleep, though she still had a hold of them. Nicholas sighed as he untangled his hair from her fingers.

Lilyan draped a strand of his hair back over his shoulder. "Why the heavy sigh, my love?"

"I was just thinking. With Mildred and Rubie here now, and guests dropping in by the wagonload, and our family growing, are you going to want me to expand our cabin or build a new one? Or two?"

She started to giggle, and soon they were both laughing until finally, they too drifted off to sleep, he thinking about the number of trees that would have to be cut, and she thanking God for His tender mercies.

Our daughter is home. Thank You, Lord.

EPILOGUE

Commodore and Mrs. Robert Westra
Request the Pleasure of Your Company
at Meadows Plantation, Camden, South Carolina
for a Grand Reception in Honor of
His Excellency President George Washington's Visit
On the Twenty-sixth of May 1791 at 7 o'clock,
Cotillion at 10 o'clock
Vitam impendere bono
(He risked his life for the good of others.)

May 1791
Camden, South Carolina

Cradled in Nicholas's arms, waiting for the room to stop spinning, Lilyan winced as her husband shouted at their seven-year-old son, "Paul, open the parlor doors. Quickly!"

"Yes, Father."

Nicholas strode into the room and gently settled Lilyan on one of the plush settees facing the fireplace. He knelt beside her, his handsome face marred by a deep frown.

"Is it the heat? What can I do?" His eyes entreated.

Lilyan glanced at the people gathered at the door, whispering among themselves.

"I should like some privacy, please, dearest."

Nicholas shot up and strode across the room. "Please, ladies and gentlemen. We appreciate your concern, but if you would be so kind, we would desire some privacy."

"Of course, my friend," said their host, Commodore Westra. "Come, Lynne, let us see to our other guests. Paul, you and Timothy come with us."

"Mother," Timothy called out in a panic.

"Nikki, let them stay," said Lilyan.

Nicholas nodded to the commodore, who herded the onlookers out and closed the doors behind them.

Lilyan craned her neck around to give her sons a reassuring smile. "Boys, where's Laurel?"

"You know Sissy. She'll be in the center of a group somewhere, talking the ears off a donkey," said Timothy, who yelped when Paul poked him in the ribs.

Nicholas, growing more impatient by the minute, frowned at his sons. "Boys! Can't you see your mother is ill?"

"Apologies, sir. Please don't make us leave," pleaded Paul.

"I'm not moving from here either, lassie, till I know what's ailing you," Callum announced and, leaning on a cane, eased onto a chair across from her.

Andrew stepped forward. "Golden Fawn and I would like to stay as well."

Lilyan sighed. "Very well."

Nicholas threw his hands up in a gesture of frustration and joined their sons to stand in front of Lilyan. As always when she gazed upon her beautiful men, she marveled at how much her sons resembled their father with their soot-black curly hair, long ebony lashes, and topaz eyes. Eyes that were all trained on her, filled with concern.

"I hadn't intended for you to find out in this very public way—"

The parlor doors flew open, and in rushed Laurel. "I ran as fast as my feet would bring me," she announced, hurrying across the room.

She wilted gracefully on the floor beside the couch, her satin and lace dress floating around her like an ice-blue confection. "Whatever is the matter?"

Lilyan smiled reassuringly at her nine-year-old, who already was showing promise of becoming a stunning beauty. She watched Laurel turn her lovely eyes up to Nicholas.

"We were about to find out, sweet girl." As always, when addressing their daughter, his countenance softened.

Lilyan observed the silent communication between her husband and their oldest child, who claimed a special place in his heart—maybe because she was their first born, the only girl, or because they had almost lost her. That was not to say he did not love his boys, because he cherished them beyond measure.

Once again, Lilyan noticed everyone's attention leveled on her. "I've seen a doctor. And I'm very happy to tell you that we're to have another addition to our little clan."

Looking as though he'd been struck by a poleax, Nicholas dropped to one knee and kissed her hand.

Callum slapped his knee and whooped.

Timothy steadily watched Lilyan. "Is that bad, Mother?"

Nicholas and Laurel stood, making way for Lilyan to gather her six-year-old into her arms.

"No, my sweet. It means that you'll have a new brother or sister."

Timothy looked relieved, if still a little confused.

Paul grinned. "Another brother. That is good news."

Laurel clasped her father's hand. "Wonderful news, Mah."

"Congratulations, Sissy," said Andrew.

"I'm so happy for you," said Golden Fawn. "Now, Andrew, Callum, I think we should take the children and give Lilyan and Nicholas some time alone."

Lilyan smiled at her sister-in-law and mouthed *thank you*.

When they were alone again, Nicholas sat on the couch and gathered Lilyan into his arms, settling her on his lap.

"You are happy with the news, sir?"

"I didn't think I could ever get much happier, my love. But my cup runneth over." He drew her hand to his lips and kissed her open palm. "I would like to go home, though. As soon as possible."

"But I don't want to interfere with your visit."

"I've accomplished what I came here to do. I've had the honor of speaking with the president. And I've traded stories with my old comrades in arms. It's more important to me that I see you home safely. It's a long journey back, aga'pi mou."

Lilyan caressed his cheek. "I'll be fine. I must admit, I would like to be back in our own house, to walk in the vineyards and watch the spring pruning."

"It's settled. Yes? We'll leave tomorrow."

The next morning, they bade good-bye to Lady Lynne and the commodore. Lilyan, Laurel, Golden Fawn, Callum, and Timothy rode in the carriage. Andrew, Nicholas, and Paul accompanied them on horseback. Their journey would be long, about two hundred miles, and over some of the same terrain Lilyan had traversed so many years ago. She closed her eyes as memories of that time tumbled through her mind. But how different this trip would be, for Cook's Road, reaching all the way from Camden, South Carolina, to Brevard, North Carolina, near their vineyard, had been vastly improved since the close of the war.

They had been on the road only a few minutes when Nicholas rode up to the carriage and ordered the driver to stop.

Lilyan stuck her head out of the window. "What is it?"

A muscle worked in his cheek. "It's General—President—Washington. He's stopped to visit de Kalb's grave."

Lilyan looked at her brother. "Shall we join them?"

Nicholas dismounted and helped her from the carriage.

Andrew strode beside them as they headed for the cemetery, past the president's entourage—a white chariot, a baggage wagon, and a troop of horsemen. They came to a halt a few yards from Washington as he approached the headstone of one of his most revered generals. He stood quietly a few moments and then knelt and bowed his head.

Sensing the deep emotions of this man who had sent men into battle to face injury and death, Lilyan pondered how he must regret that part of his responsibilities. Images of the men she had nursed back to health and those who did not make it had haunted her memories for years. Young and old, they had sacrificed everything they had. As much as they had affected her life, how much more of an impact must they have had on their Commander in Chief?

Lilyan's eyes filled with tears that spilled over unashamedly. Nicholas reached out for her hand, and as she laced her fingers around his, she glanced up to see tears rolling down Andrew's cheeks as well. How proud her husband and brother were to have fought for such an extraordinary man.

The president rose and addressed the officer beside him. "So there lies the brave de Kalb—the generous stranger who came from a distant land to fight our battles and to water with his blood the tree of our liberty. Would to God he had lived to share with us its fruits."

Lilyan, Nicholas, and Andrew withdrew and returned to their family, each humbly grateful to God, who had spared them to share in those marvelous fruits.

AUTHOR'S NOTES

Anne Bonney and Mary Read, women pirates who "pleaded their bellies"

Anne Bonney was born in Ireland in the late 1600s, the illegitimate daughter of a lawyer and his housemaid. After Anne's birth, the family immigrated to Charleston, SC. As a young woman, she eloped and married James Bonney, who took her to New Providence, Bahamas, to a pirates' lair. In 1718, Anne left James to become the mistress of Captain "Calico Jack" Rackham. Dressed as a man, she sailed with Captain Rackham to become one of the most ferocious women pirates in history. She became friends with another woman pirate, Mary Read, who also dressed as a man. According to fellow crewmembers, they had violent tempers, were ruthless and bloodthirsty, and shared a reputation as "fierce hell cats." Eventually, Anne and Mary were arrested and tried, one week after Captain Rackham's death by hanging, and were also found guilty. At their sentencing they both "pleaded their bellies," as both were pregnant by Captain Rackham. Since British law forbade killing an unborn child, their sentences were stayed temporarily. Records aren't clear, so speculation abounds. Some indicate that Mary died in prison, while others say she feigned death and was sneaked out of prison under a shroud. There's no record of Anne's hanging. Some records say her father bought her release, and she lived out her life quietly on a small Caribbean Island. Others say she moved to the south of England, where she owned a tavern.

Another report says Anne and Mary moved to Louisiana, where they raised their children together.

Catawba, flat heads

They lived in villages of circular, bark-covered houses, and dedicated temple structures were used for public gatherings and religious ceremonies. Agriculture, for which men and women both shared responsibility, provided at least two crops each year and was heavily supplemented by hunting and fishing. The Iroquois called the Catawba "flatheads" because they, as well as many of the other Siouan-speaking tribes of the area, practiced forehead flattening of male infants. Besides the Iroquois, traditional Catawba enemies included the Cherokee, Shawnee, Delaware, and several members of the Great Lakes Algonquin allied with the French. Catawba warriors had a fearsome reputation and an appearance to match: ponytail hairstyle, a distinctive war paint pattern of one eye in a black circle, the other in a white circle, and remainder of the face painted black. Coupled with their flattened foreheads, some of their enemies must have died from sheer fright.

Church Bells of St. Michael's

The bells were cast in London and installed in St. Michael's Church in Charleston, SC, in 1764. When the British took over the city during the Revolutionary War, they took the bells back to England. A Charleston merchant bought them in England and shipped them home to America. In 1823, cracks were found in some of the bells, and they were returned to London to recast. In 1862, during the siege of Charleston, the bells were moved to Columbia for safekeeping, but Sherman's army set fire to the city. Only fragments of the bells were found to be returned to London once more, where the original moulds still stood. In February 1867, the eight bells were again installed in St. Michael's steeple and on March 21st joyously rang out, "Home again, Home again from a foreign Land."

Cretan lyra
The instrument that Thanassis plays on board ship, when Nicholas dances for joy, is the Cretan lyra. A part of the traditional music of Crete and other Greek islands, it is a pear-shaped, three-stringed instrument with a series of bells attached to the bow's arc to provide accompaniment to the melody with the movement of the horsehair bow. Traditionally, the soundboard was carved using straight-grained softwood from the aged wooden beams of buildings from Venetian ruins.

Elliott Street (the street Lilyan takes from her house to her shop)
This street was laid out as a 20-foot wide thoroughfare by the agreement of several property owners through whose land the street was cut in 1683. It was known at different times as Callaibeuf's Alley and Poinsett's Alley, after Huguenot families who owned property along it. It was also known as Middle Street, and finally as Elliott's Alley or Elliott Street, for the family who owned Elliott's Bridge (wharf) and other substantial real estate in the neighborhood. During the late 18th and early 19th centuries, Elliott Street was a major retail shopping area. The neighborhood suffered the great fires of 1740 and 1778, and most of the buildings date from the 1790s. (*Charles Town/Charleston Street's In The Early Years*; By: Ill. Bro. McDonald "Don" Burbidge)

Fireflies
Annually, visitors to the Great Smokey Mountains National Park in Gatlinburg, TN, are treated to the delightful display of synchronous fireflies (*Photinus carolinus*), one of at least 19 species of fireflies that live in the park. They are the only species in America whose individuals can synchronize their flashing light patterns. Visitors to the valley liken the display to a "wave" of fans at a football game. Their light patterns are part of their mating display. The mating season lasts for approximately two weeks each year.

Since 1993, this peak date has varied from June 3 to June 21. Advanced registration is required.

Francis Marion's Men, not invited to celebration

The stated reason was lack of discipline among Marion's militia. But Marion was well known as a strict disciplinarian. All of his biographers from the early days state that. By that statement, they were all saying the city father's claim that Marion's troops were undisciplined was a lie. To say he could not control his troops or that he was not able to put together a company of properly disciplined troops out of the entire body of militia he commanded was a great insult.

Marion returned the insult by saying he did not wish to enter the city because it was diseased, and he did not want to catch anything bad. The fact is that he was in the city within a couple of days of the evacuation, as there is correspondence from him so noting.

Not getting invited to the victory party was payback. It was part fear of his power, and it was part trying to pressure (by punishment) him into going along with the confiscation and retribution policies of lesser men.

Jenny Diver, pickpocket

Jenny Diver, a notorious pickpocket, was born as Mary Young around 1700 in Ireland. She was the illegitimate daughter of a lady's maid, who, after being forced to leave her job, gave birth to Jenny in a brothel. At age 10, Jenny was taken in by a gentlewoman who sent her to school, where she learned needlework and to read and write. Once she had mastered needlework, she moved to London to become a seamstress. There she met the leader of a gang of pickpockets and learned the skills of a street criminal so well, she soon became their leader. Though she was caught several times, imprisoned in Newgate, and sent to the American colonies, she managed to return to London under assumed names. Eventually at the age of about 40, her luck ran out, and she was hanged from London's Tyburn Tree on March 18, 1740.

Lemon Castile and Bathing

Centuries ago, Arab peoples in and around Europe often used animal fat as the fatty acid to make soap. Meanwhile, people in the Mediterranean found it most convenient to use the abundance of olive trees in their vicinity. Specifically, many Mediterranean people used olive oil (fatty acid) and the ashes of the barilla tree (base) to make soap.

One of the places to do this was the Castilla region of Spain, so the soap from this area was called Castile soap, one of the first examples of hard, white soap to appear. Some say it was reserved almost exclusively for the Spanish royalty and later sought by a variety of European royalty for its mildness.

American colonists, like their European ancestors, feared that bathing would destroy their natural oils and leave them open to the ravages of diseases, so getting clean meant sponging off, usually just face and hands. More affluent people had chinaware washbasins. If they desired a full bath, their servants would heat buckets of water in the kitchen and haul them to the bedroom. There were no towels to dry with, so they used large pieces of cloth or blankets. Full baths were considered a luxury not done more than a couple of times a year.

Pudding Cap

Toddlers sometimes wore padded pudding caps, much like modern crash helmets, to protect their heads if they fell. The caps were often made of quilted cotton velvet bound with silk ribbon, stuffed with horsehair, and lined with leather.

Raven Mocker

The Cherokee call evil spirits that torment the sick *Sunnayi Edahi*, "the Night Goer." The spirits come at night to a sick person's house and stomp on the roof, beat the side of the house, knock the person out of bed, and drag him on the floor. They try to hasten death. They want the sick person to die faster and not use up any of his life span so that they can take his unused lifetime and add it to their own.

Of all the Cherokee evil spirits, the most dreaded is the Raven Mocker (*Kâ'lanû Ahkyeli'ski*), the one that robs the dying man of life. They are of either sex, and there is no sure way to know one, though they usually look withered and old because they have added so many lives to their own. At night, when someone is sick or dying in the village, the Raven Mocker goes to the place to take the life. He flies through the air in fiery shape, with arms outstretched like wings, sparks trailing behind, and a rushing sound like the noise of a strong wind. Sometimes as he flies he makes a cry like a raven and those who hear are afraid, because they know that some man's life will soon go out. When the Raven Mocker comes to the house, he finds others of his kind waiting there. Unless there is a doctor on guard who knows how to drive them away, they go inside, all invisible, and frighten and torment the sick man until they kill him. Sometimes to do this, they lift him from the bed and throw him on the floor, but his friends who are with him think he is only struggling for breath.

After the evil spirits kill him, they take out his heart and eat it, so adding to their own lives as many days or years as they have taken from his. No one in the room can see them, and there is no scar where they take out the heart, but yet there is no heart left in the body. Only one who has the right medicine can recognize a Raven Mocker. If such a man stays in the room with the sick person, these witches are afraid to come in and retreat as soon as they see him, because when one of them is recognized in his right shape, he must die within seven days.

The family will summon a medicine man to keep watch and hold it away until the person recovers. If the person dies, the medicine man will keep watch until the person is buried. After burial, the heart cannot be taken.

The medicine man drives a sharpened stick into the ground at each corner of the house. Then, about noontime, he gets ready the *Tsâl-agayû'nlï* or "Old Tobacco," with which he fills his pipe, repeating a chant. He then wraps the pipe in a black cloth. This sacred tobacco is smoked only for this purpose. He then goes out into the forest and returns just before dark, about which time the sprit will arrive. Lighting his pipe, he goes slowly around the house, puffing the smoke in the direction of every trail by which the sprit might approach. He then goes into the house to wait. When the spirit arrives, the sharpened stick on that side of the house shoots up into the air and comes down like an arrow upon his head. This causes the sprit to die within seven days.

Robbie's Long Bow / King's Forest Ranger
Forest law prescribed harsh punishment for anyone who committed any of a range of offenses within the forests. By the mid-17th century, enforcement of this law had died out, but many of England's woodlands still bore the title *Royal Forest*. The term *ranger* first appeared in 13th-century England. The justices of the forest were the Justice in Eyre and the verderers. The chief royal official was the warden. As he was often an eminent and preoccupied magnate, his powers were frequently exercised by a deputy. He supervised the foresters and under-foresters, who personally went about preserving the forest and game and apprehending offenders against the law, many of whom carried longbows. The agisters supervised pannage and agistment and collected any fees thereto

appertaining. The rangers are sometimes said to be patrollers of the purlieu. Another group, called serjeants-in-fee, and later, foresters-in-fee, held small estates in return for their service in patrolling the forest and apprehending offenders.

Royal forests usually included large areas of heath, grassland, and wetland—anywhere that supported deer and other game.

Smallpox

John Adams provided detailed descriptions of his ordeal with smallpox. In preparation for the inoculation, the nine men with whom Adams shared a room were given medicines to make them vomit. In his letters to Abigail, John made the experience seem jolly for a while. According to his April 7 letter (http://www.masshist.org/digitaladams/): "We took turns to be sick and to laugh. When my Companion was sick I laughed at him, and when I was sick he laughed at me. Once however and once only we were both sick together, and then all Laughter and good Humour deserted the Room."

Boston had so many cases that the disease helped deter General George Washington from trying to fight his way into the city last spring. He said, "If we escape the small pox in this camp and the country around about, it will be miraculous." Only after General Howe evacuated the city did Washington send in 500 of his men who had already had the disease.

Here's Adams' description of the inoculation:
"Dr. Perkins demanded my left arm, and Dr. Warren my brother's. They took their Launcetts and with their Points divided the skin about a Quarter of an inch and just suffering the blood to appear, buried a thread (infected) about a Quarter of an inch long in the Channell. A little lint was then laid over the scratch and a Piece of Ragg pressed on, and then a Bandage bound over all, and I was bid go where and do what I pleased. The doctors left us red and black

to take Night and Morning, and ordered my Brother, larger Doses than me, on Account of the Differences in our Constitutions."

Adams suffered headaches, backaches, knee aches, gagging fever, and eruption of pock marks.

It was not until 1775 that Abigail had herself and her children inoculated. After three weeks, son Charles Francis (who grew to renown as a statesman and historian) developed a pox illness and was unconscious and delirious for 48 hours.

Preparing Wool for Spinning
Soak husked rice in water for a day; change water and soak rice again until it can be squeezed into a flour; pour off water; rub with a stone until rice becomes flour; fuse picked wool into flour until it's clean; store in a covered earthen dish until ready for spinning.

Vineyards / Muscadine Mother Root
Possibly the oldest cultivated grapevine in the world is the 400-year-old scuppernong "Mother Vine" growing on Roanoke Island, North Carolina. The scuppernong is the state fruit of North Carolina.

The name comes from the Scuppernong River in North Carolina, mainly along the coastal plain. It was first mentioned as a "white grape" in a written logbook by the Florentine explorer Giovanni de Verrazano while exploring the Cape Fear River Valley in 1524. Sir Walter Raleigh's explorers wrote in 1584 that North Carolina's coast was "... so full of grapes as the very beating and surge of the sea overflowed them ... in all the world, the like abundance is not to be found." He may have been referring to Sargasso seaweed from coral reefs, which can be seen washed up on shore after a major storm off of the NC coast. The seaweed has berry-like, gas-filled bladders—looking much like grapes—

to keep the fronds afloat. However, in 1585, Governor Ralph Lane, when describing North Carolina to Raleigh, stated, "We have discovered the main to be the goodliest soil under the cape of heaven, so abounding with sweet trees that bring rich and pleasant, grapes of such greatness, yet wild, as France, Spain, nor Italy hath no greater ..."

It was first cultivated during the 17th century, particularly in Tyrell County, North Carolina. Isaac Alexander found it while hunting along the banks of a stream feeding into Scuppernong Lake in 1755. It is mentioned in the North Carolina official state toast. The name itself traces back to the Algonquian word *ascopo*, meaning "sweet bay tree."

Despite the state's reliance on native grapes, many envisioned European grape cultivars, *Vitis vinifera*, such as chardonnay and cabernet sauvignon, growing in Southern soil. But the temperate climate, with warm summer nights and late spring frosts, doomed early attempts.

Wild Ponies of Ocracoke Island
Up to a thousand wild ponies used to roam the Island of Ocracoke, located in the Outer Banks of North Carolina. Legend says that explorers De Soto or Cortez brought the horses with them from Spain. Historians say Sir Walter Raleigh brought the ponies and left them on Roanoke Island at the time of the mysterious Lost Colony disappearance. In 1953, when Cape Hatteras National Seashore was established, only twelve ponies existed. They are now kept on a range about seven miles north of the village. During times of drought, they have been known to dig shoulder-deep holes in search of fresh water.

CPSIA information can be obtained
at www.ICGtesting.com
Printed in the USA
FFOW04n2307060515
13185FF